P9-DDM-049

"You're incredible, Ben, you know that? You're an insensitive, first-class jerk, and—"

He leaned in. "And what?" he asked, voice dangerously low.

"And…" Stymied at her ridiculous and constant reaction to him, Aubrey put her hands to his chest to give him another shove, but somehow her wires got crossed and she fisted his shirt instead.

"Dare me," he said softly.

"Dare you to what?"

"Dare me, Aubrey."

Oh, how she hated how well he knew her. "I dare you to kiss me," she whispered, and then to make sure he did, she put her mouth on his first…

Praise for Jill Shalvis and Her Novels

It Had to Be You

"Engaging writing, characters that walk straight into your heart, and a town you can't wait to revisit make this touching, hilarious tale another heart-warmer worthy of Shalvis's popular series."

—Library Journal

"Four stars! A winner…Readers will laugh out loud as they rush to turn the pages."

—RT Book Reviews

"Ms. Shalvis has a gift for writing down-to-earth yet quirky heroines and swoonworthy, honorable heroes."

—HeroesandHeartbreakers.com

"Trademark Shalvis…A story and plot that keeps you turning the pages until you run out of 'em, and a sweet and sexy romance to warm the heart, all wrapped in warm fuzzies and humor. If you love contemporary romance, you'll have to read Jill Shalvis."

—DreysLibrary.com

Forever and a Day

"4½ stars! Top Pick! Shalvis once again racks up a hit…laughter is served in doses as generous as the chocolate the heroine relies on to get through the day. Readers will treasure each turn of the page and be sorry when this one is over."

—RT Book Reviews

"[Shalvis] has quickly become one of my go-to authors of contemporary romance. Her writing is smart, fun, and sexy, and her books never fail to leave a smile on my face long after I've closed the last page…Jill Shalvis is an author not to be missed!"

—TheRomanceDish.com

"It's a small-town romance of the first order…Their romance grows naturally, moving from pure physical chemistry to love in a realistic way. Watching it unfold was the most enjoyable part of the book."

—All About Romance (LikesBooks.com)

"Jill Shalvis is such a talented author that she brings to life characters who make you laugh, cry, and are a joy to read. In *Forever and a Day*, we fall for Grace and Josh and hope that their sizzling romance means the start of a future—forever and beyond."

—RomRevToday.com

At Last

"Shalvis's latest Lucky Harbor novel is a winner—full of laughter, snark, and a super-hot attraction between the main characters. Shalvis has painted a wonderful world, full of entertaining supporting characters and beautiful scenery."

—RT Book Reviews

"A sexy, romantic read…What I love about Jill Shalvis's books is that she writes sexy, adorable heroes…the sexual tension is out of this world. And of course, in true Shalvis fashion, she expertly mixes in humor that has you laughing out loud."

—HeroesandHeartbreakers.com

"A sexy, fun tale from the creative mind of Jill Shalvis…*At Last* will have you laughing, smiling, and sniffling…Another stellar read I highly recommend; pick up *At Last* for some pure reading enjoyment."

—RomRevToday.com

Lucky in Love

"Shalvis pens a tale rife with the three 'H's of romance: heat, heart, and humor. *Lucky in Love* is a down-to-the-toes charmer…It doesn't matter if you're chuckling or reaching for an iced drink to cool down the heat her characters generate—Shalvis doesn't disappoint."

—RT Book Reviews

"I read most of it with a big fat grin on my face. What can be more fun than watching Lucky Harbor's goody-two-shoes decide to stop playing it safe and begin to walk on the wild side?"

—Examiner.com

"I always enjoy reading a Jill Shalvis book. She's a consistently elegant, bold, clever writer…Very witty—I laughed out loud countless times reading *Lucky in Love*…[It] is also one of the hottest books I've read by Ms. Shalvis. Mallory and Ty burn up the sheets (and the pages) with regularity and these scenes are sizzling."

—All About Romance (LikesBooks.com)

"Whenever I'm looking for a romance to chase away the worries of life, all I have to do is pick up a Jill Shalvis book. Once again she has worked her magic with the totally entertaining *Lucky in Love*."

—RomRevToday.com

Head Over Heels

"[A] winning roller-coaster ride…[a] touching, character-rich, laughter-laced, knockout sizzler."
—*Library Journal* (starred review)

"Healthy doses of humor, lust, and love work their magic as Shalvis tells Chloe's story…Wit, smoking-hot passion, and endearing tenderness…a big winner."
—*Publishers Weekly*

"The Lucky Harbor series has become one of my favorite contemporary series, and *Head Over Heels* didn't disappoint…such a fun, sexy book…I think this one can be read as a stand-alone book, but I encourage you to try the first two in the series, where you meet all the characters of this really fun town."
—USAToday.com

The Sweetest Thing

"A wonderful romance of reunited lovers in a small town. A lot of hot sex, some delightful humor, and plenty of heartwarming emotion make this a book readers will love."
—*RT Book Reviews*

"A Perfect 10! Once again Jill Shalvis provides readers with a sexy, funny, hot tale."
—RomRevToday.com

"Witty, fun, and the characters are fabulous."
—FreshFiction.com

"It is fabulous revisiting Lucky Harbor! I have been on tenterhooks waiting for Tara and Ford's story, and yet again, Jill Shalvis does not disappoint…A rollicking good time."
—**RomanceJunkiesReviews.com**

Simply Irresistible

"Hot, sweet, fun, and romantic! Pure pleasure!"
—**Robyn Carr**, *New York Times* **bestselling author**

"4 stars!…Introduces some wonderful characters with humor, heartwarming interaction, and an abundance of hot sex. Readers will be eager for the next story."
—*RT Book Reviews*

"This often hilarious novel has a few serious surprises, resulting in a delightfully satisfying story."
—**LibraryJournal.com**

"Heartwarming and sexy…an abundance of chemistry, smoldering romance, and hilarious sisterly antics."
—*Publishers Weekly*

Once in a Lifetime

Also by Jill Shalvis

The Lucky Harbor Series

Simply Irresistible
The Sweetest Thing
Heating Up the Kitchen (cookbook)
Christmas in Lucky Harbor (omnibus)
Small Town Christmas (anthology)
Head Over Heels
Lucky in Love
At Last
Forever and a Day
"Under the Mistletoe" (short story)
It Had to Be You
Always on My Mind
A Christmas to Remember (anthology)

Other Novels

White Heat
Blue Flame
Seeing Red
Her Sexiest Mistake

Once in a Lifetime

Jill Shalvis

GRAND CENTRAL
PUBLISHING

NEW YORK   BOSTON

This book is a work of fiction. Names, characters, places, and incidents are the product of the author's imagination or are used fictitiously. Any resemblance to actual events, locales, or persons, living or dead, is coincidental.

Copyright © 2014 by Jill Shalvis
Excerpt from *It's in His Kiss* copyright © 2014 by Jill Shalvis
All rights reserved. In accordance with the U.S. Copyright Act of 1976, the scanning, uploading, and electronic sharing of any part of this book without the permission of the publisher is unlawful piracy and theft of the author's intellectual property. If you would like to use material from the book (other than for review purposes), prior written permission must be obtained by contacting the publisher at permissions@hbgusa.com. Thank you for your support of the author's rights.

Grand Central Publishing
Hachette Book Group
237 Park Avenue
New York, NY 10017
www.HachetteBookGroup.com

Printed in the United States of America

OPM

First Edition: February 2014
10 9 8 7 6 5 4 3 2 1

Grand Central Publishing is a division of Hachette Book Group, Inc.
The Grand Central Publishing name and logo is a trademark of Hachette Book Group, Inc.

The Hachette Speakers Bureau provides a wide range of authors for speaking events. To find out more, go to www.hachettespeakersbureau.com or call (866) 376-6591.

The publisher is not responsible for websites (or their content) that are not owned by the publisher.

ATTENTION CORPORATIONS AND ORGANIZATIONS:

Most Hachette Book Group books are available at quantity discounts with bulk purchase for educational, business, or sales promotional use. For information, please call or write:

Special Markets Department, Hachette Book Group
237 Park Avenue, New York, NY 10017
Telephone: 1-800-222-6747 Fax: 1-800-477-5925

To Alex Logan, because I can't imagine writing Lucky Harbor without you in my court. Thanks for all you've done and continue to do for me.

Once in a Lifetime

Chapter 1

♥

There was one universal truth in Lucky Harbor, Washington—you could hide a pot of gold in broad daylight and no one would steal it, but you couldn't hide a secret.

There'd been a lot of secrets in Aubrey Wellington's colorful life, and nearly all of them had been uncovered and gleefully discussed ad nauseam.

And yet here she was, still in this small Pacific West Coast town she'd grown up in. She didn't quite know what that said about her other than that she was stubborn as hell.

In any case, she was fairly used to bad days by the time she walked to Lucky Harbor's only bar and grill, but today had taken the cake. Ted Marshall, ex–town clerk, ex-boss, and also, embarrassingly enough, her ex-lover, was self-publishing his own tell-all. And since he'd ever so thoughtfully given her an advance reading copy, she knew he was planning on informing the entire world that, among other things, she was a bitchy, money-hungry man-eater.

She'd give him the money-hungry part. She was sinking much of her savings into her aunt's bookstore, the Book & Bean, a sentimental attempt at bringing back the one happy childhood memory she had. The effort was leaving her far too close to broke for comfort. She'd even give him the bitchy part—at least on certain days of the month.

But man-eater? Just because she didn't believe in happily-ever-afters, or even a happily-for-now, didn't mean she was a man-eater. She simply didn't see the need to invite a man all the way into her life when he wouldn't be staying.

Because they never stayed.

She shrugged off the little voice that said *That's your own fault* and entered the Love Shack. Stepping inside the bar and grill was like going back a hundred years into an old western saloon. The walls were a deep, sinful bordello red and lined with old mining tools. The ceiling was covered with exposed beams, and lanterns hung over the scarred bench-style tables, now filled with the late dinner crowd. The air hummed with busy chatter, loud laughter, and music blaring out of the jukebox against the far wall.

Aubrey headed straight for the bar. "Something that'll make my bad day go away," she said to the bartender.

Ford Walker smiled and reached for a tumbler. He'd been five years ahead of Aubrey in school, and was one of the nice ones. He'd gone off and achieved fame and fortune racing sailboats around the world, and yet he'd chosen to come back to Lucky Harbor to settle down.

She decided to take heart in that.

He slid her a vodka cranberry. "Satisfaction guaranteed," he promised.

Aubrey wrapped her fingers around the glass, but before she could bring it to her lips, someone nudged her shoulder.

Ted, the ex-everything.

"Excuse me," he began before recognition hit and the "Oh, shit" look came into his eyes. He immediately started to move away, but she grabbed his arm.

"Wait," she said. "I need to talk to you. Did you get my messages?"

"Yeah," he said. "All twenty-five of them." Ted had been born with an innate charm that usually did a real good job of hiding the snake that lay beneath it. Even now, he kept his face set in an expression of easy amusement, exuding charisma like a movie star. With a wry smile for anyone watching, he leaned in close. "I didn't know there were that many different words for *asshole*."

"And you still wouldn't if you'd have called me back even once," she said through her teeth. "Why are you doing this? Why did you say those things about me in your book? And in chapter one!" She'd stopped reading after that and maybe had tossed the book, with great satisfaction, into a Dumpster.

Ted shrugged and leaned back. "I need the money."

"Am I supposed to believe anyone's going to buy your book?"

"Hey, if the only buyers are Lucky Harbor residents, I still make five grand, baby."

"Are you kidding me?"

"Not even a little bit," he said. "What's the big deal,

anyway? Everyone writes a book nowadays. And besides, it's not like you're known for being an angel."

Aubrey knew exactly who she was. She even knew why. She didn't need him to tell her a damn thing about herself. "The big deal is that *you're* the one who wronged people," she said. It was a huge effort to keep her voice down. She wasn't as good at charm and charisma as he was. "*You* two-timed me—along with just about every other woman in town, including the mayor's wife! On top of that, you let her steal fifty grand of the town's funds—and yet somehow, *I'm* the bad guy."

"Hey," he said. "You were the town clerk's admin. If anyone should have known what had happened to that money, it was you, babe."

How had she ever worked for this guy? How had she ever *slept* with him? Her friend Ali had told her that every woman had at least one notch on her bedpost she secretly regretted. But there was no secret to Aubrey's regret. She gripped her tumbler so tight that she was surprised it didn't shatter. "You said things about me that had nothing to do with the money."

He smiled. "So the book needed a little…titillation."

Shaking with fury, she stood. "You know what you are?"

"A great guy?"

Her arm bypassed her brain and capped off her no-good very bad day by tossing her vodka cranberry in his smug face.

But though he was indeed *at least* twenty-five kinds of an asshole, he was also fast as a whip. He ducked, and her drink hit the man on the other side of him.

Straightening, Ted chortled in delight as Aubrey got a look at the man she'd inadvertently drenched. She stopped breathing. Oh, God. Had she really thought her day couldn't get any worse? Why would she tempt fate by even thinking that? Because of course things had gotten worse. They always did.

Ben McDaniel slowly stood up from his bar stool, dripping vodka from his hair, eyelashes, nose…he was six-feet-plus of hard muscles and brute strength on a body that didn't carry a single extra ounce of fat. For the past five years, he'd been in and out of a variety of Third World countries, designing and building water systems with the Army Corps of Engineers. His last venture had been for the Department of Defense in Iraq, which Aubrey only knew because Lucky Harbor's Facebook page was good as gospel.

Ted was already at the door like a thief in the night, the weasel. But not Ben. He swiped his face with his arm, deceptively chill and laid-back.

In truth, he was about as badass as they came.

Aubrey should know; she'd seen him in action. But she managed to meet his gaze. Cool, casual, even. One had to be with Ben: The man could spot weakness a mile away. "I'm sorry," she said.

"Are you?"

She felt herself flush. He'd always seemed to see right through her. And she was pretty sure he'd never cared for her. He had good reason for that, she reminded herself. He just didn't know the half of it.

"Yes, I am sorry," she said. Her heart was pounding so loudly she was surprised she could hear herself speak. "Are you okay?"

He ran his fingers through a sexy disorder of sun-streaked brown hair. His eyes were the same color—light milk chocolate marbled with gold caramel. It was difficult to make such a warmly colored gaze seem hard, but Ben managed it with no effort at all. "Need to work on your aim," he said.

"No doubt." She offered a tight smile. It was all she could do—she hadn't taken a breath since she'd hit him with the drink. "Again, I'm…sorry." And with little spots of anxiety dancing in her vision, she backed away, heading straight for the door.

Outside, the night was blessedly cold, tendrils of the icy air brushing her hot cheeks. Lucky Harbor was basically a tiny little bowl sitting on the rocky Washington State coast, walled in by majestic peaks and lush forest. It was all an inky shadow now. Aubrey stood still a moment, hand to her thundering heart. It was still threatening to burst out of her rib cage as she worked on sucking in air so chilly it burned her lungs.

Behind her the door opened again. Panicked that it might be Ben, and not nearly ready for another face-to-face, she hightailed it out of the parking lot. In her three-inch high-heeled boots, she wasn't exactly stealthy, with the loud *click-click-click* of her heels, but she was fast. In two minutes, she'd rounded the block and finally slowed some, straining to hear any sounds that didn't belong to the night.

Like footsteps.

Damn it. He was following her. She quickened her pace again until she passed a church. The building, like nearly all the buildings in Lucky Harbor, was a restored Victorian from the late 1800s. It was a pale pink with blue-and-white trim and lit from the inside. The front door was wide open and inviting, at least compared to the rest of the night around her.

Aubrey wasn't a churchgoer. Her surgeon father hadn't believed in anything other than what could be found in a science book. Cold, hard facts. As a result, churches always held a sort of morbid fascination for her, one she'd never given in to. But with Ben possibly still on her trail, she hurried up the walk and stepped inside. Trying to catch her breath, she turned around to see if she'd been followed.

"Good evening," a man said behind her.

She jumped and looked around. He was in his thirties, average height and build, wearing jeans, a cable-knit sweater, and a smile that was as welcoming as the building itself.

But Aubrey didn't trust welcoming much.

"Can I help you?" he asked.

"No, thanks." Unable to resist, she once again peered outside.

No sign of Ben. That was only a slight relief. She felt like the fly who'd lost track of the spider.

"Are you sure you're okay?" the man asked. "You seem…troubled."

She resisted the urge to sigh. She was sure he was very nice, but what was it with the male species? Why was it so hard to believe she didn't need a man's help? Or a man, period? "Please don't take this personally, but I'm giving up men. Forever."

If he was fazed by her abruptness, it didn't show. Instead, his eyes crinkled in good humor as he slid his hands into his pockets and rocked back on his heels. "I'm the pastor here. Pastor Mike," he said. "A happily married man," he added with an easy smile.

If that didn't cap off her evening—realizing she'd been rude to a man of God for having the audacity to be nice to her. "I'm sorry." It didn't escape her notice that this was now the *second* time tonight she'd said those two very foreign words. "My life's in the toilet today…well, every day this week so far, really."

His eyes were warm and sympathetic. The opposite, she couldn't help but note, of the way Ben's had been.

"We all have rough patches," he said. "Is there anything I can do?"

She shook her head. "No. It's all me. I just need to stop making the same mistakes over and over." She took another peek into the night. The coast seemed clear. "Okay, I'm out. I'm going home to have the stiff drink I missed out on earlier at the bar."

"What's your name?" Pastor Mike asked.

She considered lying, but didn't want to further tempt fate—or God, or whoever was in charge of such things. "Aubrey."

"You don't have to be alone, Aubrey," he said very kindly, managing to sound gentle and in charge at the same time. "You're in a good place here."

She didn't have a chance to reply before he'd gently nudged her into a meeting room where about ten people were seated in a circle.

A woman was standing, wringing her hands. "My name's Kathy," she said to the group, "and it's been an hour since I last craved a drink."

The entire group said in unison, "Hi, Kathy."

An AA meeting, Aubrey realized, swallowing what

would have been a half-hysterical laugh as Pastor Mike gestured to a few empty chairs. He sat next to her and handed her a pamphlet. One glance told her it was a list of the twelve steps to recovery.

Step one: We admitted we were powerless over alcohol—that our lives had become unmanageable.

Oh, boy. Aubrey could probably get on board with the unmanageable life part, but really, what was she doing here? What would she possibly say to these people if she were asked to speak? *Hi, my name is Aubrey, and I'm a bitchaholic?*

Kathy began to speak about step eight, about how she was making a list of the people she'd wronged and making amends. After she finished and sat down, a man stood. Ryan, he told them. Ryan talked about something called his fearless moral inventory and how he, too, was working on step eight, making amends to the people he'd wronged.

Aubrey bit her lip. She'd never taken a fearless moral inventory, but it sounded daunting. Nor did she have a list of people she'd wronged, but if she did, it would be long. Horrifyingly long.

Ryan continued to talk with heartbreaking earnestness, and somehow, in spite of herself, she couldn't help but soak it all in, unbearably moved by his bravery. He'd come back from a military stint overseas angry and withdrawn and had driven his family away. He'd lost his job, his home, everything, until he'd found himself homeless on the street, begging strangers for money to buy booze. He spoke of how much he regretted hurting the people in his life and how he hadn't been able to obtain forgiveness from them. At least not yet, but he was still trying.

Aubrey found herself truly listening and marveling at his courage. She didn't even realize that she was so transfixed until Mike gently patted her hand. "You see?" he asked quietly. "It's never too late."

Aubrey stared at him, wondering if that could really be true. "You don't know for sure."

"I do." He said this with such conviction that she had no choice but to believe.

She thought about that as the meeting ended and she walked home to her loft above the Book & Bean. Her aunt Gwen had run the bookstore until her death last year, and her uncle—the building's owner—hadn't been able to bring himself to lease the space to anyone else. He was dating someone new these days, but the bookstore was still very sentimental to him.

Then, last month, Aubrey had left her job at the town hall after what she referred to as the Ted Incident. Restless, needing more from her life but not sure what, she'd signed a lease, both as an homage to her aunt Gwen—the bookstore had been a refuge for Aubrey as a troubled teen—and because she was determined to bring the bookstore back to its former glory.

The Book & Bean had been unofficially open for a week now, so it could start bringing in some desperately needed income, and in a month—after some renovations—she had plans to celebrate with a big grand opening party.

She was working on that.

And maybe she should be working on other things as well, such as her karma. That was heavy on her mind now after the AA meeting. Hearing people's problems and how they were trying to change things up for themselves had been extremely intimate and extremely uncomfortable—and yet somehow inspiring at the same time. She wasn't an alcoholic, but she had to admit the whole step eight thing had really intrigued her.

Could it be as easy as that, as making a list? Checking it twice? Trying to find out if she could pass on naughty and move on to nice?

Skipping the front entrance of the bookstore, she walked around to the back of the building and let herself in without turning on any lights. Inside, she headed up the narrow stairs to the loft.

Meow.

She flipped on a light and eyed Gus, an old, overweight gray cat who thought he was king of the mountain. She'd inherited him with the store. She knew nothing about cats, and in return, he acted like he knew nothing about humans, so they were even. "Hey," she said. "How was your evening?"

Gus turned around and presented her with his back.

"You know," she said, "I understand that some cats actually greet their people when they come home."

They'd had this talk before, and as always, this prompted no response from Gus.

"A dog would greet me," she said. "Maybe I should get a dog."

At this threat, Gus yawned.

Aubrey dropped her purse, hung up her coat, and took her first real breath in the past few hours. The place was tiny but cozy, and it was all hers ever since she'd filled it with an assortment of vintage—a.k.a. garage-sale and thrift-store—furniture. Her favorite part was the dartboard she'd gotten for a buck. It was a great stress reliever, especially when she pictured Ted's smug face as the bull's-eye.

Her kitchen table was covered with the drawings she'd made—her ideas for changing the layout of the store below.

Now that the other two storefronts in this building held flourishing businesses—a flower shop and a bakery—she had high hopes her bookstore would do well, too. A pipe dream. She was working against the odds, she knew. After all, this was the age of Kindle, Nook, and Kobo. Most people thought she was crazy for facing off against the digital world. But Aubrey had made a lifelong habit of facing off against the world, so why stop now, right? Besides, there was still a place for print books; she believed that with all her heart. And it was a statement of fact that sales in indie bookstores were up about 8 percent this year.

She was going to take heart in that. She pulled the pamphlet from her pocket and thought about her karma, which undoubtedly could use a little boost. Grabbing the small notepad she used for list making, she began a new list—of people she'd wronged.

Meow, Gus said, bumping her arm.

Reaching down, she stroked his soft fur, which he tolerated even though they both knew he just wanted dinner. She poured him a small cup of the low-calorie dry food the vet had insisted she switch to.

Gus stared at her balefully.

"I promised the doc," she said.

Huffing out a sigh, Gus heaved himself off to bed.

Aubrey went back to her list. It took her a while, and when she was done, she eyeballed the length of it. Surely it would've been a lot easier to simply stand tall and face Ben tonight rather than run into Pastor Mike.

But though Aubrey had a lot of faults, being lazy wasn't one of them. She was doing this, making amends, come hell or high water.

And there was a good chance she'd face both before this was over.

Kicking off her boots, she leaned back, staring at the list. Specifically at one item in particular.

Ben.

And he wasn't on it because she'd tossed her drink in his face.

Chapter 2

♥

It was early when Ben walked out of Lucky Harbor's deliciously warm bakery and into the icy morning. His breath crystallized in front of his face as he took a bite from his fresh bear claw.

As close to heaven as he was going to get.

He glanced back inside the big picture window to wave his thanks, but pastry chef Leah currently had her arms and lips entangled with her fiancé, who happened to be Ben's cousin Jack.

Jack looked to be pretty busy himself, with his tongue down Leah's throat. Turning his back to the window, Ben watched the morning instead as he ate his bear claw. Tendrils of fog had glided in off the water, lingering in long, silvery fingers.

After a few minutes, the bakery door opened behind him, and then Jack was standing at his side. He was in uniform for work, which meant that every woman driving down the street slowed down to get a look at him in his firefighter gear.

"Why are you dressed?" Ben asked.

"Because when I'm naked, I actually cause riots," Jack said, sliding on his sunglasses.

"You know what I mean." Not too long ago, Jack had made the change from firefighting to being the fire marshal, and he no longer suited up to respond to calls.

Jack shrugged. "I'm working a shift today for Ian, who's down with the flu." He pulled his own breakfast choice out of a bakery bag.

Ben took one look at the cheese croissant and shook his head. "Pussy breakfast."

Unperturbed by this, Jack stuffed it into his mouth. "You're just still grumpy because a pretty lady tossed her drink in your face last night."

Ben didn't react to this, because Jack was watching him carefully, and Jack, unlike anyone else, could read Ben like a book. But yeah, Aubrey had nailed him—and not in a good way.

Not that he wanted the sexy-as-hell blonde to nail him. Well, okay, maybe she'd occasionally done just that in a few of his late-night fantasies, but that was it. Fantasy. Because the reality was that he and Aubrey wouldn't mix well. He liked quiet, serene, calm. Aubrey didn't know the meaning of any of those things.

"It was an accident," he finally said.

"Oh, I know that," Jack said. "Just checking to see if you know it, too."

Ben looked at his watch. "Luke's late."

The three of them had been tight since age twelve, when Ben's mom, unable to take care of him any longer, had dropped him on her sister's doorstep—Jack's mom, Dee Harper. Luke had lived next door. The three boys had spent their teen years terrorizing the neighborhood and giving Ben's aunt Dee lots of gray hair.

"Luke's not late," Jack said. "He's here. He's in the flower shop trying to get into Ali's back pocket. Guess that's what you do when you're engaged."

Ben didn't say anything to this, and Jack blew out a breath. "Sorry."

Ben shook his head. "Been a long time."

"Yeah," Jack said. "But some things never stop hurting."

Maybe not. But it really had been forever ago that Ben had been engaged and then married. He and Hannah had had a solid marriage.

Until she'd died five years ago.

Ben went after his second bear claw while Jack looked down at his vibrating phone. "Shit. I've gotta go. Tell Luke he's an asshole."

"Will do." When he was alone again, Ben washed down his breakfast with icy cold chocolate milk. *You drink too much caffeine*, Leah had told him, all bossy and sweet at the same time, handing him the milk instead of a mug of coffee.

He planned to stop at the convenience store next for that coffee, and she'd never know. It was early, not close to seven yet, but Ben liked early. Fewer people. Quiet air. Or maybe that was just Lucky Harbor. Either way, he found he was nearly content—coffee would probably tip the scales *all the way* to content. The feeling felt…odd, like he was wearing an ill-fitting coat, so, as he did with all uncomfortable emotions, he shoved it aside.

A few snowflakes floated lazily out of the low, dense clouds. One block over, the Pacific Ocean carved into the harbor, which was surrounded by rugged, three-story-high bluffs teeming with the untouched forestland that was the Olympic Mountains. Around him, the oak-lined streets were strung with white lights, shining brightly through the morning gloom. Peaceful. Still.

A month ago, he'd been in the Middle East, elbows deep in a project to rebuild a water system for a war-torn land. Before that, he'd been in Haiti. And before that, Africa. And before that…Indonesia? Hell, it might have been another planet for all he remembered. It was all rolling together.

He went to places after disaster hit, whether man-made or natural, and he saw people at their very worst moments. Sometimes he changed lives, sometimes he improved them, but at some point over the past five years he'd become numb to it. So much so that when he'd gone to check out a new job site at the wrong place, only to have the right place blown to bits by a suicide bomber just before he got there, he'd finally realized something.

He didn't always have to be the guy on the front line. He could design and plan water systems for devastated countries from anywhere. Hell, he could become a consultant instead. Five years of wading knee deep in crap, both figuratively and literally, was enough for anyone. He didn't want to be in the *right* hellhole next time.

So he'd come home, with no idea what was next.

Polishing off his second bear claw, Ben sucked the sugar off his thumb. Turning to head toward his truck, he stopped short at the realization that someone stood watching him.

Aubrey. When he caught her eye, she said, "It *is* you," and dropped the things in her hands.

Her tone of voice had suggested she'd just stepped in dog shit with her fancy high-heeled boots. This didn't surprise Ben. She'd been two years behind him in school. In those years, he'd either been on the basketball court, trouble-seeking with Jack, or spending time with Hannah.

Aubrey had been the Hot Girl. He didn't know why, but there'd always been an instinctive mistrust between them, as if they both recognized that they were two kindred souls—*troubled* souls. He remembered that when she'd first entered high school she'd had more than a few run-ins with the mean girls. Then she became a mean girl. Crouching down, he reached to help her with the stuff she'd dropped.

"I've got it," she snapped, squatting next to him, pushing his hands away. "I'm fine."

She certainly looked the part of fine. Her long blonde hair was loose and shiny, held back from her face by a pale blue knit cap. A matching scarf was wrapped around her neck and tucked into a white wool coat that covered her from her chin to a few inches above her knees. Leather boots met those knees, leaving some bare skin below the hem of her coat. She looked sophisticated and hot as hell. Certainly perfectly put together. In fact, she was always purposefully put together.

It made him want to ruffle her up. A crazy thought.

Even crazier, she smelled so good he wanted to just sniff her for about five days. Also, he wanted to know what she was wearing beneath that coat. "Where did you come from?" he asked, as no car had pulled up.

"The building."

There were three storefronts in the building, one of the oldest in town—the flower shop, the bakery, and the bookstore. She hadn't come out of the flower shop or the bakery, he knew that much. He glanced at the bookstore. "It's not open yet."

The windows were no longer boarded up, he realized, and through the glass panes, he could see that the old bookstore was now a new bookstore, as shiny and clean and pretty as the woman before him.

She scooped up a pen and a lipstick, and he grabbed a fallen notebook.

"That's mine," she said.

"I wasn't going to take it, Aubrey," he said, and then, with no idea of what came over him—maybe her flashing eyes—he held the notebook just out of her reach as he looked at it. It was small and, like Aubrey herself, neat and tidy. Just a regular pad of paper, spiral bound, opened to a page she'd written on.

"Give it to me, Ben."

The notebook was nothing special, but clearly his holding on to it was making her uncomfortable. If it had been any other woman on the planet, he'd have handed it right over. But he didn't.

She narrowed her sharp, hazel eyes at him as she waggled impatient fingers. "It's just my grocery list."

Grocery list his ass. It was a list of names, and there was a Ben on it. "Is this me?"

"Wow," she said. "Egocentric much?"

"It says Ben."

"No, it doesn't." She tried to snatch at it again, but if there was one thing that living in Third World countries did for you it was give you quick instincts.

"Look here," he said, pointing to item number four. "*Ben*."

"It's Ben and Jerry's. *Ice cream*," she informed him. "Shorthand. Give me the damn notepad."

Hmm. He might've been inclined to believe her, except there was that slight panic in her gaze, the one she hadn't been able to hide quickly enough. Straightening, he skimmed the names and realized he recognized a few. "Cathy Wheaton," he said, frowning. "Why do I remember that name?"

"You don't." Straightening as well, Aubrey tried to crawl up his body to reach the pad.

Ben wasn't too ashamed to admit he liked that. A lot.

His jacket was open. Frustrated, she fisted a hand in the material of his shirt, right over his heart. "Damn it, Ben—"

"Wait...I remember," he said, wincing, since she now had a few chest hairs in a tight grip. "Cathy...she was the grade in between us, right? A little skinny? Okay, a *lot* skinny. Nice girl."

Keeping her hold of him, Aubrey went still as stone, and Ben watched her carefully. Yeah, he was right about Cathy, and he went back to the list. "Mrs. Cappernackle." He looked at her again. "The librarian?"

With her free hand, Aubrey pulled her phone from her pocket and looked pointedly at the time.

He ignored this, because once his curiosity was piqued, he was like a dog with a bone, and his curiosity was definitely tweaked. "Sue Henderson." He paused, thinking. Remembering. "Wasn't she your neighbor when you were growing up? That bitchy DA who had you arrested when you put food coloring in her pool and turned it green?"

Aubrey's eyes were fascinating. Hazel fire. "Give. Me. My. List."

Oh, hell, no, this was just getting good—"Ouch!"

She'd twisted the grip she'd had on his shirt, yanking out the few hairs she'd fisted. She also got a better grip on the pad so that now they were tug-o-warring over it. "You could just tell me what this is about," he said.

"It's none of your business," she said, fighting him. "That's what it is."

"But it *is* my business when you're carrying around a list with my name on it."

"You know what? Google the name Ben and see how many there are. Now let go!" she demanded, just as the door to the flower shop opened and a uniformed officer walked out.

Luke, with his impeccable timing, as always. Eyeing the tussle before him, he raised a brow. "What's up, kids?"

"Officer," Aubrey said, voice cool, eyes cooler, as she jerked the pad from Ben's fingers. She shoved it into her purse, zipped it, and tugged it higher up on her shoulder. "This man"—she broke off to stab a finger in Ben's direction, as if there were any question about which man she meant—"is bothering me."

"Lucky Harbor's beloved troublemaker Ben McDaniel is bothering you?" Luke grinned. "I could arrest him for you."

"Could you maybe just shoot him?" she asked hopefully.

Luke's grin widened as he gave Ben a speculative glance. "Sure, but there'd be a bunch of paperwork, and I hate paperwork. How about I just beat him up a little bit?"

Aubrey looked as though this idea worked for her.

Ben gave her a long, steely look, and she rolled her eyes. "Oh, never mind." Still hugging her purse to herself, she turned, unlocked the bookstore, and vanished back inside it, slamming the door behind her.

"I thought the store was closed," Ben said, absently rubbing his chest where he was missing those few hairs.

"It was," Luke said. "Mr. Lyons is her uncle, and she rented the place from him and reopened the store. She's gone with a soft opening for now because she needs the income from the store, but she's wants to have a grand opening when the renovations are finished."

"How do you know so much?" Ben asked.

"Because I know all. And because Mr. Lyons called. He needs a carpenter, so I gave him your number."

"Mine?" Ben asked.

Luke shrugged. "Everyone in town knows you're good with a hammer."

"Yeah." Ben's phone rang, and he looked at the unfamiliar local number.

Luke looked, too. "That's him," he said. "Mr. Lyons."

Ben resisted the urge to do his usual and hit IGNORE. "McDaniel," he answered.

"Don't say no yet," Mr. Lyons immediately said. "I need a carpenter."

Ben slid Luke a look. "So I've heard. I'm not a carpenter. I'm an engineer."

"You know damn well before you got all dark and mysterious and broody that you were also handy with a set of tools," Mr. Lyons said.

Luke, who could hear Mr. Lyons's booming voice, grinned like the Cheshire cat and nodded, pointing at Ben.

Ben flipped him off. An older woman driving down the street rolled down her window and tsked at him. He waved at her in apology but she just waggled her bony finger at him. "Why not hire Jax?" he asked Lyons. "He's the best carpenter in town."

"He's got a line of customers from Lucky Harbor to Seattle, and I don't want to wait. My niece Aubrey needs help renovating the bookstore, and she needs someone good. That's you. Now I know damn well she can't afford you, so I'm paying, in my sweet Gwen's memory."

Well, shit.

"Oh, and don't give Aubrey the bill," Mr. Lyons said. "I don't want her worrying about it. She's going through some stuff, and I want to do this for her. For both my girls."

Ah, hell, Ben thought, feeling himself soften. He was such a sucker. "You should be asking me for a bid," he said.

"I trust you."

Jesus. "You shouldn't," Ben said firmly. "You—"

"Just start the damn work, McDaniel. Shelves. Paint. Hang stuff. Move a few walls, whatever she wants. She said something about how the place is too closed-in and dark, so figure it out. I'm going on a month-long cruise with my new girl, Elsie, and I need to know before I leave. You in or not?"

Ben wanted to say no. *Hell, no.* Being closed up in that bookstore with the beautiful, bitchy Aubrey for days and days? The reality of that didn't escape him. If he did this, surely one of them would kill the other before the work was done.

"Ben?"

"Yeah," he said, facing the inevitable. "I'll do it."

Whether he'd survive it was another thing entirely.

Chapter 3

♥

Two days later, Audrey opened her bookstore bright and early, much to Gus's annoyance. He liked to sleep in. Ignoring the curmudgeonly cat's dirty look, she took a moment to just look around. Despite her efforts, the store was still too closed-in and stuffy. She wanted to open it up by moving shelves back against the walls and adding a coffee and tea station. Definitely an Internet café and a comfortable seating area for a variety of reading and social clubs that she'd host here.

She wanted it more spacious. Sunny. Bright.

And God, please, *successful*...

Half an hour later, she welcomed her first customers of the day—a van of senior citizens. She'd coaxed the senior center into driving them over here two mornings a week for their book club.

"Hey, chickie," Mr. Elroy said, leaning heavily on his cane. He was decades past a midlife crisis, but he still managed to be quite the lothario at the senior center. "Which aisle has the sex stuff?"

He meant the how-to manuals. Anticipating him, she'd hidden any and all books on sex on the bottom shelf of the self-help aisle. No one ever went to that aisle. "Sorry," she said. "Don't have any."

"Really? Didn't anyone ever tell you that sex sells?"

Mr. Wykowski had come in behind Mr. Elroy. "You need a manual?" he asked Mr. Elroy. "All I need is a little blue pill."

And so went the morning.

When the seniors were gone, a bus full of kids showed up, as Aubrey had also made a deal with the elementary school.

The kids managed to find the sex manuals. Luckily, Aubrey was quick on the uptake and confiscated the explicit reading material before a single book spine got cracked. By the time they left, she was exhausted. In the past week, she'd learned several vital facts. One: Seniors and kids were a lot alike. And two: She wasn't making enough money for this.

By lunchtime she was back to daydreaming about the "bean" part of Book & Bean. Right now she was using a back corner, which was really a storage closet, to make tea and coffee. She wanted to remove the door and wall and replace them with a curved, waist-high counter that would create a coffee and reading niche. She ate a PB&J while perusing the Internet for affordable bar stools for the spot.

But for now, most everything she wanted was out of her budget. She knew she could ask her father for help, but she'd have to choke on her own pride to call him, and she wasn't good at that.

So instead she'd gone to the local hardware store and bought a book on renovation. She'd read it from beginning to end and thought she could handle some of the easy stuff on her own. She planned to tear out the closet herself, and she'd brought in the crowbar from the back of her car to do just that.

Clearly, it'd be far easier to suck it up and call her dad, but she rarely took the easy route. Her parents had divorced when she'd been ten and her sister, Carla, eight. Her father, William, retired from being an orthopedic surgeon, was a consultant now, but still he had a hard time talking to mere mortals. Not her mom. Tammy was an ex–beauty queen working as a manicurist at the local beauty shop, and she loved to talk. In the divorce, she'd gotten Aubrey, and William had taken the child prodigy, Carla.

An unorthodox custody arrangement, but it'd allowed the divorced couple to stay away from each other and avoid arguments. It'd also alienated Aubrey from her father, who'd recently remarried and had two new daughters now. Plus Carla had followed in his footsteps and was a first-year resident at the hospital, heading toward the same brilliant career path as her dad.

And then there was Aubrey. Living with Tammy had meant that the pressure of an Ivy League school and a medical career were off the table, but there'd been other pressures. Tammy had been the ultimate beauty queen and had turned into a beauty-queen mom, entering Aubrey in every beauty pageant and talent competition she could afford. There'd been many—at least until Aubrey had gotten old enough to put her foot down and refuse to put on one more tiara. She'd been thirteen when that had happened.

That's when the pressure to be a model had begun, but after a few disastrous auditions, even Tammy had been forced to admit defeat. Not that she'd ever given up impressing upon Aubrey the importance of beauty, the right lipstick color, and posture. Aubrey had taken every dance class known to man and also gone to grace school. Yes, there really was a school for that. Her mother'd had to work two jobs to pay for it all, but she'd been happy to do it. Or so she'd claimed every single night when she'd come home, kick off her shoes, and sag in exhaustion onto the couch.

Sugar, could you make Mama a gin and tonic?

Aubrey had hated those classes. Hated. But her mom had given up so much for her, so she'd done it. She'd learned early how to primp, walk with a thick book on top of her head—even if she'd rather be reading it—and look ready for the camera in fifteen minutes. And in spite of herself, she'd even managed to get a BA degree in liberal studies from an online institution. She had the tuition loans to prove it.

The last time she'd talked to her dad, he'd questioned her as though she were a three-year-old. "A bookstore, Aubrey? In today's day and age? Why don't you find a better use of your money—say, like shredding it?"

But she loved books. Maybe she wasn't exactly a traditional bookworm, but she could quote Robert Louis Stevenson poems, and she loved mysteries. She'd always been a big reader, back from when she'd been a child and had come here after school.

Her aunt would serve her tea and cookies and let Aubrey curl up in a corner and just be free—free of wondering why she wasn't good enough to be wanted by her own father, free of her mom's pressure to look perfect and be something she wasn't. Free of trying to fit in at school and failing. Back then, she'd huddled here in this warm place and inhaled books to escape. She'd started with the classics but had quickly found thrillers and horror, which she still loved to this day.

But back then, being here, being left in peace and quiet…it'd been her idea of heaven.

And maybe, just a little bit, she'd reopened the store hoping for that same safe place to curl up and lick her wounds.

Not exactly the smartest reason to open a bookstore. She knew better than anyone that memories and sentiment didn't a business plan make, and that a business certainly shouldn't be run from the heart.

But Aubrey had rarely, if ever, operated from her heart, and it hadn't gotten her anywhere. Time to try something new. The bookstore was new thing number one.

Her list was number two.

The door to the store opened, and Aubrey smiled a greeting at the woman who entered. "Can I help you?"

"I'm looking for some fiction. Historical fiction."

In one short week, Aubrey had learned that "historical fiction" didn't usually mean the classics. Instead, it almost always meant the romance section. She pointed the way and, a few minutes later, sold a copy of the Fifty Shades trilogy.

During a late-afternoon lull in business, Aubrey went to work on demolishing the closet wall.

Halfway through, the bell above her door rang. Naturally. Dusting herself off, she moved into view just as another woman came in.

"I'm looking for something to take with me on vacay next week," she told Aubrey.

"What do you like to read?"

"Oh," she said, "a little of everything…"

Aubrey knew this *also* meant the romance section, so she again pointed the way.

The woman leaned in close and whispered, "Do you carry that *Fifty Shades* book? And maybe…book covers?"

Aubrey was back to attempting to demolish the back wall when the bell rang again.

A woman entered with her three little kids and one of those tiny dogs that looked like a drowned rat in her shoulder bag. The thing was yapping as though his life were in mortal danger.

From his perch in a nook beneath the stairs, Gus, three times the size of the dog, growled low in his throat.

The dog immediately shut up. Probably terrified that the cat was going to sit on him. Aubrey gave Gus a warning look. They'd had this talk. There would be no bitch-slapping the customers, even the four-legged ones.

Gus stalked off all stiff-legged, with his tail swishing in the air. Aubrey reached out and stroked the little dog's head, and he pushed closer for more.

For just about all her life, she'd wanted a dog, preferably a puppy—one of the big breeds. She'd begged and pleaded her case, but her dad—pre-divorce—had always been firm.

Puppies make noise.

Puppies are messy.

No puppies, he'd always said. Ever. For a while there, Aubrey had actually believed she could get him to change his mind. She'd even rescued a dog once and brought it home, convinced her father wouldn't be able to turn away a stray.

The puppy had been gone the next day. "The owners came and got him," her dad had said. "He's living on a farm in the country."

After her mom had divorced her dad, Aubrey had gone to work on her mom. Tammy loved dogs and was on board. But they'd lived in a pet-unfriendly building, and that had never changed.

Aubrey had never gotten her puppy.

And now she had a fat, old-man cat named Gus.

Her customer, looking harassed and exhausted, sent the kids to the children's section and smiled wanly at Aubrey. "What would you recommend for me to read?"

"What do you like?"

"Anything."

Aubrey nodded. She'd found that this was rarely actually true: In fact, it usually meant that the person wasn't a reader at all. "What's the last book you read and enjoyed?" she asked, looking for a hint just in case she was wrong.

"Uh…I can't remember."

Nope, not wrong. Aubrey directed her to the latest Nicholas Sparks. After the sale, she went back to the demolition.

The other day, she'd put a bucket of books just outside the store. They were gently used cookbooks, encyclopedias, and miscellaneous nonfiction. The cookbooks had vanished almost immediately. The other books still sat out there, and despite the fact that she had a big FREE sign posted, every day at least one person would stick his or her head in the door and yell, "Are these really free?"

Today it was a twentysomething guy wearing a ski cap, down jacket, bright yellow biker shorts, and round purple sunglasses, à la John Lennon. Mikey had been a couple of years behind Aubrey in school, and by the looks of things, was still a complete stoner.

"Dude," he said. "Are these books really free?"

"Yep," she told him.

His brow went up, and he surveyed the store. "So…is everything free?"

"Nope."

"'Kay. Thanks, dude."

At the end of the day, Aubrey tallied the sales, got the day's new arrivals stocked and shelved, and locked up. Seeing the lights still on in the flower shop, she moved down two doors and knocked on the back door.

Ali opened up, wearing a T-shirt, jeans, an apron, and lots of flower petals. She smiled and pulled Aubrey in. "You're just in time. Leah brought over her leftovers, and I'm about to inhale them all by myself."

Leah operated the bakery between Aubrey's bookstore and Ali's flower shop. She was sitting on the counter near Ali's work space, licking chocolate off her fingers. "Better hurry," she said. "Ali wasn't kidding. There's two kinds of people here, the quick and the hungry."

Not needing to be told twice, Aubrey moved toward the bakery box and helped herself to a mini chocolate croissant. No one made them like Leah. "Oh, my God," she said on a moan after her first bite. "*So* good. I've been tearing up that back wall and am starving."

"I hate you," Leah said.

Aubrey felt herself go still and, out of a lifetime habit of hiding her feelings, schooled her features into a cool

expression that she knew was often mistaken for bitchi-
ness. "What?"

"You just worked for hours without getting a speck of
dirt on you?"

Aubrey looked down at herself. "Well—"

"And your hair is perfect," Ali broke in, taking in
Aubrey's appearance. "I hate that about you."

Leah nodded.

Both of them had businesses running in the black, hot-
as-hell boyfriends who loved them madly, and their lives
on track. And they were jealous. Of her.

It was just about the nicest compliment they could pay
her, and she went back to breathing. She should have
known they weren't being mean—neither of them had a
mean bone in her body. "Lifelong habit," she said. "Being
perfect."

Leah laughed and offered another goody from the bakery box. "You could at least get chunky. Or a little dirty,
just once in a while."

"I don't usually get dirty."

Ali shook her head. "Back to hating you, Wellington."

Aubrey smiled now and reached for the last mini croissant at the same time as Ali. "I'll totally fight you for it,"
she said.

Ali grinned. "I could kick your skinny ass, but since
the croissant will just go straight to my hips, it's all
yours."

Aubrey took a bite of the croissant, licked her fingers
clean, and then pulled her laptop out of her bag. "I finally
got Internet, and I'm trying to decide what to name my
Wi-Fi. I'm torn between FBI Security Van and Guy in
Your Tree. Any opinions?"

Leah snorted chocolate milk out her nose.

"How about Pay for Your Own Effing Wi-Fi, You Cheap Ass?" Ali asked.

They laughed for a few minutes, cleaned up their croissant crumbs, and then Leah dropped the bomb. "Heard about Ben," she said.

Aubrey nearly dropped her laptop. "Um…what?" Her heart was thundering, but she was telling herself that they couldn't know. *No one* knew. Not even Ben himself.

Leah was looking at her oddly. "The whole tossing-your-drink-in-his-face thing at the Love Shack the other night," she said.

Oh, *that*. Aubrey relaxed. "It was an accident. I was aiming for Ted." She took a side look at Ali because one of the most weaselly, shitty things Ted had done was sleep with *both* Ali and Aubrey while letting them each think that he was single. And they hadn't been the only women he'd done that to, either.

Aubrey had recovered quickly because…well, she knew men were jerks.

Ali had been thrown for an emotional loop, and, clearly remembering just that, she smiled grimly. "I hope you ordered a second drink and corrected your error."

Aubrey shook her head. "I got…discombobulated."

"You?" Ali asked. "Pissed off, yes. But discombobulated? That's not like you."

Yeah, Aubrey was *real* good at the tough-girl facade. But then again, she'd had a lifetime of practice. "Hard to keep it together when you toss a drink in the wrong guy's face."

"And not just any wrong guy," Leah said with a laugh.

"Ben McDaniel. Lucky Harbor's favorite son. How'd he take it?"

Aubrey shook her head at the memory. "He didn't even flinch."

"He wouldn't," Leah said. "He's pretty badass."

He hadn't always been like that. In school, he'd been the first to land himself in trouble, but he'd been fun-seeking, not tough as nails and impenetrable. Even through college. Afterward, he'd been an engineer for the city and had led a nice normal life.

Then his wife had died, and he'd taken off like a bat out of hell, living a life of adrenaline and danger as if survivor's guilt had driven his every move.

"It was his job," Leah said. "He saw and did things that changed him."

Ali was watching Aubrey carefully. "Maybe you should try to make it up to him."

Aubrey could see a certain light—a matchmaking light—in her eyes, so she headed to the door.

"Where you going?" Leah asked.

"Things to do."

"Or you're chicken," Ali called after her with a laugh.

Or that…But the truth was, Aubrey wasn't chicken. She was realistic. Nothing would, or could, ever happen between her and Ben.

No matter how much she might secretly wish otherwise.

Two minutes later, she was in her car. It was time to face the names on her list. Up first was her sister, Carla.

They weren't close. Growing up in two separate households had done that. Living with parents who didn't speak to each other had done that. Carla being told that she had gotten all the brains had done that.

But eight years ago, Carla had needed a favor. She'd found herself needing to be at her job at the same time as she'd needed to sign some documents to accept a very important internship, so she'd asked her look-alike sister to go sign for her.

Aubrey had been working her butt off full-time and trying to keep full-time school hours as well. Busy, exhausted, hungry, and admittedly bitchy, Aubrey had agreed to the favor, even though she'd known it would be a real crunch to get there in time. She'd left a little later than she should have, gotten stuck in traffic, showed up late, and lost Carla the internship.

Carla had been forced to ask their dad to step in, and she still hadn't forgiven Aubrey.

Sighing at the memory, Aubrey parked at the hospital where Carla worked and asked for her sister at the front desk. Aubrey was kept cooling her heels for twenty-five minutes, though when Carla finally showed up in the reception area in scrubs and a doctor's coat with a stethoscope around her neck, she seemed genuinely exhausted and surprised. "Hey," she said. "What's wrong? Mom?"

"Everything's fine," Aubrey said. "I just wanted to talk to you."

Carla nodded but gave her watch a quick, not-so-discreet glance. "About?"

Aubrey drew a deep breath and then let it go. "Remember the time you asked me for a favor and I screwed it up?"

Carla's gaze was moving around the room, taking in the people waiting to be called by the hospital's various departments. "Uh-huh."

"Well, I want to apologize," Aubrey said, "and find a way to make it up to you."

Carla looked at her watch again. "Wait—which time was this again?"

"The one and only time I screwed up," Aubrey said a little tightly.

Carla's gaze landed on Aubrey then, looking a little amused now. She pulled a protein bar from her pocket and offered half to Aubrey, but since it looked like cardboard, Aubrey shook her head. "It was when I was supposed to sign those documents for your internship," Aubrey said. "And I got there late."

Carla chewed her cardboard bar. "Oh, that's right. You were probably busy with Mom, having your hair or nails done. That was your life, right? Dressing up and being a beauty queen, while I had to go to the toughest school and study all the time."

Aubrey had been operating under the assumption that *she* was the jealous sister. And she *was* jealous as hell and always had been, because Carla had had it all: brains, the big fancy medical degree, not to mention their father's pride and adoration. But in feeding her green monster over the years, it'd somehow escaped her attention that Carla might have been jealous as well.

She didn't know what to make of that.

"I lost the internship," Carla said, "and had to wait an entire year to get another shot at it. Dad was fit to be tied. He'd set the interview up in the first place. He said—" She broke off, clearly tempering herself.

"What?" Aubrey asked. "He said what?"

"That I'd acted like you."

Aubrey absorbed the unexpected hit and nodded.

"Well, then, I imagine he was quite pleased to know it was me who screwed up and not you."

Carla's smile was brittle, and Aubrey wondered if she smiled like that, too. "I never told him," Carla said. "How could I? I'd gone on and on about how you were changing, how you were maturing. How I could *count on you*."

Aubrey winced. "I'm sorry," she said quietly. "I'd like to make it up to you."

Carla gave a small laugh. "How? How could you possibly do that?"

"I don't know," Aubrey said. "We still look like twins. Maybe you have another conflict of interest, and I could—"

"What? Operate for me? Meet a patient and discuss treatment?"

Aubrey met her sister's eyes. They were hazel, like her own, magnified slightly from the glasses Carla had worn since grade school. They only added to the smart image.

She wasn't going to get forgiveness—she could see that now. And she probably didn't deserve it anyway. "No," she said quietly. "I can't do any of those things. We both know that."

And there was the problem. The big flaw in her grand scheme—and there was always a flaw. She didn't know *how* to make things right. And anyway, who would forgive her? She certain didn't deserve forgiveness. Holding in the despair that this thought brought, she turned to go.

Carla didn't stop her.

It was dark outside when she got back to the Book & Bean, and she stopped short just outside the door. She'd locked up when she left and turned off the lights.

But the door was unlocked now, and the lights were

on. She went still, then pulled out her phone and dialed 911. She didn't hit SEND, but kept her thumb hovered over CALL. Taking a step inside, she paused. "Hello?"

"Hey."

The low, slightly rough voice wasn't what had her heart pumping. That honor went to the fact that there was a man on a ladder in the back of her store.

Ben.

He was in jeans, wearing a tool belt slung low on his hips, his T-shirt clinging to him. He seemed a little irritated, a little sweaty, and just looking at him Aubrey got a whole lot hot and bothered in places that had no business being hot and bothered by this man at all. "What are you doing in here?" she asked.

"I work here."

"What are you talking about? Get out."

"Sorry, Sunshine." He wasn't even looking at her, but using some sort of long, clawlike tool to pull down a ceiling tile above the wall she'd been working on. And his tool worked way better than hers.

His movements were agile and surprisingly graceful for a guy his size. Not that he was bulky in any way. Nope: That tall, built body was all lean, tough muscle, and it screamed power. And with each subtle movement, his body made it clear that it knew exactly what to do with all that power. "The owner of this building hired me," he said. "Said you were making a mess of things because your pride was bigger than your wallet."

This caught her completely off guard, both the insult and the information. "My uncle owns this building," she said.

He smiled thinly. "Yep. Happy birthday."

"It's not my birthday."

"Then happy you've-got-a-great-uncle day."

She pulled out her phone and punched in her uncle's number.

"He left on a month-long cruise with Elsie," Ben said.

Damn it. That was true. He'd just recently started dating again and was seeing Leah's grandma Elsie. Aubrey tossed her phone and purse aside and went hands on hips, giving off the intimidation vibe that worked with just about everyone. Except, apparently, Ben, who didn't even take a bit of notice. Instead, he reached down with that claw tool in his hand. "Hold this a minute," he said.

Was he kidding? "I don't take orders from you."

"I imagine not, since you don't know the meaning of taking orders."

She opened her mouth, but before she could speak, he gave the tool a very slight jiggle in her direction.

The motion was filled with such authority and innate demand that she walked toward him to take the thing before she even realized her feet were moving. It was heavy, and she let it fall to her side as he pulled himself up with nothing more than his biceps and vanished.

She stared up into the space. "Hey."

He didn't answer, and she got worried. "Ben?"

There was a slight rainfall of debris, and then he was back, lowering himself out of the hole like an Avenger, shoulder and arm and back muscles bulging and defined as he dropped lithely to his feet.

She let out a breath.

He brushed off his hands and turned, and then nearly tripped over Gus.

Meow.

"Watch out," Aubrey said. "He doesn't like—"

Ben squatted low and stroked the cat. Gus plopped onto his back with a grunt, exposing his belly for a rub.

"—to be touched much," Aubrey finished, and then rolled her eyes as Gus soaked up Ben's affection, even sending Aubrey a "be jealous, bee-yotch" look from slitty eyes.

Her cat was a man ho.

When Ben stood again, he looked at Aubrey for the first time. The briefest of frowns flashed on his face. Still dirty, still a little damp, and still complete sex on a stick, he took a step toward her.

Thinking he wanted the tool, she thrust it out at him. But he didn't take it. Instead, he stepped into her personal space and crowded her both physically and mentally.

"What's wrong?" he asked.

Chapter 4

If Ben knew anything about Aubrey Wellington, it was that she was one cool, tough, hard customer. He'd once seen her stare down an entire pack of mean girls at school with no fear—at least none showing. She didn't back down from much.

But she backed away from him and turned so he couldn't see her face. She definitely wasn't on her game at the moment. In fact, if he wasn't mistaken, she'd been...crying? Unable to imagine what could have rattled her so badly, much less bring her to tears, he moved closer to take the tool from her, tossing it aside as he turned her to face him. "You've been crying."

She looked away. He put a finger under her chin and brought her face back to his. "You've been crying," he said again.

She blew out a sigh and slapped his hand away. "You're a man. You're not supposed to notice," she said.

He took another step toward her, and he had no idea

why. Maybe because those usually razor-sharp hazel eyes were soft now. Soft and maybe even warm. She was vulnerable, and it was bringing out some crazy instinct in him to try to soothe or comfort her. And then there was the fact that he'd clearly affected her. When he'd come close, her breathing had hitched audibly.

Awareness?

Frustration?

Irritation?

A combination of all of them, no doubt, but he'd take it over her usual indifference. "Talk to me, Aubrey."

She let out a sound that might have been a laugh or a sob, and her eyes went suspiciously shiny. "I just have something in my eye, that's all."

He'd spent his formative teenage years under the authority of his aunt Dee, who'd cried at the drop of a hat. He wasn't fond of a woman's tears, but they didn't scare him. He waited her out with a pointed look.

She sucked in a breath and put her hands on his chest. The touch gave him a pure electrical jolt that stunned him stupid. He had no idea where this sexual tension was coming from, but he liked it. He didn't get a chance to figure it out before she gave him a little nudge that was actually more like a shove.

He didn't budge, and this time there was no mistaking the sound she made. Pure temper. "You're breathing on me," she snapped, and walked by him, shoulder-checking him hard enough to make him smile.

Whatever her problem, she no longer felt like crying—which worked for him.

"I can't afford you," she said.

"Your uncle's paying. Whatever you need."

That had her step faltering for the briefest second, but she caught herself. Looking touched, she said, "I'm going to pay him back."

"Not my deal."

She strode to the makeshift worktable he'd set up. Two sawhorses with a four-by-eight piece of plywood across them. He'd unrolled the set of plans he'd drawn up based on what Mr. Lyons had told him needed to be done. It was a fairly big job, actually, one that would take his mind off his own life for a while. Just what he needed.

Aubrey stared at the plans for a long moment. "This is wrong," she said, pointing to the shelving. "I want open shelves, four feet tall max, in wide rows. And this." She dragged her fingers across the half wall that her uncle had suggested to break up the room. "I want it open. And here…" She tapped a long finger on the tiny kitchen area in the back, which she'd started to demolish herself and made a mess of. "I want the half wall here."

"Half-walled shelves severely limit your product space," he said. "And without a wall there"—he nudged her finger with his, bringing it to the spot he was indicating—"your store will be noisy. And why do you want the serving area exposed to your customers?"

"Not that it's any of your business," she said, "but this is going to be more than a bookstore. It's going to be a gathering spot, where the lonely can come and make friends, where book clubs and knitting clubs alike can use the space for their meetings, where drinks and goodies can be easily served in comfy chairs and sofas while my customers read."

"How do you intend to make any money if you let them read here instead of buying?"

She shot him a grim smile that was sheer determination and grit. "Don't tell me I won't make it work," she said. "Because I will."

He looked down into her face for a long moment, then nodded. "I wouldn't bet against you."

She went still, and that's when he realized how close they were standing to each other. So close that he could see her eyes weren't just a mix of brown and green; gold swirled in their depths as well. If she'd been wearing any lip color, she'd long ago chewed it off, leaving her full mouth naked and bare—and tantalizing.

She was staring at his mouth, too, with an expression that gave nothing away, but he'd have sworn he'd seen the briefest flash of yearning. "Aubrey."

She blinked, as if coming out of some sort of dream, and cleared her throat as she tapped the plans again. "You'll have to redo these."

Shocked at how badly he suddenly wanted to taste her, he shook it off. "Anything else I should know?"

"Yeah." She crossed her arms. "I need the work done yesterday, but I don't want the work to be too intrusive on business. And also, it's probably best if our paths steer clear of each other as much as possible."

"You trying to piss me off so I'll keep my distance?" he asked.

"Would it work?"

It sure as hell should. Keeping his distance from Aubrey Wellington was of utmost importance. Wasn't it? Suddenly he couldn't remember why that was, exactly.

A tall figure appeared in the open doorway. Jack. He knocked on the doorjamb twice and then propped it up with a broad shoulder. "Ready?" he asked Ben with all his perfection of timing.

The two of them were meeting Luke for dinner. Ben shook off whatever was going on between him and Aubrey, although it took a surprising amount of effort to do so. "Ready," he said, and without another word grabbed the sweatshirt he'd left draped over the back of a couch.

"Hey," Aubrey called after him. "You never answered me."

"Because I don't answer to you, Sunshine." But yeah, he knew he'd work early and late to avoid as much interaction with her as possible.

Jack watched Ben shut the bookstore front door and then check to make sure it was locked. "Huh," he said.

"Huh what?"

"Nothing," Jack said.

"It's something."

"Okay. You've been back a month and you're already bored?"

Ben shrugged.

"'Cause if you are," Jack said, "I need help."

"With what?"

"As fire marshal, I inherited all these pet projects for town council and the like. And in all the monthly meetings, everyone always says they'll help, but then they don't answer my calls."

"What do you need?"

"Everything. There's the senior center—"

"Pass," Ben said quickly. "Those old ladies are sexually depraved miscreants."

"Afraid of Lucille?"

Lucille was a gazillion years old, and there were rumors that she'd been the first person to inhabit Lucky Harbor, around the time of the dinosaur age. She was still in town, running an art gallery and the gossip mill with equal fervor. "Hell, yeah, I'm afraid of her," Ben said.

"Me, too," Jack admitted. "Okay, no to the senior center. How about a project at the rec center? It's called Craft Corner." He smiled. "Should be right up your alley. You supervise after-school crafts twice a week."

"Crafts?" Ben asked in disbelief. "Do I look like a crafts kind of guy to you?"

Jack grinned. "You're a builder at heart, man. Figure it out. The kids really need someone, and you've got a lot of knowledge to impart."

"Uh-huh."

"And the principal of the school is a really hot, single brunette. How long has it been since you had a hot woman look at you?"

About three minutes… "Maybe," Ben said noncommittally.

Commercial Row was lined with shops, including the requisite grocery store, post office, and gas station. A few patches of snow and more than a few patches of ice lingered here and there from the last storm. With the dark had come an icy chill that had Ben shoving his hands in his pockets. The temperature tended to drop the moment the sun did.

When Jack spoke next, his voice was void of his usual good humor. "So. Aubrey Wellington? Really? You sure about that?"

"What about her?"

"You know what. She's trouble with a capital *T*."

Yeah, Jack was right. Ben already knew.

"Tell me you got that," Jack said.

"I got that."

There was a full minute of silence between them as they continued to walk toward the Love Shack. But then Jack, who'd never been real good at leaving anything alone, said, "There was something in the air between you two."

"Animosity?" Ben asked.

Jack laughed. "Not exactly."

"What, then?"

Jack shrugged, but Ben knew this wasn't necessarily an I-don't-know shrug. Because Jack knew.

Ben knew, too. But he held his tongue. It was natural for him to do so, and plus, as an added bonus, it drove Jack wild. Jack couldn't handle silences any more than he could handle leaving things alone.

And sure enough, after another minute, Jack started whistling. He couldn't whistle worth shit, and he was completely tone-deaf—which meant that hearing him whistle was far better than hearing him sing. But still, Ben wasn't in the mood for either. Especially since Jack only sang when he was being obnoxious. It was his own special brand of torture.

"Spit it out," Ben said.

Jack shook his head. "Nothing to spit out."

Ben looked at him, but Jack went silent. It was a first.

"I'm just working on the bookstore," Ben finally said.

Jack blew on his hands and shoved them into his front pockets as they continued to walk.

"You know damn well her uncle hired me," Ben said.

Jack nodded and squared his shoulders against the evening's wind.

"And we're not even going to be in the shop at the same time," Ben said.

Jack snorted.

"Damn it." Impressed that his own techniques had been used against him—and that it'd worked—Ben caved like a cheap suitcase. "Okay, so there *was* a weird vibe between us. But it's nothing."

"It was way more than nothing," Jack said. "The two of you practically melted the place down." He paused. "Do I need to give you the birds-and-the-bees talk?"

At that, Ben had to laugh. "Shut up. I lost my cherry two years before you did."

"Yeah, well, you were a real ho back then."

This was true. Ben had discovered women early. And then in high school, he'd tangled with the pretty, smart, and funny Hannah, and he'd fallen hard. He'd drawn her over to the dark side, and she'd loved it. Right up until she'd dumped him just before college.

Two years later, they'd run into each other at a party. She'd grown up a lot, and so had he. They'd gotten back together, and he'd put a ring on her finger so as not to lose her again. Then he'd lost her anyway when a drunk driver had crossed the center line and hit her car head-on.

He'd not gone back to his bad boy ways. Instead, he'd quit his nine-to-five engineering desk job and gone off the grid with the Army Corps and then the DOD.

As if reading his mind, Jack's smile faded. "It's been a while for you. With a woman."

Yeah, it'd been a while. But not as long as Jack thought. "I've been with women since Hannah."

If this was news to Jack, he didn't show it. "Just hookups."

"Yeah," Ben said. "So?"

"So what I saw back there in the bookstore didn't feel like it'd be a quick hookup."

"You're wrong," Ben said.

Jack was quiet a moment. "No one would blame you if you went for it again. For love. No one. It's just…Aubrey Wellington?"

The doubt in his voice pissed Ben off. Which was asinine. No one knew Ben better than Jack—no one alive, anyway. He knew what Ben had gone through after Hannah's death.

He knew Ben had loved her. The real kind of love. The once-in-a-lifetime, forever kind. For a guy who'd been pretty much dumped by his own parents and dropped at his aunt Dee's house at the age of twelve, it shouldn't have been possible for him to feel it at all. But his aunt Dee had mothered him relentlessly. And Jack's father—before his untimely, heroic death fighting a fire—had been a real dad to Ben. Jack had been a brother. Between the three of them, they'd taught Ben love.

And he'd had it with Hannah—a solid, soul-deep, comfortable love.

But it was long gone now, and while he missed it, he didn't want to risk it again.

Jack was looking at him, waiting for a response or reaction, and Ben shook his head. "You're reading too much into things," he said. "I'm just working at her bookstore."

"That's it?"

"That's it." And he one hundred percent meant it.

Okay, maybe ninety percent…

Chapter 5

♥

A few days later, Ben got up early and went for a hard run. He was met at the halfway point—the pier—by Sam Brody. Sam was an old high school buddy. The two of them had landed here in Lucky Harbor under shitty circumstances—Ben because his mom had dumped him and Sam because he'd been sent to yet another foster home.

And though Ben'd had Jack and Dee and a whole bunch of people who cared, none of them had ever quite understood where he'd come from.

Sam had understood.

Sam had come from worse.

They nodded at each other and fell into step, a hard, fast pace that suited the both of them. They didn't talk. They often never said a word while running. Ben wasn't a big talker anyway, although next to Sam he looked like Chatty Cathy.

Still, the silence was always comfortable, like an old

shoe. Three miles later, on the outskirts of the county, they finally slowed to their usual cool-down pace and headed back.

"How's it going with the latest boat?" Ben asked. Sam built boats by hand, and his workmanship was amazing.

"It's going," Sam said simply. "How's it going at the bookstore?"

"Just making shelves."

Sam snorted, the sound managing to convey a sarcastic "Yeah, right" and "Good luck with Aubrey, buddy" all in one.

At the pier, they separated with a fist bump, each to go on with his own day.

After a shower, Ben headed out. He and Jack shared a downtown duplex. Jack was out front walking his 150-pound black and white Great Dane, Kevin. Kevin didn't like to exert a lot of energy, so they never walked far. And mostly, his favorite walk was to his food bowl and back. But sometimes in the mornings, Kevin liked to check things out—like which dogs had peed near his territory. Kevin did his business, and then he and Jack headed off to the fire station for work.

Ben drove to his aunt Dee's house. She was working hard at recovering from breast cancer. And though it had kicked her ass, she was now kicking the cancer's ass. But sometimes she was too tired to take care of herself, and on those days, Ben and Jack took turns doing it for her. It was only fair, since she'd taken care of the both of them for the better part of their lives.

As he'd been doing several times a week, Ben let himself into her place and headed straight for the kitchen, where he'd drum up a nice, protein-rich meal.

But in the kitchen doorway, he stopped short in surprise.

Retired fire marshal Ronald McVane stood flipping sausages at the range top where Ben had created some of his best work.

Dee sat at the table, serenely sipping tea.

When Jack's dad died, a little part of Dee had died with him. Okay, a big part. In the years since, she'd battled depression and anxiety. Not once in all that time had she dated anyone.

But she was dating now. She was dating Ronald and had been for the past month, very casually. What Ben hadn't realized was that the casual part of the program had changed, because Ronald was barefoot and his shirt was unbuttoned. And, most telling of all, Dee was still in her bathrobe, with her hair more than a little wild. Not bed-head hair.

Sex hair.

He tried not to shudder at the thought of the only mother figure he'd ever known having sex.

Dee, reading his mind, smiled sweetly. "Baby, I left you a text that I was doing okay this morning."

Ronald glanced over at her, a private smile hovering about his mouth.

Dee returned the smile.

And Ben threw up a little in his mouth. "Yeah, well, you didn't define *okay*."

"Not sure you'd have liked my definition," Dee said, still all sweet-like.

Aw, Christ, Ben thought, and scrubbed a hand over his eyes.

Taking pity on him, Dee laughed, rose, and gave him a kiss on the cheek. "How about some breakfast?"

Hell, no. "That's okay, thanks." He waved vaguely at the door. "I've got a thing—"

"I heard you're helping Aubrey Wellington get her bookstore ready," Dee said.

Ben stopped. "How the hell did you hear that already?"

Dee smiled. "Do you really have to ask? It's Lucky Harbor, after all. And everyone here loves you so much. They're all so glad to have you back. You're a common topic on the Lucky Harbor Facebook page. But about Aubrey—"

"It's just some bookshelves and renovation stuff," he said quickly, not wanting to hear from anyone else what a bad idea it was. "That's it."

"Hmm," she said, not commenting on that directly. "I was just going to say, if you need any tools, you know I still have all of Jack senior's in the garage."

"Say the rest," he said.

"What?"

"The part you're dying to say. That she's a bad idea for me."

"Well, of course she is." She met Ben's gaze. "But you already know that."

He blew out a breath. "Yeah."

"She's not exactly your type."

"No one's been my type."

"She's got a reputation."

"Maybe she's changed."

She cocked her head at him. "Well, you're a big boy now. You'll have to decide that for yourself."

"But you don't like it."

"I don't." She cupped his face. "Baby, no one is ever

going to be good enough for you. Not in my eyes. You know that." She snagged a quick, hard hug and then let him go.

Ben left there like his ass was on fire. He trusted Dee with his life, but it wasn't her business whom he saw.

Or didn't see…

Back on the road, he found his zone. He liked Aubrey's plan for the bookstore, but he couldn't shut off his engineering brain. He could think of several ways to improve her vision.

Not that she'd thank him for it.

Nope—he'd have to finesse the situation, make her think everything was all her idea. He was playing around with that, working it as he would any puzzle, when two figures dashed out into the street right in front of him. "*Jesus*." He stomped on the brakes, and thankfully his truck stopped on a dime.

He couldn't say the same for his heart.

Or his coffee, which went flying, spilling everywhere.

Out in the middle of the street, the two kids had gone still as statues. Two little girls. He threw the truck into park and ran to them, crouching down to their level. "Are you okay?"

"Yes," one said while the other just stared up at him, eyes as big as saucers. They were clearly twins, maybe five years old, one wearing all pink and the other a mishmash of mismatching colors. They shared the same crazy, wild hair the color of a copper penny, which flew around their thin, angular faces. Stark blue eyes. Skinny as toothpicks.

"What are you doing in the street?" Ben asked, craning his neck, trying to figure out whom they belonged to, but the area was quiet. This was a low-income neighborhood. Yards were neglected, houses were small and close together. There was no one in sight. The hardworking blue-collar class had already left for work.

"We're supposed to stay on the sidewalk," the pink one said. "But there's lots of cracks. We're sorry, mister."

When he just looked at her blankly, trying to understand what the hell she meant about the cracks, she pointed at her sister. "Kendra's afraid of them. The cracks." She leaned in a little, like she was departing with a state secret. "She thinks trolls live in the cracks, and if she steps on one, they'll get her."

Kendra stuck her thumb in her mouth and nodded.

Ben blew out a breath and shuddered to think what might have happened to them if he hadn't seen them in time. "What's your name?" he asked Pink.

She opened her mouth, but Kendra pulled on her twin's sweater and gave her a quick head shake. Pink rolled her lips inward and looked down at her shoes—which were untied. "We're not supposed to tell strangers our names," she said softly.

Ben leaned in to tie her shoe for her before realizing that the reason it was untied was because the string had broken off on one side. "That's a most excellent rule," he said, straightening, nudging them to the side of the road. "Which house is yours? I'll see you home."

"We're not going home. We're going to school," she said.

"By yourselves?" He hated that idea. They were so young, so vulnerable.

"Billy's supposed to walk us, but he never does," Pink said. "Sometimes Joey or Nina stays with us, but today they ran ahead real fast 'cause the mean kids were chucking rocks. Kendra couldn't keep up, so I stayed with her."

Ben craned his neck and looked around, ready to rumble with whatever little asshole punk was throwing rocks at these two little girls. He couldn't believe they were on their own. The elementary school was at least another mile away. Letting out a breath, he scrubbed a hand over his jaw. "I want to talk to your mom."

"We don't got one," Pink said.

Well, if anyone understood that short sentence, it was Ben himself. "Who's in charge of you?"

Pink bit her lower lip.

Ben crouched down low again, getting as small as he could. Not easy on a six-foot-two frame. "Talk to me, Pink."

She smiled at the nickname, then sneaked a peek at a house about a hundred yards back, the corner house.

"Come on," he said, and headed that way.

"But mister, we'll be late."

"Ben," he said. "Call me Ben."

"Okay. But mister, Suzie don't like it when we're late, 'cause then the school calls her and she gets in trouble."

Then Suzie should have damn well driven them, Ben thought grimly. He walked up the narrow path and rapped his knuckles on the front door.

A fiftyish woman answered, looking harassed. "Yes?" she asked, and then frowned down at the two girls. "Oh, Lord. What did you two do now?"

"They didn't do anything," Ben said. "Though I nearly ran them over when they were in the street."

"In the street!" she gasped and glared them. "What in

the world? You know better, both of you! And now you're going to be late for school!"

"They're too young to walk to school alone," Ben said.

Suzie sent him a mind-your-own-business gaze. "They *weren't* alone. There's five of them, and the others are all older."

"Someone was throwing rocks at them," Ben told her. "The others ran ahead."

The woman heaved out a heavy sigh. "They have to learn to fight their own battles."

"They're too young to fight any battles," Ben said, beginning to get real pissed off.

"I know you," she said. "You're dating that bitchy Aubrey Wellington, not that anyone can figure out why. And you went to school with my son Dennis. You took his point-guard spot on the varsity basketball team. I know everyone thinks you're all that, but you're not."

Her son Dennis had been a first-class asshole, and he'd sucked at basketball, to boot. Ben hadn't. "The girls," he said tightly. "Can you drive them to school or not?"

"If you're so worried about them, do it yourself."

"I don't have—"

The door slammed.

"—car seats." Well, hell. Ben looked down at the two rug rats.

They looked right back, their eyes filled with worry.

"Okay," he said, making a snap decision. "Let's go." Against his better judgment, he loaded them carefully into the backseat of his truck, cinching the seat belts tight to their skinny frames and hoping to God he didn't get arrested trying to do the right thing.

"Wow," Pink said, looking around. "This is the coolest truck ever!"

His truck was a twelve-year-old Ford, and, granted, he'd had it lovingly taken care of by Jack when he'd been gone, but it wasn't *cool* by any stretch. It was functional, just the way he liked it.

In the backseat, Pink was holding her sister's hand and kicking her feet, as though her energy couldn't be contained. "Mister, are you married?"

"It's Ben," he reminded her. He pulled cautiously out into the street, not wanting to mess with his precious cargo. "And no, I'm not married."

"Why not?"

Since responding with "Well, I *was* married, but she died" wasn't exactly appropriate, he ignored the question. Not difficult, as Pink had a thousand more questions.

"You spilled your coffee?" she asked.

"Yep."

"All these tools yours?"

"Yep." Thankfully, a mile went pretty fast, and in a couple of minutes, he was pulling up to the drop-off lane in front of the elementary school. He started to get out of the truck, but Pink had herself and her sister unbuckled and out the door before he could.

"Thanks, mister!" she yelled back. "I hope you get another cup of coffee!"

Ben nodded and waved, meeting Kendra's big eyes as she gave him one last look.

She still hadn't spoken a word.

As soon as the two little redheads vanished inside the school, Ben pulled out his phone and called Luke to give him the lowdown. "What's up with that foster home?"

"It's better than most," came Luke's surprising answer.

Ben wrestled with that for a moment, knowing that if it hadn't been for Aunt Dee, he'd have ended up in a situation just like the two girls. Or worse. There were plenty of people who never got to have an Aunt Dee. Like Sam…

"Tell me you're kidding," he finally said.

"You have no idea."

Ben sighed.

"Listen," Luke said. "The kids are safe; they get a roof over their heads and three squares."

And what went unsaid…it was more than a lot of kids got. "Shit," Ben said, and hung up.

He drove himself to the car wash and took care of the spilled coffee situation. He was halfway through a three-egg-and-cheese omelet and a not-so-short stack of pancakes at Eat Me when Luke slid into his booth.

"Just heard that we're looking for an engineer to work on the new water systems for the county," Luke said.

Ben looked at him and then kept eating.

"Interested?"

"That was my old job, before I left," Ben said.

"Duh. They need an overhaul and want you back to head up the team. Are you interested or not?"

Ben shrugged.

"Let me phrase this another way," Luke said casually. "You *are* interested."

Ben's brows went up. "Is that right?"

"Yes, damn it."

"Because it'd keep me here in Lucky Harbor?"

"Your aunt and Jack missed you. And Kevin. Kevin missed you, too."

"Kevin didn't know me. Jack just got him last year."

"Whatever, man."

Ben smiled. "*You* missed me. Admit it."

"Shut up." Luke snatched Ben's plate of pancakes and pulled it toward him. He doubled the amount of syrup on the plate and dug in. "You should know that you've already turned in your résumé."

"Did I?"

"Yeah. Stole it off your laptop. They expect you to stop by this week."

"Thanks, Mom."

"Smart-ass."

It was early the next day when Ben pointed his truck in the direction of the bookstore. Halfway there he stopped at a four-way stop and saw a woman standing on the sidewalk in front of a town-house complex. She was staring at a lower unit, looking unsettled and anxious. Normally, this wouldn't necessarily have caught his interest, but the willowy, well-dressed blonde wasn't just any woman.

It was Aubrey.

She shook her head, muttered something to herself, and then began walking away. She turned the corner.

There were no cars behind him, so Ben remained there a moment, a little thrown by having seen her look so off her axis not just once, but twice now.

And then, suddenly, she was back, retracing her steps so that she once again stood on the sidewalk staring at the town house.

"What the hell?" he murmured, and pulled over.

Aubrey stood in front of a small, narrow town house, taking mental notes. The place was clearly well taken care of—lovingly so—with flowers lining the windowsills and freshly painted shutters.

You're not here to notice the care of the building. Drawing a deep breath, she looked at the list in her hand, then back at the town house.

But still, she hesitated. Yesterday she'd have said she had courage in spades, but the truth was that her encounter with the first person on her list hadn't gone so smoothly, and she was still smarting. What if this one didn't go any better?

Just do it, she told herself. Like the Nike commercials. She drew in a big breath and started forward—

"What are you up to?" asked an unbearably familiar male voice.

She nearly jumped right out of her skin. Instead, she forced herself to calmly turn.

Ben was in his truck, window down, idling at the curb, dark lenses hiding his eyes from her, looking effortlessly big and badass.

The way she wished she felt.

Chapter 6

Before Aubrey could formulate an articulate answer, Ben turned off the engine and ambled out of the truck.

Damn it. Cursing herself for getting cornered, she narrowed her eyes at him. "What are you doing here?"

"Wondering the same thing about you," he said calmly. He glanced at the building. "You seem a little fixated on number forty-three. Who lives there?"

"None of your business."

As if he had all the time in the world, Ben leisurely pulled out his phone and thumbed the screen for a moment. "Huh," he said, sounding fascinated. Then he lifted his head. "I knew this place was familiar. Mrs. Cappernackle lives here. The school librarian."

Like she didn't know. "How did you do that?"

"I have ways," he said mysteriously. "Didn't you and she have an incident? What was it?" He paused, thinking, and then nodded. "I remember now. You stole some books from the library, and she busted you for it."

No. No, no, no, that *wasn't* what had happened. Well, not exactly, anyway. "Stop it," she said. "Go away. Go put in a water system in Nigeria or something."

He actually smiled. "Already done."

Show-off.

"Why are you at the home of someone on your list?"

She went still. *Shit.* He had the memory of an elephant. And he was relentless.

And as nosy as any of the old ladies in town.

"Again," she managed to say through her teeth, "none of your business."

"You planning to off the people on that list or what?"

She whipped around to stare at him. He pulled his sunglasses off, and that's when she saw the light of amusement in his eyes. He was teasing.

Sort of.

Because the smile wasn't quite real. He didn't understand her. He was confused by her.

Well, join my club, she thought.

"Because if you are," he said, shifting closer, lowering his voice to a conspirator's whisper that shouldn't be so sexy, but totally was, "then you should be scoping the place out at night, not in broad daylight. And you should be in a vehicle with night-vision and heat-seeking goggles."

"I'm afraid to ask how you know all this," she said.

"I'd tell you, but…"

"You'd have to kill me?"

His smile went slightly more real, but his eyes were still laser sharp. "What's going on, Aubrey?"

She shook her head. What was going on was that she'd lost her mind if she thought she could really pull this off.

A million years ago, or so it seemed now, Mrs. Cappernackle, the high school librarian—the woman who lived in the town house—had tattled on Aubrey. Her claim was that Aubrey'd had sex in the reference section of the library with the principal's son.

And though Aubrey certainly had been guilty of being in the wrong place with the wrong guy before, she hadn't been that time, and not with the boy in question, either.

But in spite of her innocence, she'd gotten in big trouble, and because Mrs. Cappernackle falsely claimed she'd stolen books while she was at it, she was suspended. So when a few weeks later Aubrey realized she'd actually forgotten to return a library book she'd legitimately borrowed, she did a really stupid, juvenile thing. She claimed she *had* returned it but that Mrs. Cappernackle had only said she hadn't because the librarian had it out for her. Aubrey even managed to produce real tears and must have been convincing enough, because she'd gotten away with it, and Mrs. Cappernackle had been written up by the superintendent.

Mrs. Cappernackle had retired later that same year, and Aubrey had always felt guilty, like she'd had something to do with it.

Now, more than a decade later, Aubrey had the book she'd stolen in her purse. It wasn't the original, of course, but a new copy from her store. She wanted to hand it over as a peace offering. Or such had been her plan, but it seemed stupid now. "I'm asking you nicely," she said to Ben, "to go away."

This was hard for her, very hard, and some of that must have been conveyed, because he studied her with those assessing eyes for one long moment, then nodded and walked back to his truck.

And then he was gone.

She wasn't hopeful enough to think he'd actually completely vanish from her life, but that he'd left for now was good enough. Drawing in a deep breath, she marched up to the town house and forced herself to knock.

A moment later, Mrs. Cappernackle opened the door. She was tall, thin, and using the cane she'd once wielded to enforce her reign of terror in the library. If you got that cane pointed at your nose, you knew you were in deep trouble. Aubrey'd been at the wrong end of it often enough to vividly remember the bone-quaking, knee-shaking fear it could evoke.

Mrs. Cappernackle had aged in the past decade, and she'd been old to start with. But she took one look at Aubrey, and her expression puckered as if she'd just sucked on a sour ball. "Well, look what the cat dragged in."

"You don't have a cat, Martha," said another woman's voice, and then she poked her head around Mrs. Cappernackle.

It was Lucille. She was a senior, too, and though Aubrey had never personally had any run-ins with Lucille, the woman's gossiping prowess was legendary. So was her soft heart and kind soul. Aubrey was banking on both. "Hi," she said. *You can do this.* "Mrs. Cappernackle, I was hoping for a moment of your time."

"I have no time for you," Mrs. Cappernackle said. "And stay away from Ben McDaniel. You don't deserve him." And then she slammed the door on Aubrey's nose.

Aubrey stared at the closed door and felt her inner strength wobble a bit. Two for two…she turned to walk away, but the door opened again.

It was Lucille. Glancing back over her shoulder as if

checking for a tail, she tiptoed out and grabbed Aubrey's hand. "Honey; don't take that personally."

"Hard to take it any other way," Aubrey said.

Lucille paused as if she wanted to say something, but changed her mind. "It's not a good day," she said carefully. "Will you do me a favor and try again, real soon?"

"Sure," Aubrey said softly, managing a smile when Lucille gently patted her arm.

"You're a good girl," she said, and then vanished before Aubrey could tell her she wasn't a good girl at all.

Not even close.

Three days later, after a very long ten hours at the bookstore, Aubrey closed up shop and was dragged to a wine tasting and spa event at the local B and B with Ali and Leah. While having a free paraffin hand treatment by the spa's owner and sheriff's wife—a very lovely, very pregnant Chloe Thompson—Aubrey dodged her friends' questions about Ben. She did this because, one, she didn't want to talk about her feelings for Ben, and, two, she didn't even know what her feelings were.

Liar, liar.

On the way home, she stopped and picked up some color samples from the hardware store for the paint she couldn't possibly have been able to afford if not for her incredibly generous uncle. She'd spoken to him yesterday via Skype from his cruise and got a lump in her throat just thinking about it. He knew his wife had loved the bookstore, and he loved Aubrey enough to give her a shot at it.

It meant the world to her, but she wasn't going to spend more than was absolutely, strictly necessary. And she'd repay every penny.

The moment she parked next to Ben's truck at the bookstore, she nearly chickened out and retreated to her loft apartment for the night instead. But she wasn't a chicken, she told herself, and she forced herself to enter via the front door.

"How much do I owe you?" she heard Ben ask.

She moved in far enough to see him. He had his back to her. He held a bag of something delicious-smelling in one hand and was shoving his other hand in his pocket.

Another guy stood in front of him in a bike helmet, army fatigues, and a black T-shirt that read EAT ME DE-LIVERS. Aubrey recognized him as the man who'd been at AA the other night.

Ryan.

Ryan shook his head vehemently at Ben. "Nothing, man. You owe the diner nothing. It's on me." He paused, and his voice was filled with emotion. "It's good to see you home. Safe. Everyone's so happy to have you back." Then he stepped close to Ben and enveloped him in one of those masculine, back-slapping hugs, holding Ben for a long beat, as though he was incredibly precious to him.

Ben let out a breath and hugged him back, and Aubrey felt another lump in her throat, this one the size of a regulation football. Uncomfortable with the emotion, she let her heels click on the floor, and both men turned to face her.

Ben met her gaze, his giving nothing away.

Ryan looked at her as well, and it was clear from the way he gave one slow, surprised blink that he remembered her from the AA meeting. She braced herself for questions, but he didn't say a word. He merely turned back to Ben, clapped him on the shoulder once more, nodded at Aubrey, and then was gone.

"You know Ryan?" Ben asked into the silence.

"No."

"Sure? It seemed like you two might know each other."

"No," Aubrey said again, and bent to pet Gus, who'd come close to wrapping himself around her ankles.

Meow, he said a little forcefully and accusatorily.

She was late with his dinner.

Aubrey fed him and glanced at Ben. He was back in his tool belt, which was made of leather and crinkled all male-like when he moved. Plus, it forced his jeans a little low on his hips. She couldn't stop staring, because there was something about the way he wore his clothes that suggested he'd look even better without them.

And then she noticed…he had cat hair all over his jeans. That shouldn't make her melt, right? Swallowing hard, she forced herself to turn away. But her eyes had a mind of their own and needed one more peek, and she pivoted back.

And bumped right into him.

Chest to chest.

Thigh to thigh.

And everything in between. He'd moved silently, coming right up on her. "Did you talk to Mrs. Cappernackle?" he asked. "Did you apologize for whatever it is you did?"

She went still, then forced herself to relax. "You think you know something," she said. "But you don't." She turned to leave, but he wrapped his hand around her wrist and pulled her back.

"I don't want to talk about it," she said. Once again he was close. Too close. *So damn close.* "At all," she added, hearing with some alarm that her voice had softened.

Everything had softened, at just his proximity. "Ever," she whispered, and found her gaze locked on his mouth.

He had a really great mouth.

"I don't want to talk, either," that mouth said very seriously. And then he lowered his head. They shared a breath for a beat, just long enough for her to know what was going to happen and feel the anticipation wash over her.

Then he kissed her, deep and slow and utterly mesmerizing. His hands were firm on her back. Needing an anchor, she reached out and grasped his shirt and leaned into him. He was warm and solid, so very solid, emitting the kind of strength that she herself was a pint low on today. Leaning in more, she felt his body respond.

Someone moaned. *I did*, she realized, swamped with the sensation of being wanted, even just physically. She took in the delicious taste of him, the feel of him, the sound of his very male groan when she stroked her tongue to his.

Things got a little hazy then. A lot hazy. She felt his hands move over her, melting her bones away. She touched him, too. Her hands wandered all over his body—and good Lord, what a body.

She had no idea how long they kissed—*and kissed*—but she didn't think about stopping until she ran out of air. Breathing hard, she slowly opened her eyes and stared directly into his.

They'd heated. Darkened. And something else. He wasn't looking so relaxed now. In fact, he was looking the opposite of relaxed. He looked...feral.

And she was his prey.

It made her quiver in arousal, which was crazy, but she couldn't look away. He was still holding her. In fact, he was holding her up. And having his hands on her was doing a number on her heart rate. "I have paint samples," she said inanely.

"Paint samples," he repeated.

"Yes."

"You were thinking about paint samples just now?"

No. She was thinking about the temptation of his hard body and how he might feel on top of her, holding her down while he did all sorts of delicious things with all that...*hardness*. Not that he needed to know that. "Yes," she lied. "I was thinking about paint samples."

His lips swept along her jawline to her ear. "I could make you forget about them."

No doubt in her mind. "I don't think so," she said, having to lock her knees, what with her bones melted and all. Her palms were damp. Other places on her body were damp, too. Damn him. Realizing she was still fisting his shirt, she loosened her hands, stroking her fingers over the wrinkles she'd left.

He stepped back and let out a small smile. "I know better than to compete with paint samples." He dropped his tool belt and headed to the door.

She stared after him. "Where are you going?"

"For air."

"But...there's work to do."

"Yeah. You and your paint samples should get on it."

And then he was gone.

Meow.

Gus was still hungry. *Starving*, if his vehemence said anything.

Aubrey was hungry, too. Just not for food.

Chapter 7

♥

Ben was halfway down the street with absolutely no destination in mind when his phone vibrated.

"Don't forget," Jack said when Ben answered. "Craft Corner starts tomorrow. You need to be at the rec center between the elementary school and high school by three fifteen."

Shit. He'd completely forgotten. His brain was currently on overload.

Kiss overload.

And yeah, it'd been a while since he'd kissed a woman, but he was pretty sure a kiss had never fogged up his head the way that Aubrey's kiss just had.

It was her mouth, he decided. It was a pretty damn great mouth. "And if I've changed my mind?" Ben asked.

"I'll change it back for you," Jack said.

Ben laughed, because this was just bullshit posturing on his cousin's part. Probably. Either way, he wasn't all that worried, since he could fight mean and dirty as a snake when he had to.

But…he'd taught Jack everything he knew. "What the hell am I supposed to do with a bunch of kids at some stupid Craft Corner?" he asked.

"You've got a truck full of tools; you'll figure it out," Jack said, and then hung up.

Great. He was so *not* busy that he'd been reduced to playing arts and crafts with teenagers. He went home and barely slept—when he wasn't fantasizing about Aubrey's mouth.

He got up early and ran a few miles with Sam. "Do I look bored to you?" he asked Sam.

Sam's lips twitched. "If you're asking, you're bored."

Yeah. Shit. After he got home and showered, he formally applied for the job with the county, just to get Luke off his ass.

That afternoon, he pulled up to the rec center just as the school bus was dumping a load of kids off.

These weren't high school kids; they were much younger. Elementary school kids. Some looked as though they could be in kindergarten.

Then he saw Pink and Kendra, and he got a very bad feeling. He whipped out his cell phone and called Jack.

He didn't pick up. Fucker, he thought. Surely the older kids were already here, and that's who he'd be working with. No one, especially Jack, would think to put *him* in charge of little kids. He walked to the back of his truck. He'd loaded up a crate full of tools, figuring they'd wing it.

Pink squealed at the sight of him and ran up close,

dragging Kendra behind her. "Mister! Hi! Whatcha doing here?"

"Teaching Craft Corner."

She squealed again, confirming all his suspicions before she let out a "Yay! That's where we're headed, too!"

They walked into the classroom assigned to Craft Corner, hanging on him like they owned the place because they knew the teacher. Ben set down his crate of saws and hammers and chisels and soldering tools, and one of the grade school teachers—apparently a few of them volunteered here after school—gave him a horrified look. "What is *that*?" she asked.

"Stuff for Craft Corner." He paused. "For high school kids, right?"

The girls were jumping up and down at his side, clapping their hands in uncontained joy and excitement.

The teacher shook her head. "No. This is Craft Corner for ages five to seven."

Jack, you bastard…

The teacher heaved a put-upon sigh, pulled out a set of keys, and went to a closet. She unlocked a cabinet and gestured to it.

"What's that?" Ben asked.

"Spare materials."

He stared at the shelves stocked with things like buckets of glitter glue and popsicle sticks. "What do I do with all this?"

"I don't care, as long as you keep them busy for an hour and a half."

And then she was gone.

Ben had once been in a remote area of Somalia with two other engineers when they'd been surrounded by a group of starving rebels. They'd rounded up Ben and his two co-workers, stolen everything they had, beaten the shit out of them for good measure, and left them for dead.

That had been less painful than this—being with a group of twenty kids staring at him with excitement and hope that he was about to do something cool. Because he had nothing. To stall, he dumped out the bucket of popsicle sticks, spread them around. Did the same with the glue.

Pink tugged on the hem of his T-shirt. "So what are we doing, mister? Making something really neat, right?"

"Right." He shoved things around in the supply cabinet, looking for something—anything—to help him.

"Are we going to do it today?" she asked.

He turned to her, but she appeared to be utterly unconcerned over the long look he gave her, the one that would've had a grown man cowering in his boots. She just met his gaze straight on and smiled.

Last year in Thailand, he'd had a group of local teenagers assigned to assist him on a project. They'd been quick studies, smart as hell, and, best of all, resourceful. During their off time, they'd shown Ben how to weave. Baskets, hats, even shoes. An engineer to the bone, Ben had taken their weaving techniques one step further. He'd taught them how to extract lumber from the piles and piles of debris that lay everywhere. What had worked in their favor was the humidity, which made the wet scraps they found thin, malleable, and easy to work with. They'd been able to weave effectively with no tools at all. Using building skills they learned from Ben, they'd made a bunch of aesthetically pleasing baskets. What had started out as a fun project to cure boredom and stimulate the teens had turned into a viable way for them to actually make a living—to trade the baskets for the things they needed to survive. Ben had left there knowing that he'd truly given something back.

He held no such illusions here. These kids weren't going to remember him or these stupid sticks. But he still had an hour and twenty-eight minutes on the clock, so he had to do something. "Okay, we're going to make a picture frame."

"What will we put in the frame?" Pink asked, her cute little face upturned to his.

Good question. They didn't care about getting a photo printed. These kids had cell phones and iPads and all sorts of shit on which they could bring up a picture at the touch of a thumb. "I meant a collage," he said. "We're going to make a collage."

"What's that?" someone wanted to know.

"Stuff you collect."

"What'll we collect?" another kid asked.

He smiled as the idea came to him.

Five minutes later, he had all the kids in the rec center parking lot, finding "treasures" from his truck. Kendra was cradling a few quarters and Oreos. Another girl had claimed all the chocolate-kiss candy wrappers he'd tossed in the back. One of the other kids had found a baseball cap and a pair of flip-flops; Ben had no idea whom they belonged to. Yet another kid went through the glove compartment, making Ben damn glad he no longer kept condoms in there. But his maintenance records were now officially someone's art project. Several of the boys had gathered up the rest of his change and were making a mint off of him. One of them held up a ten-dollar bill with a whoop. Ben winced over the loss.

"Hey, this is a pretty napkin," Pink said of the—surprise—*pink* napkin she'd found. It had seven digits on it. A few weeks back, a waitress had scribbled down her number and shoved it in Ben's pocket, and he'd forgotten about it. "Uh…" he said, but Pink was cradling it as though it were gold, so he let it go.

Someone else had found several coffee cups and a parking ticket. Ben winced again. He'd forgotten about that ticket…

An hour and twenty-six minutes later, they were done. Each kid had a frame made by hand out of popsicle sticks, and inside each one was an assemblage of things they'd collected—from his now-clean truck.

Win-win, he thought.

When he'd been relieved by Ms. Uptight Teacher, he headed back to his blissfully empty truck. He slid behind the wheel and started to turn the key when he saw two familiar little redheads walking down the street.

Alone.

Shit. "Don't do it," he said to himself. But he put the truck back into park, pocketed his keys, and got out. "Hey."

Pink, holding her sister's hand, whipped around. When she caught sight of him, she beamed. "Mr. Teacher!"

"You're walking home," he said.

"Well, yeah. But on the next block we run, 'cause that's where Kelly and the mean dog live."

He sighed grimly. "Get in."

She beamed.

Kendra beamed.

And the next thing Ben knew, he'd put them both in his truck, cinched down by seat belts, legs swinging, smiles across their faces.

He pulled up to their foster home and idled a minute. "How long have you lived here?"

They both shrugged. "A while," Pink declared. "Since all the bad stuff."

He was afraid to ask, but as it turned out, he didn't have to. Pink didn't have a filter. "Our grandma died," she said. "And our daddy's up for the big one, so he couldn't take us to live with him."

Ben craned around to stare at her. "The big one?"

She shrugged again. "I'm not real sure what that means, but he's very busy doing it because he hasn't come to see us."

Ben was pretty sure he knew exactly what it meant. The guy was in prison for murder. Not that Ben was going to explain *that* to a five-year-old. He got out of the truck, unbuckled them, and waited until they were both inside their house.

While he was still sitting there, Jack called him.

"You're a shithead," Ben said in lieu of a greeting.

"You made them clean out your truck?" Jack asked incredulously. "Seriously?"

"So I'm fired, right?" Ben asked hopefully.

Jack laughed. "You're going to have to do a lot worse than that. And don't even think about it. I need you there. The kids loved you. But Jesus, figure out a craft that doesn't involve cleaning out your truck."

Ben hung up on him and put the truck in gear. On the next street he saw a teenage boy slouched against a fence, a huge mutt on a leash in his hand. He pulled over and rolled down his window. "Kelly?"

The kid sneered. "What's it to ya?"

Ben smiled at the size of the balls on the little idiot. Then he got out of his truck.

Kelly gulped but stayed in place, straightening, trying to add some height.

Height wasn't going to help him. Only brains could save him, and Ben had his doubts about even that. "We need to talk."

Kelly gulped again. "'Bout?"

"Your dog," Ben said. "You let it terrify any more little kids, especially redheaded ones, and I'll introduce you to *my* dog. And my dog eats your dog's breed for lunch."

Kelly lost a whole lot of his belligerence but tried to keep his bravado up. "Who are you, the dog police?"

"Worse," Ben said. "I'm not the police at all." He leveled the teen with the same stare that hadn't intimidated Pink much.

It worked on Kelly. The kid nodded like a bobblehead. Ben got back into his truck and called Luke. "What's up with the girls' parents?"

"What girls?"

"The two sisters from the foster home. Kendra and…" Shit. He still didn't know Pink's real name. "The one who wears pink all the time."

Luke laughed softly. "The one who wears pink?"

"Yeah," Ben said impatiently. "From head to toe. You can't miss her. What's their story?"

"I don't know," Luke said.

"But you could find out."

"Well, yeah."

"Call me back when you do."

Luke paused. "You do remember you don't like kids, right?"

"It's all Jack's fault."

"Of course," Luke said without missing a beat. "It's always Jack's fault."

Ben disconnected and then, in need of fortitude, drove to the diner. He hadn't even gotten out of the truck when he saw the flash of a willowy blonde standing in front of the beauty salon.

Aubrey.

As he watched, she stuffed that damn notepad into her purse, turned, and walked away. Quick, sure steps. Determined. She walked the same way she'd kissed him.

A woman on a mission.

He couldn't imagine what she was up to, but he'd bet his last dollar it involved her list. The one with his name on it.

Aubrey stopped short, said something to herself, and walked back to the salon. She strode inside, back ramrod straight.

Fascinated, knowing he'd seen this game before, Ben waited. While he did, Luke called back.

"Records on the kids are sealed, so I went to the source," he said.

"Child services?" Ben asked.

"Lucille."

Ben had to laugh. If anything had happened in Lucky Harbor that Lucille didn't know about, it wasn't worth knowing. "And?"

"She knew their grandmother. The kids' mom is gone. Their grandmother died, too, in a car wreck. The girls were four at the time and in the car. Minor injuries only. Father's a mechanic in Seattle."

"What?" Ben asked. "He's not in prison?"

"Not according to Lucille."

Ben absorbed the unexpected shock—and the anger. Also a shock. But he *was* angry. He was furious. The girls had lost a mother and grandmother, and their prick of a father was working less than two hours away while letting them think he was in prison?

Aubrey came out of the beauty shop. "Gotta go," he said, and disconnected. He studied Aubrey. She didn't look devastated this time. She looked…well, he wasn't sure. He looked her over again and then realized what it was.

She was relieved. There was a lightness to her carriage, and damn if she wasn't almost smiling as she got into her car, without even looking his way, and drove off.

He had to try damn hard not to follow her.

Chapter 8

♥

When the alarm went off several days later, Aubrey had trouble getting out of bed, and she hit SNOOZE on her alarm clock about four times. Finally, Gus sat on her chest and refused to budge until she promised to feed him immediately.

She'd gone to her mom's the night before and stayed late. They'd had dinner, and then Aubrey had helped paint Tammy's bathroom a sunshine yellow for "cheer," as her mom had called it. Aubrey thought it was okay, but if it'd been her bathroom, she'd need sunglasses to take a shower every morning.

She'd planned to beg off early, but then Carla hadn't showed up, which had saddened her mom. Carla was invited every week and rarely, if ever, showed up, but it still got to Tammy. So it'd been midnight before Aubrey had gotten home, and she'd been shocked to discover that in her absence, the renovation fairy had finished demolition of the closet area.

Ben had come back and worked, and standing there alone in her dark store, in the middle of the night, she'd smiled. And been so grateful.

And confused.

How was it she only liked Ben when he wasn't here, or when he had his tongue in her mouth?

Now, in the light of day, standing in the same spot, she looked around again. Already so many changes had been made. There was little left of Aunt Gwen's store—except the heart. The heart was here in spades.

Meow.

And Gus the cat.

Her phone buzzed, and she pulled it out of her purse. It was Leah.

"Why are you starting your day without stopping in?"

Leah and Ali had a morning ritual that involved Leah feeding Ali breakfast and Ali putting up a fresh bouquet in Leah's bakery. "I didn't know I was part of the equation," Aubrey said.

"Well, you are. So get your skinny ass over here. I've just created a brand-new batch of raspberry Danishes, and Ali's going to eat them all if you don't hurry."

"I don't have anything to give you in return."

Meow, Gus said.

"Well, except the cat," Aubrey said. "And I don't think you can have a cat in a bakery."

"I'd take that fat sweetheart in a hot minute if I could," Leah said.

Aubrey looked down into Gus's annoyed green eyes and felt her heart squeeze. Nope, even she couldn't give up the grumpy old man.

"And anyway," Leah said, "it's not about what you can

give us in return, though you do have books now. I can download right from your website to my e-reader, right?"

"Right," Aubrey said.

"Well, then, that makes you my new crack. Hurry." And then she disconnected.

One of the things Aubrey was most proud of was her website, where people could download books to read on any digital device. They could do it from right inside her store or from the comfort of their own homes. She walked out her back door, down the alley about fifteen feet, and into the back door of Leah's bakery.

Inside the kitchen, Ali was leaning against the work-station, double-fisting Danishes.

"See?" Leah said. "Oh, and be careful when you take one from the box. Sometimes she bites, and I don't know if she's had her shots."

"I've totally had my shots," Ali said. "And anyway, I only bite Luke."

Aubrey carefully took a Danish, keeping an eye on Ali just in case Leah wasn't kidding. She took a big bite and then realized both Ali and Leah were looking at her.

"Now," Ali said to Leah. "Ask her now. While she's sugar-loading. It's hard to dodge people when you're on a sugar high."

Leah nodded and turned to Aubrey. "So…you've been busy."

"Very," Aubrey said warily.

"Busy kissing Ben."

And just like that, Aubrey choked on the Danish.

Leah pushed away from the counter, went to the refrigerator, and poured Aubrey a tall glass of milk.

She drank down the milk. She was no longer choking.

Mostly she was stalling for time. "Went down the wrong pipe," she said.

Ali and Leah were both watching her, waiting, and she sighed and set down the remainder of her Danish. "So this wasn't really about including me as part of your morning ritual. You wanted to hear the gossip."

"Actually," Ali said, "we were hoping for both."

Leah nudged the Danishes back toward Aubrey. "You always going to be so defensive?"

"Maybe," Aubrey said, and then caved. "Okay, probably."

"Listen," Leah said. "You're a friend. I think you're going to be a really good friend. But…"

"But Ben is family," Aubrey finished. "You're marrying his cousin. I get that. You're worried about him."

"Always," Leah said. "Even though he's a big boy, and he's going to do whatever he wants to do."

She'd noticed.

"Actually, to be totally honest, we're a little more worried about you," Ali said.

This surprised her. "Why?"

"Ben's not exactly a long-term bet right now," Ali said.

"And you think I am?"

"Of course," Ali said. "You had a rough patch and an unfair deal over Asshat Teddy. We both did."

Leah nodded, and Aubrey realized that what they'd said was true: They were worried—for her. Touched, she set aside her glass. "It really was just a kiss." Even saying it made her wince a little bit on the inside. First of all, it *hadn't* been just a kiss. It'd been the kiss of all kisses. And second, she shouldn't have allowed it to happen. No matter what she'd told Ben, he *was* on her list. This meant she had to try to make amends with him, not kiss him. Because when he found out why he was on her list, he wasn't going to want to kiss her. He was going to want to never see her again...

"I saw the kiss," Ali said. "I just happened to be outside, on the front sidewalk, talking to Olivia, who runs that very lovely vintage clothing store down the street. And bee-tee-dub, that was no 'just a kiss' kiss," she said. "That was a...wow kiss. I went home and jumped Luke's bones."

Aubrey had to laugh. Ali was right: It *had* been a wow kiss. But it'd also been a fluke. "It's not happening again," she insisted, and faced both their doubt and her own. "It can't."

A few minutes later, Aubrey was back inside the Book & Bean. She unlocked the door, turned on all the lights, and flipped over her OPEN sign.

Gus, asleep in his bed beneath the stairs, cracked open one eye and meowed at her. The nocturnal creature was annoyed by daylight.

Aubrey went to stand in what would soon be her little service niche. Ben had cleaned up after the demolition, but she went over it, sweeping and dusting to keep the store spotless. When she was done, she stood looking at the place where Ben had pressed her up against his long, leanly muscled, warm body.

At just the thought, her lips tingled in memory of their kiss. And if she was being honest, other parts tingled, too. In the bright light of day, she couldn't imagine what the hell she'd been thinking to slide her hands up his chest and into his silky hair and pull his head down to hers for more.

Okay, so she hadn't been thinking…

It'd been a mistake, albeit a delicious one, and she needed to move on. She was good at that—moving on. And she'd proven it with the first success on her list. Smiling just thinking about it, she pulled the notebook from her purse, then took out a pen.

And then, with a smile she couldn't contain if she'd tried, she very carefully, very purposefully, crossed off number three.

Melissa.

Back in high school, the two of them had been rivals who'd gotten off on one-upping each other. Melissa had been pretty and funny and incredibly charismatic, and whenever she'd set her mind on a guy, she'd gotten him.

Even when Aubrey had wanted him.

Aubrey'd had the fattest crush on one guy in particular. Ben, of course. It didn't matter that he had a longtime high school sweetheart; she'd still yearned and burned for him. Secretly, of course. She hated to remember those days, when she'd been a lowly freshman, garnering a lot of unwanted attention from the junior and senior boys because of her looks. This had, in turn, made her a target for the popular girls, of course. Hannah being one of them. One time Aubrey had been in the school parking lot, surrounded by a couple of aggressive, obnoxious boys. Ben had chased them off, and Hannah had been with him.

"She asks for that attention, Ben," Hannah had said when a grateful Aubrey had started to walk away.

The humiliation of that had burned deep, but it was chased away by Ben's defense of her.

"No girl asks for that, Hannah," he'd said.

Aubrey had never forgotten it. It'd been the start of her terribly painful crush, that one moment of kindness, and she'd hated, *hated*, that he'd been with Hannah.

In any case, Melissa had sensed Aubrey's crush and loved to torment her about it. One summer night Melissa had a bonfire on the hidden beach past the pier, a spot only teenagers and the homeless ever bothered to hike to. Melissa had brought some alcohol that she'd pilfered from her parents and had plied Hannah with it until she'd fallen asleep by the fire. Melissa had then sat down next to Ben and pulled out every trick in Aubrey's own arsenal. The *I'm-so-cold* accidental snuggle. The *scared-of-the-dark* accidental snuggle. The *wow-you're-really-strong* accidental snuggle. By the time Melissa had moved on to the *there's-a-big-bug!* accidental snuggle, Ben was cranky from fending Melissa off, and Aubrey was cranky knowing she wasn't going to get a shot at Ben herself.

So she'd one-upped Melissa.

She'd dared everyone to go rock climbing on the cliffs and jump into the water—a stupid, dangerous stunt. She'd been neck and neck with Melissa all the way up to the top. They'd been neck and neck at the jump into the water, too. Aubrey had landed safely.

Not Melissa. A wave had slammed her up against a rock, and she'd broken her arm. They'd dumped her at the hospital and deserted her, not wanting to get in trouble for the illegal bonfire, the alcohol, or the cliff jumping.

Melissa had been treated and then cited for public intoxication and reckless endangerment.

Aubrey had gotten off scot-free.

She'd have written it off as a silly, juvenile stunt, but

Melissa had been on course to play softball at a junior college. But with her arm requiring two surgeries, she'd been dropped from the team.

She'd never gone to college.

Aubrey's path had crossed Melissa's a few times here and there. After all, Tammy worked at the same salon. But Aubrey and Melissa had never talked about that night, which had changed Melissa's life forever. But this morning, Aubrey had driven by the salon and got lucky, finding Melissa there early working on stock, and she brought up the past for the first time in all these years.

Melissa had told Aubrey that not too long after she'd broken her arm, her parents had cut her off because of her partying ways. It'd been a wake-up call. She'd gotten herself together, gone to beauty school, and was now running her own hair salon. She swore up and down that she was actually grateful for the path she'd ended up on. And happy.

Happy…

Aubrey shook her head in marvel. But Melissa had been sincere. She'd hugged Aubrey and told her to come in for a cut sometime and they'd talk about old times.

"Wow, she smiles."

Aubrey stifled her startled shriek. Ben stood in the doorway, propping up the doorjamb with a broad shoulder, arms crossed over his chest. A casual pose.

But there was nothing casual about the assessing look he was giving her. "I smile plenty," she said, irritated at herself. Just the sight of him used to remind her of her mistakes. Now the sight of him reminded her that he'd kissed her.

And he kissed amazingly…

That knowledge was damned distracting. She needed to find a way to get rid of it, but she couldn't. She thought about it every waking moment. And also during her sleeping moments, what few there'd been.

Meow.

Gus had gotten up for Ben. He never got up for Aubrey, but there he was, on all four legs, rubbing up against Ben as though he were catnip.

She was beginning to see how it was that Ben might have gotten cat hair on his pants.

Ben crouched low and gave the cat an allover body rub that had Gus rolling in ecstasy on the floor, the low, loud rumble of his rarely heard purr filling the room.

She rolled her eyes and then realized Ben was looking at her, really looking at her, and she went on guard. "We going to talk about it?" he finally asked, straightening.

"No." Hell, no.

He gave an almost smile, as if that had been the answer he'd expected, and yet there was a flash of something else as well. She dismissed it, because there could be no way he wanted to talk about it, either.

Another man came up behind Ben in the doorway. "Knock, knock," he said, rapping his knuckles on the doorjamb. "Am I interrupting?"

"Pastor Mike." Aubrey immediately looked around herself guiltily, as if she'd been caught doing something wrong. She stopped herself and added a mental head slap. *Good Lord, woman, get a grip.* "No, you're not interrupting anything. How can I help you? Do you need a book?"

"No, I don't need a book," he said. "But thank you."

Aubrey didn't know what to make of this. People came here for books. Or, in Ben's case, to drive her crazy.

"I just wanted to see how you were doing," Pastor Mike said, his smile casual. Easy.

"I'm…" She didn't dare look at Ben. "Good. Thank you." She had no idea why he was really here. Were there AA rules she didn't know about? She hadn't signed up for anything. She'd been careful not to make any commitments that night. She hadn't wanted anyone getting into her business.

And she especially didn't want *Ben* getting into her business.

Mike looked at Ben and held out a hand. "Good to see you home safe. There were lots of candles lit for you. Your aunt Dee lit one every week."

Ben shook Mike's hand. "She likes to hedge all her bets."

The pastor smiled. "It worked. Heard you were sticking around this time. You helping our girl out?"

Ben's mouth quirked at the "our girl." "Yeah. So you and Aubrey are close?" he asked Pastor Mike.

Aubrey jumped in before Pastor Mike could give her secret away, on purpose or otherwise. "Yeah, we're close," she said, moving toward Ben. "We're…buddies." She tried to nudge him out the door—to no avail, of course. The big lug couldn't be budged.

"What are you doing?" he asked, effortlessly resisting her efforts.

"You've. Got. To. Go."

"Do I?"

"Yes!" She flashed a we're-all-family-here smile over her shoulder to Mike. "He was just saying he had to go," she told the pastor. "He's a big sinner, you know. Maybe you should go with him. Keep him from sinning further today."

Pastor Mike laughed. Why he was laughing Aubrey had no idea, because this wasn't funny.

"I don't have to go," Ben said. "I've got all day."

Great. He had all day. "No, really. You're a busy guy, so—"

"I'm all yours," he said easily.

Oh, for God's sake.

"Aubrey," Mike said gently.

"Just a minute, Pastor." She gave up trying to shove Ben out the door and went hands on hips, blowing a strand of hair from her face. She gave him a dirty look before turning back to Mike.

"It's okay," he said quietly. "I can't stay. I really did just want to see how you were doing, or if you needed anything."

Oh. Well, that was a little sweet, she could admit. "I don't. I'm fine, thank you."

Mike looked as though he knew better than to believe that, but he didn't argue with her. He simply nodded. "You know where to find me if you need anything."

And with that, he was gone.

"So," Ben said into the silence. "You and Pastor Mike. You're…buddies."

"Yep."

"From…?" he asked.

She gave him a look. "Maybe I go to church every Sunday."

He flashed a heart-stopping grin, and she sighed. "Yeah, that was probably a stretch, believing I'm actually good enough to go to church."

His smile faded as his gaze touched over her features. "Good's way overrated," he said. "But you're doing okay, I'd say."

The combination of that and the way he was looking at her had her heart squeezing uncomfortably, so she took a few steps back. "What are you even doing here?"

"I work here," he reminded her.

She sighed. "And thanks for that, by the way. It's really amazing how much you got done last night. It looks good."

He nodded in acceptance. "My turn to ask a question now," he said, and pushed off the wall, closing the distance between them.

"Uh…okay. But maybe we should set limits—"

"No limits. Here's my question. When are you going to tell me what's going on with you?"

Oh, boy. "That's a pretty widely scoped question."

"You're right," he said. "Let me narrow it down for you. Start with the list, and why you're going around town talking to people. Did you become a Jehovah's Witness or something?"

That startled a laugh out of her. "I think that's two questions."

His eyes warmed a little. "And?"

"And…no. I'm not a Jehovah's Witness."

Chapter 9

♥

Ben laughed, and when he did, Aubrey took another step back—right into the wall. She frowned at him as though it were his fault, which made him want to laugh again. Instead he studied her, a little surprised to realize that she was truly flustered by him.

This was fascinating. He knew it wasn't often that she allowed her feelings to show. Hell, he'd have said it wasn't often that she actually felt anything. She was one tough, smooth cookie. She always had been, all through school, even when she faced off against the mean girls or the stupid guys who thought she'd put out just because of how she looked.

She'd gotten even tougher. Inscrutable.

But then he'd kissed her. He'd had her in his arms, and he knew damn well she'd been feeling plenty.

So had he.

But today it was more than lust. He was making her

nervous, and he decided he liked that, too, much more than he should.

Mostly because she made him a whole hell of a lot of things, including—of all the ridiculous possibilities—jealous of a happily married pastor. He had to wonder what the connection was between Mike and Aubrey. The list?

And why did he care so much? The answer to that was unsettling, to say the least. She was getting under his skin—big-time.

He shouldn't have kissed her.

She was wearing a pretty dress, some silky forest green wraparound thing that hugged her curves and brought out her eyes.

And Christ, how it was that he was noticing such shit, he had no idea. She was a job to him right now, nothing more, nothing less.

Which didn't explain why he couldn't take his eyes off her mile-long legs when she turned and put some distance between them. She walked to the open space between the last row of bookshelves and the closet he'd removed and then squatted down and began to set out a bunch of squares.

A layout, he realized as she arranged them. She was working on a layout now that she had the funding she'd so desperately needed.

He looked around and realized something else. After he'd made a bit of a mess last night, she'd swept up. Dusted. And gotten rid of the last of the shit lying around from the old bookstore. She'd been working hard.

Really hard, he realized, getting a closer look at her, seeing the signs of exhaustion beneath her eyes and in the tightness of her mouth. Exhaustion and worry. "You've been busy," he said.

"Why do you sound surprised? It's my store."

He didn't know why he was surprised, exactly. "I guess I don't see you as the local friendly merchant type," he said.

"Should I even ask how you *do* see me?"

He knew better than to touch that one.

At his silence, she made a low sound of annoyance. "You don't know me, Ben," she said, making him feel like an ass as she went back to her little squares, toeing some things around, giving off an *I'm-very-busy* vibe.

But he did know her. Or he was starting to. He knew how very much this store seemed to mean to her. Knew that whatever that list was, it, too, meant a lot.

And he knew she kissed and tasted like heaven on earth.

Not that she wanted to hear any of *those* things from him. "Are you sure you want things so open?" he asked, and she jumped, clearly startled to realize he was right behind her now, looking over her shoulder down at the arrangement.

"I want to encourage socializing," she said stiffly. "I want people to have a place to go." She didn't look at him. "I want people to feel comfortable hanging out here so they won't be alone."

This made his heart squeeze, because he thought maybe she was the one who felt alone. "Why do you think people are so alone?" he finally asked, sincerely curious.

"Everyone's alone at some point." She glanced back at him. "You know that."

Because he'd lost Hannah. Holding her gaze, he gave a slow nod. "And you think a bookstore can make people feel…not alone?"

"I think having a place to go can help."

"Getting unlonely isn't about a physical place," he said.

"Well, I know that." Breaking eye contact, she once again went back to her layout. "But it's a start."

He watched her play with the arrangement of the squares for another moment. "Why such a wide path between the seating areas?" he asked. "You could have more merchandise in here if you close it up, even a little."

"I know what I'm doing."

"Yeah? Care to share?"

"I'm going to be hosting bingo night. And the knitting club. And the cookie and book exchange. And, I hope, a whole bunch of other stuff. A lot of that includes seniors, and they need the extra space to maneuver with canes and wheelchairs and things. The other day, Mr. Elroy took out an entire book display with his cane and then blamed in on Mr. Wykowski. They nearly came to blows, like a couple of twenty-year-olds, but Lucille stepped in, telling them they couldn't have any cookies if they didn't zip it."

Ben smiled. "Remember the time that you danced at the senior center and put three seniors into cardiac arrest?"

"*Near* cardiac arrest," she said, correcting him. "And it was a beauty pageant. I wasn't dancing. I was baton twirling for the talent competition."

He fought a smile and lost. "Whatever you say, Sunshine." He stepped into her space then, all the more amused when she went still, like Bambi in the headlights, unsure of whether to move clear, or stand firm.

She stood firm.

He pushed the squares around a bit. "How about this? You get an extra wall, which we'd make a half wall, as you wanted. That divides up the space so you can have two different groups at the same time and yet still gives you an open feel. Also, if you make the wall a shelving unit, you acquire additional product display or storage space."

She stared down at the squares for a long moment, saying nothing.

"Or not," he said with a shrug. "Your space."

"No, it's…good. You're good."

"Sometimes."

Her gaze jerked to his, and for a moment, hunger and yearning was heavy in the air between them.

Then she rolled her eyes. "And so modest, too."

He smiled, then pulled back the edge of the carpet, revealing what he'd discovered last night—hardwood floors beneath.

"Oh, my God," she said, and dropped to her knees, bending low to see the wood more closely. "Score!"

He eyed the way her dress pulled tight over her perfect ass and said, "Definitely." He tore his gaze off her. "I'll pull up the carpet for you tonight if you'd like."

"I'd like." She stood up, dusted her hands off, and pulled out a stack of paint samples. "I was thinking this one for the walls, and this one as an accent color."

He spread out the samples and nudged two colors over the top of her choices.

She stared down at them. "Lighter?"

"Yes. It'll make your space appear bigger."

"Warmer, too," she noted.

"You wanted comfy," he reminded her. "Your word, not mine."

She stared at his colors for a long moment. "You going to help me paint?"

"I can do it myself," he said, thinking a little space between them might be warranted.

"I want to be involved."

Perfect. "Painting's messy," he said.

"I'm good at painting."

He looked at her for a long moment, then shrugged. If she was willing to get burned, why the hell wasn't he?

"Besides," she said. "I don't tend to get messy."

He smiled, a real one. "Where's the fun in that?" he asked, and was rewarded by her blush.

The next night, Ben entered the bookstore after closing. He hadn't necessarily set out to avoid Aubrey.

Okay, he'd totally set out to avoid her.

As a result, he'd managed to go several hours today without thinking about her at all. Which was completely negated by the fact that she'd been starring in his dreams…

Yesterday, he'd pulled up the carpets in the bookstore. He'd swept afterward, but the hardwood had still needed some TLC. But as he looked the place over now, he realized Aubrey had scrubbed the hell out of the floors, getting up years of grime and scuffs. He didn't know what he'd expected from her, or why he'd assumed she'd have him do as much of the dirty work as possible, but she was working her ass off, and he found that…appealing. Wildly so.

"My aunt loved this place," she said from behind him. She was in sweats, eyes sleepy, as if maybe he'd woken her up. "I'd come here after school, and she'd have a snack waiting," she said. "She was always so busy, because she did all the work herself, but she made time for me. No matter what her day looked like. She'd put me in that big, soft chair"—she pointed to a huge overstuffed chair in the corner—"and then she'd bring me a stack of books to read, and for a little while, I'd escape."

"Escape what?" he asked.

She shrugged as if embarrassed and then looked out at the store. "I want to bring that magic to others."

He had no idea why his gut tightened, or why in that moment he wanted to give her whatever she needed. "We can do that," he said.

She turned to him. "We?"

"Your uncle hired me," he reminded her. "I don't leave a job just because the customer drives me insane."

She gave a little smile. "But why is this your job in the first place? Why are you even back in Lucky Harbor?"

Good question. Loaded question. Here felt like... home. Here was where he felt most like himself, but he shrugged. "Maybe I missed it," he said, testing the waters by saying it out loud.

"Sentimental, Ben? You?"

"You don't know me," he said, repeating the words she had said to him. "Or who I am."

She didn't smile, but she did nod in acknowledgement. "Is it getting easier?" she asked quietly. "Being here without her?"

He paused. No one ever asked him that. Where he'd been, most people had no idea he'd lost his wife. Only the people here in Lucky Harbor knew it. And the people here tended to tiptoe around the subject, not wanting to upset the grieving widower.

But five years was a long time, and he'd learned that as much as you loved someone, you couldn't keep her memory alive in your head for five years. Much as you loved someone, her laugh, her smile, her voice…it all faded a little with time. "I'm not on the edge of a cliff, if that's what you're asking," he finally said.

"What are you?"

He shrugged. "Tired, mostly."

"Given where you've been and what you've done, I can only imagine," she said softly.

Uncomfortable with this very real conversation, he turned away and walked the length of the room, pulling out his tape measure. "I bought the wood for the shelving units. I'll get more for the half wall if you want to go that route."

"I do," she said. "I scrubbed the floors, and since I like them scarred, I'm not going to do anything else to them. You're good at changing the subject, you know that?"

He did know that. She wanted to talk about the past five years, which made her as interested in him as he was in her.

She lifted a shoulder and gestured around her. "A bookstore is my favorite place. It shouldn't surprise you that I read—a lot. Research a lot. Your last project saved the lives of thousands, providing not only water for farmers and their crops but also giving them a means to keep providing those things on their own for generations to come."

His brows went up, both surprised and uncomfortable with the close scrutiny. "Are you actually giving me a compliment?"

"Maybe. Just a little bit."

"Why?"

"Why? What do you mean, why?"

He moved toward her, noting with some amusement that she sucked in a breath but held her own and stood firm.

They bumped. Front to front.

She appeared to stop breathing and tilted her head up, her gaze going to his mouth. "You know why," she whispered. "Because we're…attracted to each other."

"That's one word for it." Slowly he lifted a hand, watching her pupils dilate as he reached toward her…

And then past her to the counter, where he flipped open her notebook.

She blinked, whipping around to see what he was after, and went from soft and dreamy to pissed off in the blink of an eye. "Hey—"

"You've got someone crossed off," he said, teasing her. "Should I call the police?"

She narrowed her eyes. "Ha-ha." She snatched back her notebook. "Maybe you can be a funny carpenter and actually get some work done. I need those shelves, like, yesterday."

"What else do you need?"

She was at the door already but stopped to turn and look at him. "Excuse me?"

"A minute ago, it seemed like you needed a man."

"I don't *need* anyone," she said. "But if I did, it'd be someone...*sweet*," she said pointedly. "Sweet and... beta."

"Beta," he repeated.

"That's right," she said. "I'm over alpha men. And you, Ben McDaniel, are as alpha as they come."

Well, she had him there.

Chapter 10

♥

Two days later, Aubrey pulled up to her mom's house and checked herself out in the rearview mirror. Pale. Serious.

Stressed.

She put on some shiny lip gloss and then smiled—a big fake smile that didn't reach her eyes. One could fake anything, she knew, including happiness.

She was a pro at that.

But it was important to her that her mom really believe she was happy. Tammy had been through a lot in life—too much. So keeping the smile in place, Aubrey headed up the walk to her mom's condo. The evening was chilly but gorgeous. Clear and sharp, without a cloud in the sky. The stars lit her way.

She didn't even have to knock. With uncanny mom radar, Tammy sensed her daughter coming home to the fold and threw open the front door. "My baby!" she squealed with an ear-to-ear grin, yanking Aubrey in close for a tight hug. "Come in! I've got chicken frying, and now that you're here, I'll make mac and cheese, too, the way you love it, with the crusty bread crumbs and extra cheese on top."

Comfort food. Once upon a time, Aubrey had lived for such meals. Until the day she'd gone headfirst into puberty and couldn't fit into her jeans. After that, she'd secretly starved herself, pretending to eat her mom's food but really feeding it straight into the trash compactor.

Tammy had often expressed her pleasure at passing her "good metabolism" to her own flesh and blood, but the truth was Aubrey had her father's metabolism. She had to watch every calorie and work her ass off at the gym for every single indulgence she took. "I'm not hungry, Mom."

"Nonsense! You have to eat. I hope Carla comes tonight."

"Mom," Aubrey said slowly, not wanting her to be disappointed, as she always was. "Carla's not coming."

"Yes, I am." Carla came in behind Aubrey, still in scrubs. "But I've only got half an hour before I have to be back."

"Of course!" Tammy said, beaming at her two girls. "Your job's very important; I know that. Come in!"

Aubrey stepped into the living room. There was a lot of furniture there for the small space, but Tammy didn't like to throw anything away. And on every end table and coffee table there was…stuff. Candy dishes, frames, knickknacks. It was clustered and crowded, but to Aubrey, it was also home.

Carla had never spent much time here. She looked around now, and though she didn't say anything, Aubrey knew she was thinking that the place was a hoarder's dream.

And Aubrey could admit that they pretty much were a reality show waiting to happen.

Carla settled for sitting on a corner of a couch. Aubrey took the other far corner. "So…" She searched for a safe topic. "How are you?"

"Exhausted," her sister said, leaning back, closing her eyes. "Two straight shifts, and I'm a zombie. Haven't had time to go food shopping, get my mail, or water my poor plants, much less brush my hair. My neighbors probably think I'm dead."

Tammy tsked. "Honey, you've got to at least brush your hair. What will people think?"

Carla let out a low laugh. "They'll think I'm not dead after all, but that I do need a hairdresser."

"I could do those things for you," Aubrey said to her.

"What?" Carla asked. "Brush my hair? Or tell my neighbors I'm not dead?"

"Get you some groceries. Get your mail." Aubrey shrugged. "Water your poor plants."

"Why?"

"Because I'm your sister."

Carla opened her eyes and looked at her. "Is this about last week?"

"No," Aubrey said. But it was. A little. She had something to offer, damn it.

"That's so sweet of you to want to help, Aubrey," Tammy said. "Look at us, getting along like a real family."

"We *are* a real family, Mom," Aubrey said. She looked at Carla. *Tell her*, she said with her eyes. *Tell her we're a damn family*.

Carla met her gaze, paused, possibly rolled her eyes briefly, and then nodded at her mom. "We are family, Mom. We're just not always that good at it."

"Hey, we're better than some!" Tammy put her hand to her chest and her eyes filled. "No one move, do you hear me? I need a picture of this." She scrambled through the crap on the coffee table and came up with her phone. "Move closer to each other."

Aubrey and Carla shared an awkward grimace and then shifted closer.

"Yeah, like that. Perfect! Now hug." She gestured with one hand, the other holding the phone. "Oh, and smile! Goodness. This isn't a funeral."

Aubrey and Carla put their arms around each other, held the uncomfortable pose, and smiled.

And…smiled.

"Mom," Carla said, a little strained. "Take the picture already."

"I'm trying!" Tammy said, fumbling with her phone. "Crap! I can never find the damn camera on this thing."

Aubrey's smile was feeling more than a little brittle. "It's on your home page, Mom. Top left app. It says CAMERA."

"Oh." Tammy laughed. "Yes. Got it."

When Tammy finally took the shot and lowered the phone, Aubrey and Carla immediately broke apart.

They ate at the tiny table in the kitchen, practically elbow to elbow.

"Just like old times," Tammy said. "Remember when you'd come visit, Carla? We'd sit here just like this and talk about school. Hey, we could talk about work!"

"I live my work," Carla said. "I don't want to talk about it. How about yours?"

Aubrey watched as Tammy happily told Carla all about the salon and her clients. She remembered every single one, and every single thing they ever told her. It was part of what made her so popular.

"And you?" Carla asked Aubrey. "How are things at your work?"

"You know she's running her own business now," Tammy said, voice bursting with pride. "She took over Aunt Gwen's bookstore."

"You stopped working for the town hall?" Carla asked, surprised.

"Honey," Tammy said on a laugh. "Don't you ever read Facebook? Her boyfriend dumped her and she got fired."

"Well, not exactly," Aubrey said to a gaping Carla. "I dumped *him* and then *I* quit." Important difference, at least to her.

There was an awkward silence while everyone processed this.

"A bookstore," Carla finally said. "I thought those were all going out of business these days."

"This one's different," Aubrey said. "I'm selling digital books, too, and opening the place to all sorts of clubs, like knitting clubs and tea clubs…" She broke off because Carla wasn't looking impressed.

"How will that sell books?" she asked.

"Because it's going to be a place where people want to come and hang out. And buy their reading material," Aubrey said, trying to sound more positive than hopeful. "Don't you and your fellow surgical residents have a bunch of reading and studying to do? I could give you guys a place to meet and get together, and give you a discount on your materials."

"A discount," Tammy said. She loved a good bargain. "Well, isn't that nice?"

A few minutes later, Carla's cell phone buzzed. She read a text and stood. "Sorry, I have to get back." She looked at Aubrey. "I'll let people know about your store and the discount. We get together on Sunday nights and Wednesday mornings at the ass crack of dawn."

"My store is closed during those times, so you'd have the store exclusively."

Carla hesitated. "We meet in the cafeteria now, and it's not ideal. Their tea sucks."

"My tea never sucks, and I'll bring in goodies for you guys from the bakery next door," Aubrey said.

Carla nodded, and then was gone a few minutes later.

"That was really sweet of you, looking out for your sister like that," Tammy said. "You have such a big heart, honey."

Aubrey looked at her as if to say *Yeah, right*.

"No, it's true," Tammy insisted. "Carla may have gotten the brains, but you got all the heart."

Aubrey laughed. Okay, *that* she'd heard before, but there was no use in being insulted. Not when her mom meant it as the highest of compliments. Her gaze snagged on a stack of bills in the mess on the table. "How are you doing, Mom? Really?"

"I'm great, honey."

Aubrey tapped the stack of bills.

Tammy shrugged. "Oh, those," she said. "Don't you worry about those. They'll get paid in good time."

"I've got a little savings left," Aubrey said. Emphasis on *little*. "Let me—"

"No, no. I've got it, though you've proven my point

about heart." Tammy stroked Aubrey's hair. "You're still using that stuff I gave you from the salon, right? It's a miracle worker, isn't it?"

"Yes. Mom—"

"But you're not wearing any lipstick."

"I'm wearing gloss. And I was working."

"You should *always* have lipstick on beneath," Tammy said. "Especially when you're working. It gives you color and pizzazz."

"Carla wasn't wearing any," Aubrey said, "and you didn't bug her about it."

"Yes, well, I'm a little afraid of Carla, to be honest."

Aubrey laughed.

"Are you telling me she doesn't scare you?" Tammy asked, smiling.

"She scares the crap out of me," Aubrey admitted, and they *both* laughed. And then her mom went back to her favorite topic. "There's really no reason to slack off on how you look, you know. Even if you're working your tush off. How many times have I told you: If you look good, then life *is* good."

Aubrey suppressed her sigh. "I look *fine*."

Tammy looked pained at this. "You know how I feel about that word."

Fine was reserved for bad hair days. "I'm not on a modeling job, Mom."

"Well you *should* be," Tammy said. "You'd make a fortune. Goodness, you were on such a roll with the beauty contests. You could've gone all the way, honey. You could have become a model."

"I love what I'm doing now," Aubrey said, shuddering at the memory of her modeling days.

"That's wonderful," Tammy told her. "But I'm just saying. You're so pretty, baby. And your figure! You could have done catalogs. You could have been one of those angels for Victoria's Secret."

Aubrey laughed.

"I'm serious!"

Sad thing was, Tammy *was* serious. And she could have no idea, but Aubrey *had* given modeling a try. There'd been some lowbrow modeling, which had led to some lowerbrow modeling, which had led to some things that Aubrey tried very hard not to think about, though she had managed to pay for most of her college tuition that way. "Modeling isn't for me," she said firmly.

Tammy sighed. "If you say so."

"I do."

"I just want you to be taken care of," Tammy said.

"I'm perfectly taken care of, Mom. By myself."

Tammy smiled. "Oh, I know. You're so strong, Aubrey. So independent. I know you've had to be. Sometimes I worry we did the wrong thing, your dad and I, splitting you two up like we did the furniture and silver."

"You did what you had to," Aubrey said.

"For me," Tammy agreed. "I loved you both so much, but your father and I…we were on track to kill each other. I just figured the best thing was to split everything up, including you girls. And when it worked out so well, your sister with your daddy and you with me, it just got easy to not switch around so often."

"Or at all," Aubrey said mildly.

Tammy sighed. "Or at all."

"Dad wasn't much for following the rules."

"Your daddy isn't the only one at fault," Tammy said

softly. "I know it hurt you that he didn't have much time for you, but he was so busy working at the hospital, and his work was so important. Your sister is so much better suited to that life. I always meant to get me another man so you'd have a father figure, but that never really worked out."

"Mom, it's fine. It's all water under the bridge."

"Well, now, that's what I've always thought," Tammy said. "You were so popular at school."

More like notorious...

"You had boyfriends. And you dated in college. You always seemed to have a date."

Aubrey loved her mom, she truly did, but Aubrey had gone to college in Seattle while working at various admin jobs. Not very far away in the scheme of things, but since Tammy rarely—if ever—left Lucky Harbor, Aubrey might as well have been on the moon. In all honesty, Tammy had no idea what Aubrey's college life had been like.

"And then you got that fancy job at the town hall. I thought for sure you'd find yourself a fancy man to go with it and finally give me grandchildren."

"Mom—"

"No, honey, let me finish. Every job you've ever had, you excelled at. Anything you've ever wanted, you got for yourself. You're so capable. So strong. But you're acting like...what do they say? An island."

Every once in a while, a shockingly deep and wise kernel of wisdom came out of her mom's mouth. "There's nothing wrong with relying on myself," she said in response. She couldn't be disappointed in someone else that way. "I'm really okay, Mom. I promise."

"Well, I have eyes in my head, don't I? I can see that you're good. But it's okay to let someone in sometimes, you know. Being independent and strong and having to do everything yourself is one thing. But you shouldn't have to be all on your own, always. You can let people in, let down your guard. Have more friends. Be less stressed…"

Aubrey smiled. "I'm not stressed. I love the store. And I'm not alone, either. I have you."

"Aw, honey." Tammy's eyes went shiny, and she tilted her head back and blinked rapidly while waving a hand near her face. "Don't you dare make me cry—I'm not wearing waterproof mascara today."

Aubrey left her mom's place feeling like a stuffed sausage—reminiscent of a time years ago when she'd felt that way every night. She took the long way back to the shop, by way of the bluffs—which actually wasn't on her way home at all. It was at least ten miles out of her way.

The houses up here were expensive. Ritzy. Gorgeous.

Her dad lived at the end of a cul-de-sac in a huge, sprawling two-story house he'd had built to spec a few years ago, designed for his second wife.

Aubrey didn't pull all the way down to the end of the street; she didn't want to give herself away. Feeling like a ridiculous stalker, she eyed the lit-up house and felt her pulse kick. On the big front porch, with all the pretty hanging lights, sat a huge dollhouse. A big, perfect, gorgeous, fancy, clearly outrageously expensive dollhouse.

And it was forgotten on the porch, looking a little wet from the elements and dirty.

Her heart squeezed. Not hers, she told herself. Not anything like hers.

Hers had been much smaller, made of cheap plastic and cardboard. But she'd loved it. She'd loved it so much. Somehow it'd gotten lost in the divorce shuffle and subsequent move, and she'd mourned its loss more than the loss of her family's togetherness. How silly was that?

But seeing this perfect dollhouse, neglected, unloved, brought it all back. That's how she'd felt after the divorce, too. Neglected. Unloved.

Suddenly there was activity in the yard, which was lit by the house and porch lights, and she went still as stone, as though *that* would make her invisible.

But the three occupants on the frozen grass didn't so much as turn her way or pay the slightest bit of attention to her.

It was her dad and Aubrey's two half sisters, Brittney and Katrina, ages four and six. They were in matching dresses and wool coats. Her dad was in a suit and overcoat, looking neat and unruffled as ever, and they were all chasing around after a little puppy.

Aubrey felt sucker punched in the gut. She actually bent over with the pain, her hands on the steering wheel, her mouth open and gaping as though she were a hooked fish.

A dollhouse *and* a puppy. They had her dollhouse and her puppy. Okay, okay, not *hers*. But she felt as if part of her had just been stolen. Peals of laughter were coming from her half sisters, and then a sound she didn't recognize at first.

Her father's laugh.

By the time Aubrey got home, she was feeling the need to put on her ugliest sweats, swipe off all her makeup, and fill a Big Gulp cup with wine.

Make that vodka. She let herself in through the shop and inhaled the scent of freshly cut wood.

Then she heard Ben's clipped voice.

"Fuck that," he said. "The guy's working less than two hours away? At a decent-paying job? And yet he's not providing for his kids, much less even *seeing* them? They're rotting away in that foster home, Luke."

Aubrey stepped farther inside and found Ben at the far window, facing outside. He held the phone up to his ear with one hand while the other was shoved into his hair, holding it off his forehead. His feet were planted wide, in an aggressive stance that was dialed to pissed-off badass.

"No, I'm not backing off on this," he said, and then paused, clearly listening. Whatever he heard made him relax and let out a breath. "Say that to my face and we'll see how pretty your fiancée thinks you still are afterward," he growled, though now he sounded a whole lot less pissed off.

"At least contact the asshole," he said. "Those girls deserve that—yeah, yeah, I look at them and see me. Jesus. Neither of us needs a shrink to know that. But they're *five*, Luke. I was twelve, and already knew how it was. These girls, they're…*shit*. They have no idea. They need him. Tell the asshole that. They *need* him." He disconnected and shoved his phone in his pocket.

And didn't move. Just stared out into the night…

Aubrey didn't know what to do—an unusual feeling for her. She was intruding on a private moment, and yet this was *her* place. She dropped her purse to give him warning of her presence, and when he still didn't move—not a single, tense, muscled inch—she realized he'd known she was there all along.

"If you're looking for an argument," came his disembodied voice in the low light, "forget it. I'm not in the mood."

But that was a lie. He was absolutely in the mood for a fight, and that suited her just fine.

Because she was in the mood, too.

Chapter 11

What's the problem?" Aubrey asked Ben.

"I said I wasn't in the mood for you, Aubrey."

Given the conversation she'd just overheard, she decided to cut him a break on the serious 'tude. "I can see that. Maybe you should cut out for the night."

At that, he turned to her, his gaze narrowing as he took in her face. "What's the matter?"

Unfortunately, she was still embarrassingly close to tears, so she didn't dare go there. "Just go home, Ben."

And to make sure he—or she—didn't do anything stupid, she left first. She walked to the small back hallway, which opened to an even smaller office space and a very narrow set of stairs that led to her loft.

She took the stairs at a quick pace, closed the door behind her, and stood in the middle of the room. The only light came from the moonlight slanting in through the slats of the window blinds. She didn't need to hit the light switch to see the four hundred square feet, which consisted of a love seat, a square table and two chairs, a kitchenette, and her one indulgence…a soft, plush bed piled with softer, plusher pillows.

She resisted, barely, the urge to throw herself face-down on it and assume her favorite thinking position.

Meow.

Oh, good. A purpose. Without so much as shedding her coat, she strode over to Gus, who was sitting by his empty bowl, staring at her accusatorily. She poured him a scoop and petted him while he ate.

"You ran away before you decided on colors."

With a gasp, she whirled. Ben was standing right there. Of course he was. He was in faded, loose jeans and a T-shirt, snug across his chest and arms. He looked a little dusty, a little sweaty, and his eyes glittered with the same temper she felt coursing through her.

"You need a damn bell around your neck," she said.

He didn't smile. He simply held out two color samples. "Pick one."

"There were more than two choices."

"There's only two *good* choices."

She'd picked out five decent colors, but decided not to push him. "What was your phone call about?"

"What call?"

"The one that pissed you off when I walked in."

He gave her an assessing look. "Why do you look like you've been crying?"

"What was your phone call about?"

"You first," he said.

She crossed her arms.

He gave her a grim smile. "Yeah, that's what I thought."

She sighed. "I don't like to talk about it."

He shook his head. "Listen, maybe I don't know what's going on. Maybe I can only guess it has something to do with your list. But have you considered that I might be worried about you?"

"Worried? Whatever for?"

"Maybe you're involved in something bad or dangerous."

She looked at him for a beat. His eyes were solemn, his mouth grim. He was serious. Dead serious.

He was worried about her. That had never crossed her mind. "I had dinner with my mother," she said. See? She could share. She wasn't always an island. "I ate enough comfort food for three people for a week. Then, for shits and giggles, and because I didn't feel bad enough about myself, I drove by my father's house and found him playing in the yard—in a suit, no less—with his new family and a puppy." She closed her eyes and admitted the most painful part. "And the girls had a dollhouse on the porch."

"A dollhouse."

"Yeah, like...I don't know." She gestured with a hand to waist height. "About this big. I had one when I was little, but when my parents divorced, somehow it got in with my sister's stuff. When I asked my dad for it back, he said it was Carla's." She laughed a little at herself. "It's dumb how much I loved and missed that thing."

"Why didn't you ask your sister for it back?"

"Because what if she loved it as much as I did?" Aubrey shook her head. "My mom felt really bad, but she couldn't afford to buy me one." She hated that memory and wished she'd never said anything. "It's silly, letting that get to me. It wasn't mine. It was a new one, a brand-new one, all pretty wood and fancy."

And unused…

Shaking it off, she said, "Your turn."

He just looked at her for a long beat. "You didn't say why you've been crying."

"Does it really matter?"

"You wouldn't think so," he said softly, coming close. He stroked a strand of hair from her temple, tucking it behind her ear. "And I'm not all that thrilled to tell you, but it does. Matter."

She closed her eyes. Not to savor his touch. Because it wasn't *his* touch she was reacting to, she assured herself. Anyone's touch would have reached her tonight.

Okay, that was a big fat lie.

"When I was growing up," she said softly, eyes still closed, "there was no playing in the yard with my dad, and he certainly never would have done so in his suit. He might've gotten dirty. And a puppy…well, I was more likely to take a spaceship to the moon than be allowed to have a pet."

"Ah," he said quietly. "Daddy issues."

Her eyes flew open, but there was no mockery in his face. Instead, he let out a long, slow breath. "I nearly hit two kids who ran out in the street in front of my truck last week," he said.

"Oh, my God."

"Yeah. Twin five-year-old girls. They were walking to school."

"Alone?" she asked.

"Well, not after I found them."

She felt her heart melt over this big tough guy facing

an emotion as sweet as protectiveness for two little girls he didn't even know.

"They're foster kids," he said. "And their foster mother is supposedly one of the better ones, but…" He shoved his hand through his hair and shook his head. "I saw them again later when I worked Craft Corner—"

"Wait," she said, stopping him. "*You're* working Craft Corner?"

He scowled. "Yeah. So?"

She smiled. "You're working Craft Corner," she said again, and laughed. "I'd like to see that. Mr. Tall, Dark, and Grumpy-Ass working with little kids."

"Now, see, how is it that everyone but me knew it was little kids? Jack conned me into it," he admitted.

She laughed again.

"Not funny."

"You being conned into anything is pretty funny."

"You think I'm impenetrable?"

"I think you're a fortress."

He blew out a breath, but didn't deny it. "Pink told me their mom is dead and their dad's in jail for the big one."

She was beginning to see why this had gotten to him. "Murder?" she asked.

"That's what I assumed. I had Luke run them."

"And?"

"And mom *is* dead, but their dad's working at an auto shop in Seattle."

She gaped at him. "That fucker."

"My thought exactly."

He looked extremely pissed off again. Unusual for him, but she understood now and ached for the girls *and* him. "I didn't have the greatest childhood," she said quietly. "But I know it could've been so much worse." She met his gaze, knowing that his childhood *had* been worse, maybe as bad as the girls'. After all, his dad was rumored to be in jail, too, and his mom had just dropped him off one day at his cousin Jack's and had never come back for him. She couldn't even imagine the ways that haunted him. "I know you had it rough," she said softly.

He met her gaze and then stepped into her a little bit more, so they were sharing air. "I don't feel like talking anymore."

His voice and proximity gave her a whole-body shiver. "Sure. What do you feel like doing?" she asked.

He just looked at her, eyes blazing.

"No," she said, lifting a hand, not sure if she was warding him off or really just trying to keep herself in check. "I meant what I said earlier."

He caught her hand in his. "When you said you didn't need a man, but if you did it wouldn't be me?" he asked. "When you said you wanted sweet? And...*beta*?" This last was said with more than a hint of mockery.

"That's right," she said, standing by her words, however stupid they sounded now. "Beta."

They were toe-to-toe now, and their bodies brushed. His was tough as nails. Hard. Warm.

Strong.

Male.

He smelled like freshly cut wood and like whatever soap he'd used. Like overheated man.

And everything within her tightened in desperate need, just to be...taken. To let go. To forget, just for an hour...

"You'd better say it again," he said very quietly.

"What?"

"That you don't want me." He gave a slow shake of his head. "Because you're looking at me like I'm dinner and you haven't eaten all day."

She let out a shaky breath, and her breasts brushed his chest.

His eyes darkened, but he didn't move. "Aubrey. Say it."

"I said I don't *need* a man," she said softly. "Need and want are two different things. I *don't* need a man." She blew out a breath. "But I want one. I want you. Damn it." She was so on edge that she was already trembling, dying for his first touch. For the taste of him.

For the oblivion she knew he'd bring.

But he still didn't move.

She raised her chin, looking him straight in the eye. "Don't play hard to get, Ben. It doesn't suit you."

His jaw tightened, and she couldn't help but be a little maliciously pleased at making him as frustrated as she was. "I've just said I want you," she murmured. "So what's the problem?"

"The problem is—" His eyes dropped to her coat, the one covering her from neck to thigh.

"Yes?"

"*Shit.*" He shoved his fingers through his hair again, the muscles in his arms taut as he stood before her, the image of hot and temperamental, with testosterone and pheromones pouring off of him, and her stomach cramped.

He was going to refuse her.

Reject her. She started to turn away, but he slapped both palms on the wall on either side of her head, caging her in. "I don't need you," he said succinctly.

"Already established," she managed, her body already

humming, yearning, aching for him. Her body was a hussy.

Still holding her caged against the wall, his gaze dropped to her mouth. "This changes nothing," he said. "We do this, we're over it."

"*So* over it."

He nodded, gaze on her mouth. His own quirked very slightly. "You want me."

"In spite of yourself," she said, annoyed all to hell. "Yes."

He stared down at her for what felt like an eternity. "Lose the coat."

Chapter 12

♥

Aubrey's bones liquefied. "What?"

"You heard me," Ben said, voice so low and rough as to be a growl.

She had no idea what it said about her that she reacted to this with a shudder that was a mere millimeter below orgasm. Not taking her eyes off Ben, she reached up and slowly began to unbutton her coat. There were a lot of buttons. Each one she popped open made his eyes darken further.

After the last one, she let the coat fall. Before it hit the ground, Ben slid a hand on the nape of her neck and drew her in, his mouth closing over hers. Soft, then sure and demanding, and the hunger consumed her, hot and terrifying.

As if he felt the same, he let out one low, mirthless laugh and whispered, "Damn, you drive me insane" against her mouth.

There was a note of dazed frustration to his tone, and Aubrey absolutely knew the feeling. He wasn't in her future, and yet he tasted better than her wildest fantasies. And God help her, but she wanted more.

Leaning in again, his mouth hovered near hers as his gaze raked down her body, sending sparks racing along every nerve ending. "In those fuck-me boots, you're as tall as I am," he said.

"Is that a problem?" she asked.

"Hell, no. I like it. We're all lined up." Proving it, he hauled her in against him, one hand sliding up to sink into her hair, the other low on her back, nudging her even closer. She let out a low moan at the contact, and his lips curved in a sinful smile. His mouth should be illegal in all fifty states, but she bet he could do things with it. Things she wanted.

Bad.

He nipped at her lower lip, and she parted for him, but then he bypassed her mouth, skimming along her jaw. She heard a needy whimper. Hers, of course. Her eyes fluttered closed as he kissed a hot path to her ear and ran the tip of his nose along her lobe. "You sure this is what you want?" he asked.

Was he kidding? She was clutching him, her hands fisted in his shirt, rubbing against him like a cat in heat.

"Aubrey."

She didn't know why, but the sound of her name on his lips did something to her. Something sinfully wicked, but more, too. She took a deep breath, wrapped her arms around his neck, and melted into the planes of his hard body. "Yes. This is what I want."

"I'm not sweet," he reminded her.

"Or beta," she said. "But I'm not looking for that kind of man right this very minute."

"What are you looking for?"

"You. This."

He traced her spine with his fingertips, leaving a trail of fire that she felt all the way to her toes. Holding her gaze prisoner, he brushed his lips across hers, his hands sliding with purpose from her back southward, until he was cupping a cheek in each hand, rocking her into a most impressive erection. There was a jolt of electricity as he skimmed further south, beneath the hem of her dress.

She arched back as his clever fingers traced the edge of her thong, teasing, stroking up, and then down, and then further, between her legs.

Less clothes. She needed less clothes between them and more full frontal contact. As if reading her mind, he gave a quick yank and her thong tore free and slithered to the floor.

His eyes were black with desire. "Do you have a condom?" he asked.

"Bathroom."

He scooped her up so that she could wrap her legs around him and carried her there. He set her on the counter and flicked on the light.

"Bottom drawer," she managed.

He found the box, not commenting on the fact that it hadn't been opened. In return, she didn't comment on the fact that he obviously didn't have a condom on him. She reached out to turn off the light but he put his hand over hers. "On," he said.

Contrary to what anyone might think, she hadn't actually done this in a while. She assumed it was like getting back on a bike, but just in case it wasn't, she wanted room for error. "Ben—"

"On," he said firmly, and before she could say another word, he pulled off his shirt and she found herself sighing in pleasure at the sight of him, all lean, tough planes delineated with muscle born of years of hard physical labor.

Watching her watch him, he kicked off his work boots and finished stripping with easy, economical movements.

He was hard.

Everywhere.

Okay, well, if *this* was her view, he was right—the light could absolutely stay on.

"We good?" he asked, clearly amused by the fact that he'd just caught her drooling over him.

Yeah, she was good. So damn good…"I didn't know I was going to be so attracted to you naked," she admitted.

"Liar."

Yeah, he was right. She *was* a big fancy liar. She'd known she was attracted to Ben for a very long time. Possibly forever.

"Now you," he said, reaching for the zipper on her dress.

She held him off. "Maybe we should move to my room." *Which would have more forgiving light than these harsh fluorescents…*

In answer, his mouth came down on hers. She opened to him completely, not that he gave her a chance to do anything less. Still kissing her, he shifted to stand between her legs, opening them wider, then wider still. She lost herself in the way he devoured her mouth, so that when her dress fell to her waist, she gasped in surprise. She opened her eyes and looked into his.

"I wish you could see yourself the way I'm seeing you," he said hoarsely. Her heart clenched because she caught something in his gaze she didn't often find when people looked at her.

Raw desire.

This worked for her, but there was something else as well, possibly affection—not that she wanted to acknowledge it. Still, it was there, as apparent as the racing of her pulse. Then he leaned down and brushed his lips across hers as his hands stroked her heated flesh.

Her plan had been to infiltrate his defenses, get him naked, and—she hoped—get an orgasm while she was at it.

Stick to the plan, Aubrey.

But…but what if this was his first time since Hannah? She opened her mouth to ask, but he kissed her until she lost her train of thought. He kissed her as though he knew *exactly* what he was doing. If he was just getting back on the bike, he was having no problems. "Ben?"

He dragged that hot, talented mouth down her throat, along her collarbone, to a breast. She stopped breathing. But when he sucked her nipple into his mouth at the same time he slid a hand between her thighs, she cried out, arching back, giving him full-pass access without even realizing what she was doing.

She completely forgot what she'd wanted to ask him.

He teased her until every thought left her brain, and then he dropped to his knees and ran his hands up the inside of her legs. Holding her in place right where he wanted her, he leaned in and continued the torture with his lips, his tongue, his teeth, groaning his approval when she gasped out his name and slid her fingers into his hair. Her eyes strained to stay open because there was something about seeing him get so turned on by pleasuring her. But her eyes drifted shut in sheer, lustful bliss.

"Watch," he said, and she tried to, but he did something diabolical in tandem with his tongue and fingers that had her writhing mindlessly into him. He was taking her apart one lick at a time, and she was already quivering, on the edge, toes curled. She knew that she could give herself a somewhat satisfying orgasm in about ten minutes. A man, when she chose one, could usually get her off in about twice that.

But Ben had her shuddering in less than five minutes.

She was still lost in the throes and thinking she'd never had such an erotic experience in her life when he entered her with one hard stroke and reminded her there was more.

So much more…

She opened her eyes to find him watching her, unwavering and intense. She slid her hands up his chest and around his neck, pulling him closer as they moved together.

Unbelievably, she started to tighten around him again, though she tried to hold back. She wasn't sure why, but before she could think about it, he stroked a thumb over her swollen, wet flesh and she was gone, gone, gone. Her cry of pleasure seemed to push him over the edge. Fisting one hand in her hair, the other on her ass, holding her in place, Ben buried his face in the crook of her neck and came with her.

She didn't move for a long moment, couldn't. Ben didn't, either, and she wondered if he was as stunned as she was by the sheer sexual power they held over each other. When she finally shifted to get up, he tightened his grip on her. Face still pressed against her throat, she felt him just breathe her in. After a few minutes, he gave her a

slow, lazy nuzzle, then kissed her with surprising tenderness before raising his head.

She took stock. Her dress was bunched around her
waist, her only item of clothing. Well, except for her
footwear. "I'm still wearing my boots," she said inanely.

He smiled. "The memory of how you look, just like
this, is going to fuel my dreams for a long time to come."

She gave him a little nudge. Taking the hint, he disentangled their bodies with care, but she couldn't control
the needy little gasp that escaped her at the loss. He went
still for a beat, but she nudged again. Her torn panties
were useless, but she managed to twist her dress back into
place.

Ben hadn't made a move to get dressed. He unselfcon-
sciously dealt with the condom disposal and then offered
her a hand to help her hop down from the counter.

Life was simple for guys, apparently. No complicated
emotions to think about. They could walk around naked
without worrying what they looked like.

Of course, she thought, Ben didn't have to worry. He
looked…edible.

The bastard.

She bent for his clothes and shoved them at him.

Taking his sweet-ass time, he pulled on his pants and
straightened, and she did her best not to stare at him. But
she failed. She couldn't help it; he was just so damn…hot.
She let her eyes soak him up, from his still-bare chest
to the fact that though his pants were on, they were unbuttoned and riding low, and he was still semihard. He
looked…dangerous, she decided. And primed for another
round.

Her body was game.

He flashed her a smile. He knew what she was thinking. She turned her back while he finished getting dressed, which made him laugh softly and pull her around to face him again. "Okay?" he asked.

She swallowed her half-hysterical laugh. "Well, let's see. I just had wild monkey sex with a man I can't get along with to save my life, in the bathroom above my shop, no less—which, by the way, I don't even think is locked." She tossed up her hands. "Why wouldn't I be okay?"

He studied her a moment. "We got along just fine in the past hour, I'd say."

She felt the blush race up her face. "You know what I mean."

"Yeah, I suppose I do. Do we need to talk about it?"

"Hell, no."

He looked relieved. "We said this wasn't going to change anything," he said. "We both got what we wanted."

"Yeah," she said. But what if she suddenly couldn't remember what she'd wanted?

And suddenly, he wasn't looking so relieved. He was looking…wary. "Did you change your mind, Aubrey?"

"No." Not that she would admit it anyway, not even over the threat of death and dismemberment.

"Good," he said with quiet steel. "Because I don't want a committed relationship."

"Ever?"

He hesitated. "Not any time soon, anyway."

She absorbed the unexpected shock of disappointment, and, she hoped, kept it from her face. "Then we're good."

He paused again, as if searching that statement for

honesty. "I locked the shop before I came up here," he said. "The flower shop and bakery are long closed." He smiled, his voice light and teasing when he added, "So no worries. No one could have heard you."

Oh, hell, no, he didn't just say that. She opened her mouth to tell him that they'd *both* been loud, but she shut it again.

Because he was right. *She'd* been the noisy one.

Damn. She should really have orgasms with other people more often. She moved from the bathroom to the door of her loft and not so subtly opened it for him to leave.

Ben looked amused but didn't say one word as he crossed the room. As he came up even with her, he cupped her jaw and planted one hell of a kiss on her. If she hadn't still been trembling from what they'd just done, she'd have pushed him away. But as it was, she had to fight her limbs, which wanted to cling to him like Saran Wrap.

Lifting his head, he sent her one last look of wicked promise, and then he was gone.

Alone, she shut and locked her door and then leaned back against it. *What had she just done?* There was really only one man in town who had the power to hurt her. And she'd just had sex with him.

Chapter 13

♥

Ben dreamed about Aubrey writhing in ecstasy in his arms. Best dream ever. He was late getting out of bed, but it was worth it, he thought, hitting the road running as he headed along the harbor. The icy ocean air—so cold it felt like hell had frozen over—sucked the breath from his lungs, but the discomfort was nothing compared to what he'd felt in some of the places he'd been.

Sam was waiting for him at the pier, running in place, his breath puffing out in little white clouds. "Thought maybe you weren't coming," he said, and looked Ben over carefully. "Rough night?"

Yeah, not exactly. "I'm good," Ben said. And he was. Possibly a little too good.

Sam let it go, and they ran hard, as usual. No words necessary.

An hour later, Ben was in the bookstore when Aubrey stormed in with eyes flashing, boots clicking as she moved across the floor, anger coming off her in waves.

She was wearing yet another businessy dress, this one made of soft, sweater-like material that covered her from chin to knee but nicely hugged the curves he now knew intimately.

He was pretty damn sure he should have been over her enough not to get hard at the sight of her. "What's up?" he asked.

Like he didn't know...

"My car won't start," she said animatedly, furious and beautiful. "Something happened to it overnight."

Yeah. *He'd* happened to it. He'd pulled the coil wire late the night before after a drink with Luke. The coil wire was still in his pocket, as a matter of fact.

Aubrey stalked across the store, straight to Ben's still-steaming to-go cup of coffee, which Leah had poured for him. She drank from it as though it were her lifeline.

All without making eye contact with him. "Black. Blech." She sighed. "I don't know what I'm going to do. I can't afford a mechanic."

She wasn't going to need one.

"It's always something," she said, sounding tired. Frustrated. At the end of her rope.

Still not looking at him directly.

Another man might have felt guilty as hell, but Ben told himself he wasn't another man. He wanted to know what she was up to, what was wrong, and he'd meant it when he'd said he wanted to know if she was okay. And yeah, after last night, he was more curious than ever. There was no better way to figure her out than to drive her around. "Where do you need to go?" he asked.

She looked down at her phone, thumbing through screens with dizzying speed.

He put a hand on her. "It can't be far," he said. "You need to open the store in an hour and a half, right?"

She finally looked at him and then blushed. He figured that was the "wild monkey sex," as she'd called it. The best wild monkey bathroom sex he'd ever had. "Do you need a ride?" he asked.

"No," she said quickly. Too quickly.

"Look at you, lying so early in the morning."

She blew out a breath. "Okay, so I have a few…errands to run."

"I'll take you."

She drank some more of his coffee and just stared at him. "Why would you do that?" she finally asked.

Because he was a jerk. "It's the neighborly thing to do," he settled on.

"We're not neighbors."

"Okay, it's the thing to do for someone who screamed your name as she came."

She sputtered. "I so did *not* scream your name."

"The mirror practically shattered," he said.

"I can't believe—that is just so rude of you to say."

"I loved it," he said simply, and watched as a good amount of her defensiveness drained away. "Come on," he said. "Let's hit the road. I've got an errand, too. The stain came in for your shelves. Oh, and I need to buy more condoms."

"You do *not* need more condoms. Remember? We decided we were a one-time thing—" Then she seemed to finally catch his drift and realized, belatedly, that he was just yanking her chain. "Shut up," she said.

He gave her a slow, long, hot look, and the last of her temper appeared to vanish. She squirmed a little bit, and with that little telltale move, made his entire day—though he couldn't have said why to save his life.

"What are you going to do while I'm...doing my stuff?" she asked suspiciously.

"I've got my own stuff to do in the truck while I wait."

"Yeah?" she asked. "Like what?"

He pulled out his phone. "Like kicking Jack's ass on a game we're playing."

"*Call of Duty*, or something equally alpha and macho?"

"Something like that," he said.

She finished his coffee and handed him the empty cup. "Fine," she said. "Let's go. I need to hit the grocery store first."

Two minutes later they were on the road, huddled up to the heater vents in his truck.

"You need a newer vehicle," she said, squinting through the foggy windshield.

"Shh!" He lovingly stroked the dash of the truck. "Don't listen to her, baby. You're perfect just as you are."

Aubrey rolled her eyes. "A little attached, are we?"

"Very," he said. "This was my uncle Jack's truck, you know."

She glanced at him. "No, I didn't know."

"I helped him rebuild her."

"He died while fighting a fire, right?" she asked.

"Yeah." Ben and Jack junior had been fourteen at the time. It had devastated the both of them—Jack, who'd lost his dad, and Ben, who'd lost the only father figure he'd ever known. His aunt Dee had given Ben the truck, though officially he'd had to wait several years to be old enough to drive it.

Unofficially, though, he and Jack had used it to make

more than a few illegal and illicit late-night trips. The truck had seen him through some pretty hairy times. He'd never get rid of it.

"That must have been a terrible loss for you," Aubrey said quietly.

It hadn't been his first loss, and even at age fourteen, he'd known shit happened. But yeah, it'd sucked hard. "I had Dee," he said. "She kept me on the straight and narrow." Even when he'd only added to her grief, she'd never given up on him.

"I've met her," Aubrey said. "She's a wonderful woman. Strong, too."

Ben smiled. "She had to be to keep a rein on Jack and me."

"I bet," Aubrey said on a soft laugh. "I can only imagine the holy terrors you guys must have been. Are you in contact with your parents at all?"

"No." And what went unsaid was that his dad refused visitors and he didn't even know where his mom was.

Aubrey turned from him, looking out her passenger-side window. "I was raised mostly by my mom," she said quietly. "She was twenty-one when she had me. My dad was a few years older, but still not ready for a family—though he took my sister in the divorce."

Ben glanced over at her, but she still wasn't looking at him. "They split you up like two pieces of furniture?" he asked.

"Yep," she said lightly, but the tenseness in her shoulders gave her away.

"And you don't see him much, right?" he asked.

"No." She shrugged. "He's pretty busy," she said. "He has two new daughters now."

"And a puppy." He paused. "And a dollhouse."

She turned her head and met his gaze, looking surprised that he remembered.

Didn't people listen to her? Care about her? He hated the idea that it was probably far more likely that she rarely opened up and *let* anyone listen to her. "Parents can really suck," he said.

She choked out a short laugh. "Yeah."

The coil wire in his front pocket was starting to weigh him down now, big-time, but he pulled up to the grocery store.

"Be right back," she said.

Good as her word, five minutes later she was back with a mysterious brown bag, and then directed him to a town house complex. "Be right back," she said again.

When she reappeared a few minutes later, he once again slid his phone away and looked at her.

"What?" she asked. "Do I have something in my teeth?"

"Can't tell unless you smile."

She flashed him a very fake smile, and he made a big show of looking at her teeth. "Perfect," he said, and flashed her a *real* smile. "Are you going to cross a name off your list?"

She studied him a moment. "Not yet."

He looked at the town house she'd just come from. "Who lives there?"

"Carla. My sister."

"You bring your sister groceries?"

Aubrey shrugged, a little embarrassed, he thought. "She's a resident at the hospital and working crazy hours," she said. "She's exhausted and doesn't have time to do stuff like get food."

"That's...sweet of you."

She looked at him. "You and I both know I'm not sweet."

It was true that he'd never thought of her as particularly sweet, but he was beginning to change his mind. "Your boots are wet."

"I watered her plants."

Yeah, he was definitely changing his mind about her. "Where to now?" he asked.

She hesitated.

"We can just sit here if you'd rather."

She was turned away from him, staring out into the gray morning so that he couldn't see her face. He didn't have to; he could sense the eye roll. "The pier," she finally said. "And this time, *no questions*."

Aubrey's nerves were high and getting higher. She didn't wait for Ben to turn off the engine at the next stop. The moment he pulled into the pier parking lot, she slid out of the truck and then paused, glancing back at him. "You're waiting here, right?"

"Right."

She didn't trust him. "Promise?"

"What are you so worried I'm going to see?" he asked in that lazy, calm voice that made her want to crawl into his lap and cajole him into taking her to the same place he'd taken her last night in her bathroom.

But that wasn't going to happen. That had been a one-time thing.

The best one-time thing ever...

Shaking that off, she looked at him. It hadn't escaped her notice that he *hadn't* promised. He was in dark reflective glasses, so she couldn't see his eyes. His hair was finger-combed at best, and he had sawdust on his jeans from working at her bookstore. "I mean it, Ben," she said. "This is my business."

"Whatever you say, Sunshine." He pulled out his phone, presumably accessing whatever shoot 'em up, kill 'em game he was playing with Jack.

It was as close to a promise as she was going to get, and she knew it. She blew out a breath and then caught sight of his screen. Not a shoot 'em up, kill 'em game at all. "*Words with Friends*?" she asked. "*That's* the killer game you play?"

"It can be killer," he said lightly, his manhood apparently not threatened in the slightest. "Hey, do you know a seven-letter word that's got the letter *X* in it? I've got a triple-word opportunity here."

"Extinct," she said, "which is what I'm going to make you if you follow me." She shut the truck door on that ridiculous threat and walked off.

The Ferris wheel was lit up but not turning. It was icy cold outside, but she ignored the wind as she walked past the diner and then the arcade. Between the arcade and Ferris wheel were two kiosks. One sold ice cream, another sold locally made items.

Both were closed now. The ice cream shop was actually boarded up. The two brothers who ran the place didn't work during the winter months. One of them, Lance, suffered from cystic fibrosis, so they usually— providing Lance's health allowed it—took off somewhere south for warmer weather.

The other kiosk wasn't closed for the season. In fact, the woman who ran it was there right now, getting ready to open up for the day. She was busy flipping through a stack of receipts and not paying any attention to the pier around her until Aubrey stopped right in front of her.

Her name was Cathy, and she sold beautiful handmade scarves, hats, and throws she and a few other local women created.

Looking up with a friendly smile, Cathy said, "I'm still closed, but if you see something you like, I could probably be talked into a quick deal."

Aubrey reached out and ran her fingers over a knitted infinity scarf the color of a rich ruby. Soft as heaven. "It's beautiful. They're all beautiful," she said.

"That one would look good on you, with that coat and your golden hair."

Aubrey pulled it off the rack and draped it around her neck. She peered into one of the mirrors hanging on the side of the kiosk.

"Pretty," Cathy said.

Aubrey looked at her reflection and met Cathy's eyes in the mirror behind her. "You don't remember me."

"Oh, I remember you," Cathy said. "We were in PE together. And cooking class."

Aubrey let out a breath. "I came here to see you."

"Why?"

"Because I've never been able to forget how I teased you for being so skinny," Aubrey said quietly. "It was rude, and so wrong." It'd haunted her all these years.

"Well, I *was* skinny," Cathy said, and adjusted Aubrey's hair so it fell better over the scarf in the back. "And I've always thought you did it because you were jealous."

"Definitely jealous," Aubrey said. "I had to run off my

nightly junk food every single morning and I was *still* curvy. I was unbearably jealous of how you looked, but it's no excuse."

Cathy once again met her gaze in the mirror. "I was anorexic. Did you know that?"

"No." *God.* Aubrey closed her eyes. "I'm so sorry, Cathy."

"I was anorexic," Cathy said again. "And no one noticed that I was starving myself. Except you."

Aubrey opened her eyes and once again met Cathy's.

"You got me to eat one of the cheeseburgers we made for cooking class—do you remember?" Cathy asked. "It was our midterm, and we were required to eat what we cooked. I tried to throw mine away, but you told on me and then I had to eat the burger in front of the whole class."

Aubrey winced at the memory. "Yeah, I remember. I—"

"No, listen to me." Cathy's voice shook a little now. "I hadn't eaten in a week, Aubrey. That burger was the best thing I'd ever tasted. It helped me to start eating again."

Aubrey let out a breath. "I'm glad. So glad. But I shouldn't have done any of that to you. Not that I'm trying to excuse myself, but I was trying to lose weight. I needed to fit into a stupid pageant gown for an upcoming beauty contest, and I couldn't. I was starving myself, too, and so hungry and angry all the time—but I wasn't anorexic. I was just a bitch."

Cathy smiled. "Yeah. You were that." She cocked her head and studied Aubrey's reflection. "I was going to overcharge you for this scarf, you know. Because I'm a bitch, too." She smiled. "But you know? We didn't turn out so bad after all."

*　*　*

Ben was leaning against his truck, sipping the coffee he'd purchased from the diner with one hand and beating Jack's ass in *Words with Friends* with his other hand when Aubrey stepped off the pier and headed his way.

It'd only been about fifteen minutes, but she looked like she'd lost a little bit of the chip on her shoulder. He didn't say a word as he opened the door for her.

"Pretty scarf," he said, and watched her hand fly to the material now wrapped around her neck.

But she said nothing.

"How'd it go?" he asked.

More nothing.

"Do you have any gum?" he asked.

"Yes." She opened her purse, and he reached in and smoothly grabbed her notebook.

"*Hey*," she said.

He flipped it open. "We crossing anyone off yet?"

She snatched it back and hugged it to herself.

Reaching past her into the glove compartment, he pulled out a pen and handed it to her.

She glared at him for a beat and then snatched the pen. She opened her pad and very carefully crossed off number four.

Cathy.

He smiled at her. "Where to now?"

She reached for his coffee, but he got to it first, lifting it out of her reach. "You could do me next. Seeing as I'm sitting right here."

"I could *do* you? You think I'm going to *do* you right here in your truck?"

He had to work hard to keep from laughing. "I meant the list. I'm on your list."

"Oh." She narrowed her gaze at him, her cheeks flushed. "I've told you, you're *not* the Ben on my list."

"Prove it," he said.

"What?"

"If I'm not the Ben on your list, then who is?"

She just looked at him for a long moment. "You have a shovel?" she finally asked.

"In the back. Why?"

"Can you go back to the store?"

"Sure. On the drive there, you can tell me what your definition of 'do me' is."

She blushed some more and ignored him. At the store, she was gone for less than five minutes, and then she climbed back into the truck a little breathlessly. "Head out on Route Ten," she said.

"You should feel free to show me this bossy side of you in bed anytime."

She sent him a baleful glance as he pulled out of the parking lot and headed to Route 10. The highway turned inland—not up into the mountains, but east, to the far end of the county. The houses out here were few and far between. There were a few ranches, but mostly these places were older and run-down.

"Turn right," Aubrey said, looking down at her map app.

Ben followed her directions onto a dirt road, and then onto a dirty driveway. The mobile home there was a double-wide. Sitting on the porch was an old guy in a rocking chair.

Ben stopped the truck. "Is that…Mr. Wilford?"

"*Ben* Wilford," Aubrey said smugly.

"The mean old science teacher?"

"He's retired now, but yes. And mean is an understatement," she muttered under her breath.

"*This* is the Ben on your list?" he asked in disbelief.

"Yes, Mr. Egomaniac, this is the Ben on my list. Stay here," she said, and started to slide out of the truck.

He caught her arm. At the touch, she went still as if prodded with an electrical current.

He knew exactly, because he felt it as well. And it told him something, something he hadn't been prepared for. They *weren't* done with each other.

Not by a long shot.

This wasn't good news. Neither was the fact that he was playing with her. He'd tricked her into needing a ride from him and he'd justified it because he wanted to know what she was up to.

But the joke was on him, because he realized the truth—he just *wanted* to be with her.

That wasn't good news, either.

"What?" she asked.

More than a little unhappy with his epiphany, he shook his head. "Nothing." And then he let go of her, gesturing for her to have at it. Whatever "it" was.

She slid out of the truck and headed to the back to pull out his shovel. Then, carrying the shovel, she walked up to the double-wide in her fancy dress and coat, as though she belonged there.

Mr. Wilford stood, eyes narrowed and nearly hidden behind his white, bushy brows. Ben rolled down his window, but he still couldn't catch any words. He didn't have any trouble at all catching Mr. Wilford's bad attitude, though. Ben braced to get out of the truck, but the old man got up, limped to his front door, and vanished inside—but not before slamming the door, practically on Aubrey's nose.

Damn it, that pissed Ben off. But Aubrey merely squared her shoulders and vanished around the back of the trailer.

Ben waited a minute and then followed. He couldn't help it if he wanted to make sure she was okay. And that Mr. Wilford didn't shoot her for trespassing. He risked Aubrey clobbering him over the head with the shovel for not staying in the truck, but he'd deal with that when he got closer. He wasn't actually too worried, but he'd discovered something about his odd relationship with Aubrey. He preferred kissing her to arguing with her.

Not that he was exactly comfortable with that…

Chapter 14

♥

Twenty-five minutes later, Aubrey slid back into Ben's truck. The ground had been frozen and was almost impossible to break apart, forcing her to work her ass off. As a result, she was hot and sweaty, but she felt good about the morning's progress. Very good. Lowering the truck's sun visor, she studied her reflection in the small mirror there. Not too bad. She swiped at her slightly smudged mascara. Then she pulled out her notebook and, with great ceremony for the man seated next to her, she crossed off BEN. "There," she said to Ben. "All taken care of."

"Uh-huh," he said.

"Yep. Ben's off my list." It wasn't the *right* Ben, of course. The right Ben was seated next to her, but he didn't need to know that.

Nor did he need to know how much it was killing her, how she was sleeping less and less at night, worried about exactly that.

His being on her list.

Not to mention his reaction when he found out. She couldn't bring herself to tell him, not yet. He'd walk away, and even knowing that's what she deserved, she wasn't ready for it.

"Well, if you're righting your wrongs," he said—clearly fishing but coming so uncomfortably close to the truth that she held her breath—"then don't forget Kristan. Remember how mean you were to her in high school when she took your spot in the school play?"

Kristan wasn't on Aubrey's list. Nor would she be. "She tripped me at rehearsal, and I sprained my ankle so that I couldn't dance the lead. If I were making a list of wrongs to right, which I'm not"—she paused when he snorted, and she sent him a glare—"then *I* should be on *her* list." She swiped her sweaty brow and sat back, arms still trembling from exertion.

He started the truck and took them back to the highway. "You want to talk about it?" he asked casually.

No. She didn't want to talk about last night and the best sex she'd ever had. She was afraid she'd beg for more. "Talk about…?"

He glanced at her. "You were out there digging for something—or attempting to, anyway, since the ground was pretty frozen."

Damn it, he'd sneaked a peek. "A pumpkin patch," she admitted. She leaned back and sighed. "And if you were spying on me, the least you could have done was come help."

He gave her a slow, lazy grin that did things to her girl parts. Each and every one. And thanks to him, there were more of those parts than she'd remembered. "You looked like you were doing all right," he said.

Trying to ignore her annoying reaction to him, which she was helpless to prevent, she sighed. "Gee, thanks."

"So why were you digging Mr. Asshole a pumpkin patch in the off-season?"

She looked at him. "It's the off-season?"

He grinned. "Little bit, Sunshine."

Damn. She'd not even thought of that, and she hadn't looked at the seed packet when she'd bought it earlier at the grocery store. "How about I answer a question, and then you answer a question?" she suggested.

"Fine," he said. "You first. What the hell was that back there?"

She slid on her sunglasses. "Mr. Wilford gave me an F in eighth-grade science because he didn't like me."

"He didn't like anyone."

"But I'm the only one he failed. He said I was cheating when in fact I wasn't." She paused. "Okay, so I *was* cheating, but only to help Lance."

"The kid with cystic fibrosis? The one who runs the ice cream joint on the pier in the summer?"

"Yeah. He'd been going through a rough patch and had missed a week of school. He couldn't catch up, so I was feeding him the answers to the test. Mr. Wilford caught me." She'd never forget how he'd stood over her, those bushy brows—which were black then—bunched together. And how he'd said so harshly, *You're a selfish girl, Aubrey Wellington. No one likes a selfish girl.*

She'd heard *No one likes you*, and she'd reacted with predictable bad behavior. "Lance tried to tell Mr. Wilford the truth," she said, "but he wouldn't listen. He thought I was a bad seed, and his mind was made up. So he failed me."

She'd then been disqualified from two beauty contests that her mom had already paid for and bought gowns for, and it'd been a huge drama in the house. "I tried to talk to him about it after school," she said. "I found him in the school garden, working on his pumpkin patch with the garden club." She blew out a breath and a low laugh. "I can still see him standing there among his prize pupils and his equally prized pumpkins, pointing a dirty, bony finger in my direction. He said"—she adopted a low baritone—"*You, Aubrey Wellington, will* never *amount to anything.*"

"He thought we were all miscreants," Ben said quietly. "But he shouldn't have said that to you."

"Actually, in hindsight I probably deserved it," she said. "I was a total shit. But there was something in his tone that got me. And then he just walked away, like I wasn't worth his time."

"He spoke like Darth Vader," Ben said, "and walked like he had a stick up his ass."

She laughed. "Yes," she finally said. "But at the time I didn't think about that. I was embarrassed and humiliated." She paused and then admitted the rest. "I kicked one of his pumpkins and broke it loose from the stem. I didn't find out until the next day that it'd been one of his award-winning pumpkins, the one he'd planned on taking to the annual pumpkin contest—which had a thousand-dollar prize."

"Ouch," Ben said.

Aubrey sighed. "He cried. Mr. Wilford cried." She was still staring out the side window, so she was surprised when she felt his warm fingers close over hers.

"You were just a kid, Aubrey."

"Yeah, but not really. And I cost the school garden club that grand. I've always felt so bad about that."

"So you dug him a new pumpkin patch," Ben said. "What's your plan, to grow him another award-winning pumpkin?"

She bit her lower lip, and he laughed. "It is," he said, and laughed again.

"Stop that."

"It's cute," he said.

"Cute?" She almost choked on the word. No one had ever called her cute before, not ever. Her phone rang, and she pulled it out, frowning at the unknown number. "Hello?"

"Aubrey Wellington," said Darth Vader's voice. "What did you do to my backyard?"

"Mr. Wilford?" she asked, glancing over at Ben in shock.

"Well, how many other people's yards did you decimate today?" he asked testily. "What the hell did you do?"

"I…dug you a pumpkin patch," she said. "I planted pumpkin seeds."

Ben smiled.

"You *what*?" Mr. Wilford asked.

"I ruined your prize pumpkin all those years ago, remember? And how did you get my number?"

"Of course I remember what you did. You cost me a thousand bucks and ruined the best pumpkin I ever grew. And this is Lucky Harbor. It was easy to get your number; I called Lucille."

"I'm going to grow you new pumpkins," she said.

"Off-season?"

She sighed. "Okay, so I didn't plan that part so well.

But maybe one of them will be a prize pumpkin," she said. "It's my way of apologizing."

"Fat lot of good that's going to do me now," he said. "I'm too old to be worried about the watering."

Well, crap. She hadn't thought of that, either. "I'll do it," she said.

Ben laughed and then choked it off when she glared at him.

"*You're* going to water the pumpkins?" Mr. Wilford asked in disbelief. "You, Miss Fancy Pants?"

"Yes," she said through her teeth. "I am."

"Pumpkins like to be watered regularly," he warned.

"Fine. Um, how often is regular—" But he'd hung up. She slid her phone away.

Ben was still grinning.

"Not a word," she said, Googling "pumpkin patches." "Unless you know how often to water pumpkins."

That night, Aubrey closed up the bookstore after a decent business day and smiled as she walked across the scarred hardwood floors. They'd been a surprising find beneath the carpet. The wood was nice and light, and it seemed to open up the store.

Happy, she headed up to her loft. There, she pulled out her notebook and eyed the crossed-off items, including BEN.

She'd improvised there, and she thought maybe she'd actually pulled it off. But now, without Ben's prying eyes watching her, she added one more item to the bottom of her list.

THE HARD ONE.

Chapter 15

♥

The next morning, Ben went to work on the countertop for the serving area of the Book & Bean.

Aubrey was two weeks away from her grand-opening party.

Though it would be close, the renovations would be done on time. Ben thought of the coil wire in his pocket. He'd hoped to get at least one more day of driving Aubrey around, even though he was pretty sure he knew exactly what she was up to now.

And it wasn't trouble. In fact, it was the opposite of trouble. She was working at righting her wrongs, and it was tugging at a part of him that didn't want to be tugged.

He hadn't planned on feeling anything for her and was now trying to resign himself to the fact that they had more than just some seriously explosive chemistry. He'd told himself that they could get past that by spending some quality naked time together, but they'd already tried that, and it'd backfired because he'd gotten past exactly nothing. In fact, now all he wanted was more. A lot more.

It was 7:00 a.m. before he heard signs of life from above, and thirty minutes more before the telltale *click, click, click* of her boots alerted him that she was coming down. And, like Pavlov's dog, he started to go hard.

He was ridiculous.

"Ben?"

And just like that, the sound of her husky voice finished the job. He wondered what she'd say to a second round of wild monkey sex, right here, right now. If he just stripped her out of her clothes and sat her on the stack of wood he still had to measure and cut, he could then step between her legs. He'd slide his hands beneath her sexy ass, of course, to prevent splinters. Or they could use her couch. Better yet, he could bend her over the stack of boxes of new stock that'd come in, shove up her dress, and take her from behind.

Yeah. *That* was the ticket.

She came around the corner, and he unbuckled his tool belt, letting it fall to the floor. They were going to do this, and it was going to be good—

"I've got company," Aubrey said. She went to the front door of the store and opened it.

And then one, two, three…*eight* women came in behind her, one of them his own aunt Dee.

Lucky Harbor's resident hell-raisers.

Dee smiled and waved at him, giving him a sweet kiss on the cheek as she passed him.

"What are you doing here?" he asked. Croaked.

"Aubrey's invited my book club to meet at her store," Dee said. She frowned at him. "You sick, honey?"

"No." Dee's book club was a weekly event—"club" being a loose word for a bunch of women who got together, drank too much wine, laughed so loud they could break windows, and talked about everything *but* books. The "club" had been kicked out of the diner, the bar and grill, *and* the senior center. They'd been talking about having to disband.

He glanced at Aubrey.

"I wanted them to have a place to go," she said.

"You're going to need a 'crazy' permit," he said.

Dee smacked him upside the head. "We're trying something new," she said. "Meeting in the early mornings. You know, before people get…feisty."

Ben sent Aubrey a *good luck* look that she ignored. Instead, she walked her guests through the bookstore and sat them in the chairs and on the couch that he'd just made nefarious plans for.

"So," she said, looking to the seniors' ringleader—Lucille, of course. "What do you think?"

"It's perfect," Lucille said. "We're so honored that you'd have us, honey."

Ben shook his head, cleaned up, and left out the back door. Then he stared at Aubrey's car in the lot.

Which was minus its coil wire.

He wrestled with his conscience and lost. Blowing out a sigh, he popped open the hood and began to put it back.

"Whatcha doing?"

He nearly jumped out of his skin, then gave Luke a long look across the engine compartment.

Luke grinned. "Scared ya. You committing a misdemeanor for any reason in particular?"

"I'm not committing anything. And why are you here?"

"Got a call that a suspicious-looking character was lounging around back here and screwing up cars that belong to pretty blondes."

"Bullshit."

"Okay, I didn't get a call," Luke said. "I stopped by Ali's shop to say hey."

No, he'd stopped by the shop to get laid. Because Luke had an unmistakable I-just-got-laid look to him. Ben sighed. He'd like to have that look…

"So want to tell me what you're up to?" Luke asked.

"Hell, no."

Luke grinned. "That's okay. I already figured it out."

"No, you didn't."

"Sure I did. You kissed Aubrey last week, and now you're doing something stupid to fuck it all up."

Ben narrowed his gaze. "Let me guess how you know about the kiss. Facebook?"

"Ali." Luke shrugged. "You were the one stupid enough to do it up against the wall and visible through the window. Rookie mistake," he said, and tsked.

"Don't you have somewhere to be?" Ben asked.

"Nope. So. You and Aubrey, huh? You two going to…?"

Well, at least he didn't know *that* much. Ben didn't answer. Instead he made sure the coil wire was back in place and shut the hood. Then he headed toward his truck.

"Hey," Luke said. "Waiting for the details here."

"Ask your fiancée."

Ben did a morning run with Sam, who, unlike some of his nosy-ass friends, did *not* press him for details on the Aubrey situation.

After their run, Ben headed to Seattle. He found Bob's Auto Shop, parked, and walked to the first open bay. A linebacker-size guy rolled out from beneath a lifted truck, wearing overalls and no shirt. He didn't need one; he had tat sleeves down both arms and over his chest. The patch on his overalls read BIG ED. "Can I help you?" the giant asked.

"I'm looking for Dan Ingalls," Ben said.

Big Ed gave a chin jerk toward the next car over. The guy working on it was built the same as Ed the Linebacker, though he was wearing a shirt. He had tats, too, including a teardrop beneath his eye.

The patch on *his* overalls read BIG BOB.

Ben was sensing a pattern here. "How you doing?" he asked Big Bob.

Big Bob didn't smile, just looked at him as he slowly cracked his knuckles.

A real friendly bunch. Terrific. "Looking for Dan Ingalls," Ben said again.

Big Bob did the same chin jerk Big Ed had done, toward the back of the shop this time. Ben headed back there, very aware that he now had the two guys at his back and most likely yet another one in front of him somewhere. He found a truck, hood up, and indeed there was a guy standing on a step stool, head buried in the engine compartment, torquing something.

"Dan Ingalls?" Ben asked.

Dan didn't stop what he was doing or even look up. "Who wants to know?"

"A friend of your kids."

Dan went still, not even pulling his head out of the compartment. "What?"

He didn't repeat himself. Still keeping track of the big boys, Bob and Ed, at his back, Ben kept his voice low. He wasn't too worried; he'd been in worse spots—far worse—but there was no reason to be stupid.

Dan straightened. He was easily one-third the size of his two co-workers. No muscles. No tats. What he did have was crazy, wild hair, the exact color of a copper penny, flying around his thin, angular face and stark blue eyes. He was skinny as a toothpick and short enough to barely meet Ben's shoulder. "Who are you?" he asked.

"Ben McDaniel. I live in Lucky Harbor, where your girls live in a foster home. A *shitty* foster home," Ben added harshly. "And I wanted to see why they aren't with you."

Dan looked a little shaken. "I don't have kids."

Ben arched a brow.

Dan came down off the stepladder and hitched his chin to indicate Ben should follow him out of the garage. They passed the very large Big Ed, and then the equally large Big Bob, both of whom were watching Ben with stony expressions.

Ben ignored them completely.

"Sorry about that," Dan said when they were outside. "They're…protective of me."

"Why? Are you in some kind of trouble?"

Dan looked away for a moment, then gained a slight measure of Ben's respect when he met Ben's gaze straight on. "I was."

"And your kids?"

Dan shook his head. "I told you, I don't have any."

"Odd, since you have two mini-me's in Lucky Harbor who are your spitting image."

Dan gave a sharp exhale and walked away, going about ten feet before pacing back. "I waived my rights so that they could get adopted."

"Then why are they in a foster home?"

"Because their mom died," Dan said.

"And you didn't feel the need to take them?"

"I couldn't."

"Why?"

"I'm not father material."

"Should have thought about that before you had them," Ben said.

Again Dan paced. "What do you mean, the foster home is shitty?" he finally asked.

"You don't know what 'shitty' means?"

Dan sank to a concrete planter that had nothing it in but dirt and cigarette butts. He shoved his fingers through his hair and studied his knees. "I didn't want this life for them."

"Well, what the hell did you think would happen when their mom died and you didn't step up?"

"I—I don't know. I…I was in jail for a while."

"Yeah, your daughters told me."

He looked sick. "They know?"

"I'm not sure what they know, but they said you're up for, and I quote, 'the big one.'"

"Jesus." Dan rubbed a shaky hand over his mouth. "They're five."

"They're growing up fast."

"Jesus," Dan said again.

"What did you do time for?"

"Being in the wrong place at the wrong time," Dan said.

Ben gave him a *go on* look.

He let out a long breath. "They got me on armed robbery and involuntary manslaughter."

"Christ." Ben shook his head. "Never mind, then. I've got the wrong guy for those girls." He turned to go.

"Wait."

Ben turned back. "What?"

"How are they?"

"What do you care?"

Dan winced but held eye contact. "Listen, you have no reason to believe me, but the whole arrest…it was a mistake, okay? But regardless, I did the time. I paid the price. I'm out. Making myself a life."

"Without them," Ben said harshly.

"I thought they were safe. Happy. Why would I mess with that?"

"Because they need their dad."

"I'm not equipped to handle kids," Dan said. "I wouldn't know what to do with them."

"How about caring about their welfare? You have a job. You're a mechanic, so I assume you have wheels. You could get visitation. Hell, you should have custody."

"I have visitation rights. But I'm not good with kids."

"You're their dad," Ben said again, voice hard. "That means it doesn't matter that you're a pussy—you man up."

"Hey," a low, angry voice said. "You don't talk to him like that."

Ben turned to Big Bob and got sucker punched in the eye.

It was the only punch Bob landed.

Five minutes later, both Bob and Ed were on the ground, Bob holding his ribs and Ed holding his jaw. Ben brushed off his hands. Ed had landed a good blow to the kidney, but Ben was okay. Still, he should probably get back to a gym. Breathing a little hard, he turned to Dan.

Dan, eyes wide, raised his hands. "Hey, I warned you. I told you they were protective of me."

"Yeah." Ben touched his already aching eye. "Thanks."

"You're pretty fucking *badass*," Dan said, impressed. "You were in prison, too?"

"No. I was in hell. Go see your kids."

Chapter 16

♥

Aubrey woke up to a grumpy Gus staring her down. She got up, fed the demanding cat, and then went to work. She unpacked and shelved her new stock. She placed next week's order and spent an hour on hold with her phone company to complain about having Internet only in the western half of the store.

Afterward, a customer came in and spent half an hour walking the aisles and occasionally lifting a book up and looking to Aubrey. "What's this one about?"

Aubrey had ceased to be surprised about the fact that people actually assumed she'd read every book in the store. She'd also learned that the people who browsed the way this woman did almost always left without actually buying a book at all, so she'd started amusing herself by making up plots on the spot. Still on hold with the phone company, she covered the receiver and said, "That one's about an alien who comes to the Wild, Wild West."

The woman nodded and put the book back. One aisle later, she picked up another.

Aubrey searched her brain's database. After half an hour, she was beginning to run out of material. "That one's about a guy who goes a little crazy after a failed marriage and ends up in a dancing contest with another woman."

The woman put that book back, too, and Aubrey told herself she really needed to find a new hobby. But finally the woman came to the front. "Do you have anything like that *Fifty Shades*?" she asked.

"Now, that I do have," Aubrey said, and led her to the romance section.

After the woman left—without buying anything—Aubrey began doing what she'd put off doing all day yesterday: searching for a mechanic. Her selection was limited, as there were only a few in Lucky Harbor, and most likely she couldn't afford any of them. At that thought, she went to her brand-new coffee nook, which she'd already stocked. There was a small flask there for Lucille, who liked brandy in her tea. Aubrey preferred a little tea in her brandy, but she didn't touch either one of them now. No, she went straight for the box of sugar cookies she'd put away for a high-stress day.

Breakfast of champions.

"Hey."

At the sound of Ben's voice behind her, she jumped. "Where did you learn to walk so quietly?"

"Work."

She thought about what that might mean, given that he'd been working in places far more dangerous than she could possibly contemplate. She craned her neck to look at him and gasped. "What happened to you?"

"Nothing."

"*Nothing* gave you a black eye?"

He shrugged.

She went to the freezer beneath the counter and pulled out a small bag of frozen peas.

He looked at the bag. "Why do you have frozen peas in a bookstore?"

"They're for cramps." She placed the bag over his eye, smiling when he sucked in a breath at the cold. "Baby," she said.

His look might have had another man wetting his pants and any woman on the planet licking her lips, but she told herself she was unmoved.

But she wasn't. "What happened?"

"Nothing," he repeated. "What are you doing?"

"I don't answer questions for people who answer a question with another question."

He smiled. "How about we each answer a question?"

She opened her mouth, but he put a finger to her lips. "With a twist," he said.

Her stomach fluttered. "What's the twist?"

"If you don't answer, you get a dare."

Her brain went off the rails at the thought of what a dare might include. But curiosity won over self-preservation. "Deal. Tell me what happened to you."

"I went to talk to Pink and Kendra's dad."

"So…he punched you?"

"Nah. He's just a little guy."

"Then who punched you?"

"Dan and I were having a private little chat and his two linebacker buddies decided they didn't like me much."

"So *they* punched you?"

He shrugged. "One of them got a shot in before."

"Oh, my God, you are the worst storyteller ever," she declared, tossing up her hands and making him smile. "Before *what*?" she demanded.

He watched her, still clearly amused. "Before they decided they were done tangling with me," he finally said.

"Yeah?" she said, eyes narrowing. "And what made them decide that?"

He just kept looking at her.

"You took them *both* down?" she asked, horrified.

"Your turn to talk," he said enigmatically.

"Oh, no," she said. "I had to dig that story out of you. You owe me a dare by default."

"Sure," he agreed too easily in that low, gruff voice that made her nipples harden. "Anything."

She nearly swallowed her tongue. "You can't promise me 'anything,'" she said, annoyed to find she sounded breathless.

He didn't look worried. "Why? Are you going to take advantage of me?"

Her entire body tightened at the thought of all she could do to take advantage of him and the pleasure they could both get out of it.

He took in her expression and laughed softly. "Hold that thought. Now answer my question or face a dare."

"I'm hiring a mechanic."

"Thought you couldn't afford one."

"I can't," she said, trying not to notice that his hair was still wet from a recent shower, and that he smelled really good. Guy good, like soap and deodorant and Ben. She wanted to press her face to his throat. Especially since he'd clearly skipped shaving that morning—and maybe the day before, too—and had the exact right amount of scruff on his face to make him look hot as hell.

He came closer, giving her a better view of the way his broad shoulders stretched the material of his shirt and how his long legs were encased in denim worn to a buttery softness by myriad washings, lovingly cupping certain parts—

He shut the laptop she still had open on the counter.

"Hey," she said.

"Hay is for horses." He hauled her close, making her breath catch in her throat as her gaze drifted to his mouth.

The mouth she'd been dreaming about.

Damn him.

Then she realized that mouth was moving, and the words sank in. "*I* sabotaged your car," he said.

She blinked. "What?"

"Yeah. I removed your coil wire. It's back in now, though. Your car's fine, Aubrey."

When this computed, she went from the good kind of hot to the very bad kind of hot in the blink of an eye. She couldn't even speak. All she did was sputter. A minute ago, she'd wanted to press herself to him like white on rice. She still wanted that. But she wanted to smack him more. She settled on giving him a good shove.

He didn't budge.

"I wanted to see what you were up to," he said. "I wanted to make sure you were okay."

"It was none of your business!"

He shrugged, and that just pissed her off even more. "Why?" she managed. "Why does anything I do even matter to you?"

He scrubbed a hand over his jaw. The sound of his palm scrapping over several days' worth of whisker growth had her belly quivering. *Keep it together.* "Why, Ben?"

He shook his head.

"Not good enough," she said. "Tell me why what I do matters to you."

"It shouldn't," he said, meeting her gaze steadily.

She just stared at him. "You're incredible, you know that? You're an insensitive, first-class jerk, and—"

He leaned in. "And what?" he asked, his voice dangerously low.

"And…" Stymied at her ridiculous and invariable reaction to him, she put her hands to his chest to give him another shove, but somehow her wires got crossed and she fisted his shirt instead.

"Dare me," he said softly.

"Dare you to what?"

"Dare me, Aubrey."

Oh, how she hated how well he knew her. "I dare you to kiss me," she whispered, and then to make sure he did, she put her mouth on his first.

He yanked her in hard, so that she fell into him. It was crazy, but she slid her hands up his chest and into his hair to hold him to her. He had one hand up the back of her sweater on bare skin, his fingers spread as if he wanted to touch as much of her as possible. His other hand slid down, cupping her bottom, which made him groan.

"You drive me crazy," he said against her mouth. "You taste so fucking good. You always taste so fucking good."

She might have said *ditto*, but then his tongue stroked hers, and they both moaned. Then he was trailing hot, open-mouthed kisses along her jaw to her ear, which he nipped, and her knees melted. "Damn it," she sighed.

She felt him smile against her skin before he kissed the spot just beneath her lobe. She shivered and knew she was a goner. She was even hearing a ringing in her head—

The store's phone.

She must have missed four rings, because it clicked over to the machine, and they heard her own voice saying, "Book and Bean. Leave a message, and I'll get back to you as soon as possible."

And then came Mr. Wilford's voice.

"Listen, missy. You dug this pumpkin garden; you need to get your skinny ass out here and water it. I'm too old for this. You hear me?"

"Why does everyone call my ass skinny?" Aubrey asked the room.

"It's a good ass," Ben said, hands on it. He squeezed. "*Really* good."

There was a knock at the door, and she pushed free. "Oh, my God. I have work." She poked him with a finger. "Stop distracting me with your mouth!"

"I could distract you with another body part instead. Say the word."

"Oh, no, you don't. You're done distracting me. I don't sleep with guys who sabotage my car. And why did you do it?"

At the second, more persistent knock, he gestured to the door. "You're ignoring a paying customer."

"We're not done with this," she warned him.

"No doubt."

Chapter 17

♥

Mornings were easier these days, thanks to the new routine of hitting the bakery before opening the bookstore.

Aubrey was sitting on Leah's back counter, inhaling powdered doughnut holes left over from the day before. She'd just told them how Ben had pulled her coil wire and had paused, expecting a suitable level of outrage from her friends.

Instead, Leah laughed. She laughed so hard she slid down the cabinet and ended up sitting on the floor.

Ali laughed, too, though she managed to remain upright. "So cute," she said.

"*Cute?*" Aubrey repeated, outraged all over again. "How in the world is that cute?"

"He likes you," Ali said simply, and popped another doughnut hole in her mouth.

"What is this, high school?" Aubrey muttered, reaching for another doughnut hole, too. "And he doesn't like me. And I don't like him. He just did it so he could figure out what I was up to."

Leah nodded. "No doubt. But I bet this entire box of doughnut holes that he also did it because he has a protective streak a mile long regarding people he cares about." She smiled when Aubrey didn't have a ready retort. "And in any case, you could just tell him what you're up to, you know. Or tell us."

Aubrey let out a breath. "I haven't told anyone."

"All the more reason to tell *us*," Leah said. "This"—doughnut hole in hand, she gestured to the kitchen around them—"is the cone of silence. Nothing you say here can be repeated outside this room without permission from the tellee."

"Tellee?" Aubrey said.

"You," Leah said.

Aubrey looked at Ali. Ali nodded and held up two fingers, as though she were making an oath.

"Were you a Girl Scout?" Aubrey asked.

"No," Ali said. "But I totally could've been. I can make all kinds of knots in ropes. And I look pretty good in khaki."

Leah nodded. "This is true."

Aubrey sighed. "Okay, fine. It's my karma. It's…shaky at best. I needed to fix some things from my past, so I made a list."

"A list?" Ali asked.

"Of people I wronged."

"Well, hell, Aubrey," Leah said. "We *all* could make a list."

"Really?" Aubrey asked. "Did either of *you* sleep with your married professor in college? Because he's number seven."

"Okay, that's pretty bad," Ali said after a moment of silence. "But I've made some pretty damn spectacular mistakes myself, so there's no judgment here. Would you like my opinion?"

"Could I stop you?" Aubrey asked drily.

Ali laughed. "Probably not. I told you that I saw you and Ben through the window of your store, right?"

For a beat, Aubrey's heart stopped, until she realized that Ali was referring to the kiss, not the…deed.

"What I saw was really hot," Ali said. "So hot you nearly steamed up the glass. But it was more than just lust. He cupped your head, Aubrey."

"Aw," Leah said on a dreamy sigh. "He did? Really? God, I love that man."

Aubrey shook her head to clear it, but nope, she was still confused. "What does it matter that he cupped my head?"

"It means it wasn't just a kiss," Ali said. "It was more. And we"—she gestured between herself and Leah—"having recently found the loves of our lives, can tell the difference between sex and love."

Leah nodded in agreement.

"When you do it with Ben," Ali went on, "it won't be just sex. It'll be *love*."

Aubrey inhaled wrong and got a bunch of powdered sugar down the wrong pipe.

Leah jumped up to get a glass of water.

Ali helpfully pounded Aubrey's back. When she could breathe without wheezing, both her friends were looking at her rather seriously.

"So you *already* slept with him," Leah guessed.

Aubrey took a moment with that one, because in all

truth, there'd been no actual sleeping involved. "Was it only okay with you when I was just kissing him?"

"No." Leah covered her hand with her own. "No, it's not like that. I think you'll be fantastic for him."

"We're not together," Aubrey said. "Not like that. It was just a one-time thing."

Ali laughed. "Yeah, okay."

"No, really."

"I saw you," Ali said. "I saw the chemistry. Remember when the town hall caught fire, and the entire town was covered in smoke?"

"Yeah."

"Well, I saw more smoke generated between you two than I did at that fire."

At that, Aubrey rolled her eyes.

"I'm serious," Ali said. "Whether you like it or not, you and Ben have something."

For the record, if this was true, she didn't like it. Not one bit.

"Which means you should really tell him about the list," Leah said.

No one was more aware of that than Aubrey. That damn list was starting to eat her alive. "He's seen it. He's guessed about it." She let out a breath. "But he doesn't know that he's on it. I'm *not* telling him that part."

"You could tell us instead," Ali said, fishing.

Aubrey shook her head, and Ali sighed.

"I still think you should tell him," Leah said.

"No," she said firmly.

"That might come back to bite you on the ass," Leah said.

No doubt. "The grudge he earned from me with that

whole coil-wire stunt is currently scheduled to last years," Aubrey said. "So there won't be any more…smoke. And we're done talking about this."

Like good friends, they dropped the conversation and ate some more doughnut holes.

"These are amazing," Ali said. She smelled like roses today, which made sense, since she was looking like she'd rolled in them. They clung to her clothes, as did the scent of the petals.

Aubrey agreed with her friend's assessment of the doughnut holes, but her mouth was too full to talk.

Leah was pulling pies from her oven. "These should go like hotcakes—"

The door out front opened, and the bell rang, signaling a customer. "Damn it," Leah said, and eyed both Ali and Aubrey. "Aubrey. You get it."

"What? Why me?"

"Because you look the most presentable. Just tell whoever it is I'll be right out. Or better yet, serve them."

Ali grinned. "This is why I dress in flower gunk."

Aubrey sighed and jumped off the counter, heading out front. She stopped short at the sight of Ben. She was still mad at him, really mad, but some of that anger faded without her permission at the sight of him standing there with a little girl clinging to each of his hands.

The girls were tiny, a little scrawny, and one of them was dressed in pink from head to toe. The other's hair was falling out of her pigtails, and her dress was smudged and dirty. Also, she had the beginnings of a black eye. It matched Ben's.

His eyebrows went up at the sight of Aubrey. "You take a second job?"

"Yes," she said. "It's called eating doughnut holes." She smiled at the girls, her heart melting a little. They were a little bedraggled and so damn precious. "Hey, there," she said to them. "What'll it be?"

"We don't got any money," the one all in pink said, eyes locked on the display case.

"I'm buying," Ben told her. "Whatever you want."

"Wow," Pink said reverently, nose pressed up against the glass. "Whatever we want? Really? What about those pretty red cupcakes? Oh, wait, no—look at those cookies; they're black and white with little pink dots! Oh, oh! Those pink-and-chocolate thingies! Look at all the pink—"

Ben held up a finger, and she stopped talking. "Whatever you want," he repeated.

"Any of it?" she asked in awe.

"*All* of it, if that's what you want."

The little girl said "Wow" again and very carefully surveyed the displays. "We gotta be sure to get something that won't spill on the car seats you got for us."

"They're borrowed," Ben said. "And they can be washed."

Aubrey stood behind the counter, ostensibly waiting for the kid to make a choice, but really watching Ben with the girls. He wore dark jeans, an untucked button-down shirt, and work boots. His hair was just a little tousled, either from his fingers or the wind, and he looked like a rock star. A really sexy one. He was relaxed, hands in pockets, head tilted down, listening politely to the girls' chatter.

Or the girl. Singular. Because only one of them talked—the one all in pink. She pointed to the cookie section. "Can we pretty please each have one of those big fat chocolate chip cookies?" she asked Aubrey.

"Of course." Aubrey handed one to each twin. The one in pink smiled and said, "Thanks." Her twin didn't smile; she just stared at Aubrey, eyes large and red-rimmed and shimmering, the bruise standing out starkly against her pale skin.

"She says thanks, too," the one in pink said, and hugged her twin.

Her twin nodded and solemnly took a bite of her cookie.

Aubrey gestured to the girl's eye, wondering what had happened to her. "Looks like it hurts."

She nodded again.

"Someone got her with an elbow on the playground," her twin said. "It was mean."

Aubrey's heart squeezed. "Wait here." She ran through the bakery kitchen, past her two startled friends, out the back door, into her bookstore, and to the freezer, where she grabbed her second bag of peas. When she dashed back to the bakery and handed it to the little girl for her eye, Ben smiled.

"Thanks," he said. "Have Leah add the cookies to my tab." He dropped a five into the tip jar. He turned the girls to the door, and then they were gone.

Aubrey was still standing there, staring at the closed door, when Ali and Leah flanked her.

"Isn't he adorable?" Ali asked.

Ben was a lot of things, but Aubrey was pretty sure adorable wasn't one of them.

Chapter 18

♥

With a week and a half left until her grand-opening party, Aubrey stood in the crap-food aisle of the grocery store, trying to decide between cool ranch and salt-and-vinegar potato chips. It was an important decision, and one she took very seriously. Whichever flavor she picked would be keeping her company through tonight's TV session. She went back and forth for a ridiculously long moment before deciding the hell with it and tossing both in her cart. That's when she saw the barbecue-flavored chips as well. Damn. She wasn't supposed to be able to choose between them all, was she? She was reaching for a third bag when she heard her name.

Turning, she came face-to-face with Pastor Mike, smiling his easy smile.

She quickly backed away from the barbecue chips and briefly wished she had fruit and vegetables in her cart. Which was silly. Pastor Mike was a man, not God. He didn't care how many bags of potato chips she consumed.

And probably God didn't care, either. Still, she moved to stand in front of the cart so he couldn't get a good look at its contents, which so far consisted of Advil and the chips.

"How are you?" Pastor Mike asked.

"Great." She wanted that third bag of chips.

Pastor Mike smiled. "Is that why you're chip-loading? Because you're great?"

She sighed and glanced at her cart. "Saw that, did you?"

He smiled. "I love those salt-and-vinegar chips."

"Yeah, me, too."

"So," he said in that calm voice. "How are you really?"

"Well, as you can clearly see, I just loaded about ten thousand calories of chips into my cart, so…" She shrugged.

"I've been hoping you'd come to another meeting."

"Oh, I don't think—"

"There's one tonight." He flashed a charming smile. "Better for you than chip therapy."

"Is there *anything* better than chip therapy?"

"No," he admitted. "But this would be really close. We'd love to see you there. It's at eight thirty."

Well, hell. "Maybe." She paused. "And thanks. You've been so kind—and helpful, too."

He cocked his head, eyes curious. "I haven't done anything."

She thought about the list and how she was working her way down it. And how, in spite of having about a fifty-percent success rate at the moment, it'd felt really good to face those ghosts. "You did a lot," she said. "You motivated me."

He smiled. "Well, then, I'm glad. You've got my number if you need a ride. Otherwise I hope to see you tonight."

She nodded and then went through the checkout. And if she added a candy bar from the evil, *evil* rack right before the cash register, no one but she had to know.

She had one more stop to make before heading home, and suddenly she needed the candy bar to face it. Chocolate courage, she decided. She inhaled it and then headed to the Love Shack. She knew that someone from her list went there every night for a quick nightcap before heading home.

Sue Henderson.

Back when Aubrey had been eighteen, Sue had been an assistant DA. She'd moved up the ranks in the years since. She was a judge now, which only made her all the more intimidating. She was at the bar nursing a white wine when Aubrey approached. The only reaction Sue gave was a simple narrowing of her critical gaze over the rim of her glass.

"Well, that answers the question of whether you remember me," Aubrey said, and gestured for the bartender. She was going to need a drink for this.

"Rumor is you're working your way through town and making apologies," Sue said.

Aubrey stared at her, stunned. "Well, that was quick."

Sue shrugged. "It's Lucky Harbor."

True. Aubrey accepted her wine from the bartender. It was Jax serving tonight. He co-owned the bar with Ford. Jax was handsome and charming—and sharp enough to take one look at Aubrey and Sue sitting together and bring them each a second glass. "On the house," he said, shooting Aubrey a quick wink before moving off.

Sue finished off her first wine and reached for her second. "So."

"So," Aubrey said. Her heart started pounding. This was always the worst part, getting started. But then Sue started for her.

"You put green food coloring in my pool on the day I was hosting a huge, important town hall luncheon," she said. "The luncheon I was hoping would get me from ADA to DA. I spent a fortune decorating my backyard that day, bringing in gorgeous tables and flowers. The caterers had set up around my pool—which, thanks to you, looked like a toilet tank. A really *disgusting* toilet tank."

"Yes," Aubrey said, nodding. "I did that."

"I didn't get to be DA that year."

Aubrey knew that, too. Sue had been her father's neighbor. They were still neighbors, actually. And on the few occasions when Aubrey had been invited to visit, Aubrey had run across Sue, as she and her father had been friends.

Sue hadn't approved of Aubrey's beauty contests and general upbringing. She'd been fond of saying things like "Looks will fade, Aubrey, and you'll find yourself fading along with them" and "I guess your sister really did get all the brains."

Aubrey hadn't really minded hearing the looks-fading thing; she'd known that. But she had minded being held up against her sister and found lacking. Or maybe she'd just been plain tired of all of it by then. Regardless, she'd done Sue wrong. "I shouldn't have put the green food coloring in your pool," she said.

"*And* my pond," Sue added.

"And your pond," Aubrey said in agreement.

Sue stared at her. "That's it? That's my big apology?"

"You did eventually get promoted," Aubrey pointed out. "And you're a judge now. A good one."

Sue looked slightly mollified. "I *am* a good judge. But you stained the pool's finish—did you know that? We had to drain it and redo it. And the pond…you killed my fish."

"I know," Aubrey said. "It was a rotten thing to do." She paused. "You work with troubled teens."

"Yes," Sue said, looking suspicious. "Aren't you a little old to be a troubled teen?"

Aubrey ignored the jab. "You've funded a special program for them at the teen center. You bring in career women once a week to meet with the girls and talk with them about their options. Doctors, lawyers, chefs—"

"I do."

"I thought maybe I could volunteer to do that," Aubrey said casually, even though she felt anything but casual. She felt…nervous. Sick with it, actually. But it was something she wanted to do to help others, especially those who were as emotionally adrift as she had been.

"You want to talk to troubled teen girls," Sue said dubiously.

"Well, who better than a once troubled teen girl?" Aubrey asked quietly.

Sue looked at her for a long moment. "The people I have working with those teens are no longer troubled."

"*I'm* no longer troubled," Aubrey said.

"Just a few months ago, you slept with your boss and lost your job because of it."

When would that stop following her around? "No," she said. "I slept with my *date*, who turned out to be screwing half the town. I quit my job because he also turned out to be slime."

Sue just looked at her.

"Okay, so he was also my boss," she admitted. "But…" Aubrey started to say it wasn't what Sue thought, but the truth was…it'd been exactly as Sue thought. She met the judge's gaze. "You know what? Never mind. It was a ridiculous idea."

Ben had been eating nachos and nursing a beer with Jack and Luke when Aubrey had walked into the Love Shack. She'd gone straight to the bar without seeing him, her gaze locked on someone already there.

At his table, Jack was telling them the story of having to rescue one of the world's dumbest criminals on the job yesterday. Some guy had climbed a tree outside the convenience store to reach the second-story window, where the office was. Presumably the idea was to break in from above, but he got stuck in the window, half in and half out, hanging twenty-five feet above the ground, screaming for help.

Ben laughed at this right along with Luke, but his gaze kept being drawn back to the bar.

And Aubrey, as she'd sat sipping a wine, talking to Judge Sue Henderson.

The two women had looked incredibly cool and calm, but Ben knew Aubrey—knew the telltale signs that revealed the real Aubrey beneath the veneer. Her smile wasn't reaching her eyes. Her legs were crossed, her body still, except for the slight movement of her fingers nudging her glass back and forth. She appeared to be taking a breath every two or three minutes. He supposed that's how she'd survived her rough patches—by going into hibernation mode.

But he'd also seen her looking very much alive and breathing, like she'd just run a marathon, and he much preferred that look to this brittle one.

She seemed to be near a breaking point. How was it that no one but him saw that?

Then the judge had said something, and though Aubrey didn't move, he could tell whatever it'd been, the barb had hit deep. Aubrey nodded, tossed back her wine, and stood. She said something. Sue didn't respond, and Aubrey walked off.

And right out the door.

Ben stood and tossed some bills on the table. "Gotta go."

Luke, gaze also on the door, just nodded thoughtfully.

Jack, having never been particularly thoughtful, said, "Anything to do with the beautiful leggy blonde that just left?"

"No," Ben said.

"Bullshit."

"Leave it alone," Ben told him.

"Did you leave it alone when I was making a fool of myself over Leah?" Jack asked, leaning back lazily in his chair.

"Hell, yeah," Ben said. "I left it plenty. And no one's making a fool of himself here tonight, especially me."

"First of all," Jack said, lifting a finger. "You delivered Leah to my doorstep drunk as a skunk and then left her with me. How was that possibly 'leaving it alone'?"

"Okay, you know the real truth, which is that Leah delivered *herself* to you that night," Ben reminded him. With Aubrey's help, in fact. "I just helped her find you and then made sure neither of you drunk idiots drowned."

"And second of all," Jack went on, as if Ben hadn't spoken, "you are *so* about to make a fool of yourself. I can tell these things." He looked to Luke for confirmation.

Luke lifted his hands. "Don't look at me. I can't tell shit."

"Says the guy who found himself wrapped around Ali's little finger before he could so much as blink," Jack said in disgust. "Never mind him," he said to Ben.

"I'm *not* going to make a fool of myself," Ben said testily.

Jack just grinned. Luke toasted him with his beer.

Ben swore, flipped them both off, and walked out into the night. It was a mild one as far as winter nights went. A little chilly, but dry for a change.

He'd expected Aubrey's car to be long gone, but it was still in the lot. Empty. He walked through the lot to the street and looked both ways.

No tall, willowy, enigmatic blonde in either direction.

He walked to the church, one block away, but tonight the building was dark. Ben stood there, the cold, salty air blowing over him, and suddenly he knew where she'd be.

He crossed the street and hit the pier. Far below, the waves smashed against the pylons and rocks. Everything was closed, but strings of white lights had the entire length of the pier glowing into the dark night. He stilled to listen and heard the soft *click, click, click* of heels. Gotcha, he thought, and followed.

He didn't catch up with her until the very end of the pier. She'd sunk to a bench, pulled her legs up, and had her arms wrapped around her knees. Facing away from him, she was looking out into the inky night.

When he sat next to her, she jumped a little and then glared at him. "I swear I'm going to buy you a bell for your neck."

He didn't smile. Couldn't, because her face was wet, and her mascara was smeared slightly beneath her eyes. The sight made his heart stop. "You're crying."

"No, I'm not."

"Aubrey—"

"Damn it, I told you sometimes I get something in my eyes." She swiped angrily at her face.

Sighing, he slid a little closer and put an arm around her.

She resisted, but he simply held on, and then suddenly she sagged against him. "You really piss me off," she murmured, and turning to him, buried her face in his chest.

He wrapped both arms around her and pressed his head to hers. "I know."

She fisted her hands in his sweater and gripped him tight. "You're still insensitive and a first-class jerk," she said soggily, reminding him of the things she'd said to him when he'd pulled her coil wire.

"I know that, too," he said.

She shuddered and tightened her hold on him.

Something deep in his chest squeezed. It was never easy to watch a woman cry, but when a really strong woman like Aubrey let go, it was even harder. He stroked a hand down her hair. "What's wrong, Aubrey?"

She laughed mirthlessly against him. "You mean you don't already know? You know everything."

He didn't say anything to this, just held her while she cried for a few minutes. Then she sniffed, and if he wasn't mistaken, wiped her nose on his shoulder. "I need to walk," she said, and got up.

He went with her. He could have gone back to Luke and Jack. He could have gone home. He had no reason to stick with Aubrey. No reason except that he wanted to.

They walked off the pier, and she kept going. Past Eat Me, the Love Shack, the post office, the flower shop, the bakery, her own bookstore. They walked the length of Commercial Row and ended up at the rec center.

"You've been working here," Aubrey said. "With the kids."

He nodded.

"I heard you've turned Craft Corner into a huge success," she said. "Leah said more kids show up each time."

He wasn't comfortable with taking the credit. "I've gone twice. And it's all Jack's doing."

Her expression said she wasn't fooled. "You're enjoying it."

What the hell. "Yeah," he said. "I'm enjoying it." He was still surprised at that. But when he'd gone for the second time a few days ago, the director had found out he was certified as an EMT and had asked him to be a staff member. They'd given him a key to the building and a big welcome in lieu of a stipend. Which was fine. His old job—the one that was now going to be his *new* job—would provide a surprisingly decent salary.

"And you took your old job back," Aubrey said, as if reading his mind. "You start soon."

He laughed low in his throat at the power of Lucky Harbor's gossip mill. "Leah?" he asked. "Or Ali?"

She laughed, too, a little guiltily, he thought. "Facebook," she admitted. She paused for a long beat, studying the rec center quietly. "If Hannah were still alive, you'd probably have a bushel of kids enjoying this place by now."

A few years ago, just the thought would've given Ben a stab of pain. But whoever had said that time heals wounds had actually been right. His wounds were healing. Their gazes met. "Most people tiptoe around the subject of my dead wife."

"I don't tiptoe very well."

No, she didn't. It was wrong of him to even try to compare the two women. It was wrong to compare anyone to Hannah. Especially since, with her death, her image had changed in his mind, and her imperfections had faded. He knew that it was simply a coping technique, and that it probably wasn't all that healthy. But Hannah had always been his calm, his eye in the storm, his refuge. She'd had such a quiet, soothing energy, and it'd suited his adventurous soul well.

He hadn't been lying when he told her he'd been with women since Hannah, but his attention wasn't captured. He'd not been tempted to go for another relationship.

Not once in five years.

So the fact that he was suddenly, irrationally tempted by Aubrey made absolutely no sense to him, not a single lick. Aubrey was…not quiet. Not soothing. She was wild and unpredictable.

Hannah's virtual opposite.

Aubrey was watching him now, with those hazel eyes that seemed to see far more than he wanted anyone to.

"Show me what you've done with the kids here," she said.

He grimaced. "It's not all that impressive."

"Show me."

He pulled a set of keys from his pocket and opened the door for her. The place was empty, closed up for the night. Leaving the lights off, he took her hand and led her down the darkened hallway to the room he'd been using. The moonlight slanted into the classroom through the wall of windows, illuminating a series of hanging dream catchers. He'd been taught how to make them by the children on a Native American reservation in Montana when he'd been there several years ago after a devastating flood.

"Pretty," she whispered, standing there in the dark room.

Sadness seemed to come off her in waves. Sadness and…loneliness. God, she was killing him. "Aubrey."

"You give back," she whispered. "You were gone for five years, and still you came home to a place that loves you and you found a way to give back to your town."

"You're trying to give back," he said.

She didn't respond to this, didn't confirm or deny. Or even move. So he moved instead, closer to her, putting a hand low on her back, letting her know he was there. "Tell me what happened tonight."

"It's not important," she said, and shifted to move away, but he caught her.

"It is to me," he said. "Talk to me."

"Sometimes," she murmured quietly into the night, her head turned away from him, resting on his shoulder. "I feel like a really bad person."

He stroked a hand down her back, physically aching for her. He'd like to tell her she was a really *great* person, but she wouldn't believe him. The only thing he could do to coax her out of this mood was to do something he was really good at—which was annoy her. "You're not all *that* bad," he said.

She went still, and then snorted. "And maybe you're not a *total* first-class jerk."

"Oh, I'm still a first-class jerk."

She lifted her head. "No," she whispered.

"*Yes*. Here's why." And he kissed her.

Chapter 19

♥

Aubrey was never prepared for what Ben's kiss did to her. It was like she spent ninety-nine percent of her time walking around in a black-and-white world, and then when he kissed her, colors bled into her vision like a painting.

Not that she needed a man in order to see or feel. No, she had the ability to do those things all on her own, but it was as if being with Ben reminded her of that.

"I love kissing you," he breathed, holding her close against his warm, hard body.

And hell if that didn't melt her bones. "You don't need to work at charming me," she said a little breathlessly.

"No?" His mouth made its way to her ear, giving her a delicious shiver when he licked at the sensitive skin just behind her lobe. "Are you already charmed, then?"

"Just about everything you do charms me," she admitted, goose bumps breaking out all over her body, thanks to his questing mouth. "And we both know I'm a sure thing here tonight. You don't have to work so hard."

He met her gaze, his own filled with amusement. "You're a sure thing? Well, damn, woman, you could've told me."

She laughed, and something about the way joy surged through her, shoving back all the sadness, made her throw herself at him. Literally. She just…jumped him. Fortunately, he had quick reflexes and caught her, though they practically fell to the floor, kissing and groping. Twining her arms around his neck, she pressed her breasts against his broad chest as he kissed her long and deep, with wild, fast abandon. She returned the favor, the both of them panting in the quiet, dark night as they rolled, fighting for the top. She won and straddled him. "This doesn't change anything," she panted.

"Agreed," he said so fast her head spun. Apparently, a small part of her had hoped he'd protest and possibly even say he was rethinking his no-commitment stance. The way *she* was starting to rethink hers…

"We have to hurry," she said, remembering Pastor Mike and tonight's AA meeting.

Ben rolled her beneath him. "I don't like to hurry."

No kidding. She already knew he liked to take his sweet-ass time. He liked to stop and kiss every inch of her skin, tasting her. Licking her. Kissing her…just the memory made her hot. She had no idea what it was about him that flipped her switch every time, but he did it seemingly without trying. She closed her eyes, but she wanted to see his expression, wanted to let his gaze tell her all the things that his mouth never did, so she opened them again.

Yeah, she flipped his switch, too. A relief. "I have an appointment," she said. "We *have* to hurry."

"An appointment?"

Damn Pastor Mike and his charming smile. She checked her watch. Eight o'clock. "I have half an hour," she said. "So no stupid, wussy foreplay. Just fast, hard action." She saw his amusement again. "I mean it, Ben."

"Okay," he said. "We'll table the stupid and…*wussy*?" he asked, seeking clarification.

"Yes," she said impatiently. "Wussy."

"No stupid, wussy foreplay, then," he said. "Just fast, hard action. Got it." He was out-and-out smiling now, but when his gaze settled on her face, he went serious. Intense.

And she went hot, like molten lava. "Now, right?" she asked breathlessly against his mouth.

"Hell, yeah, now." He rose off her, picking her up with him. Reaching out, he hit the lock on the classroom door.

The bolt sliding home was the only sound in the room other than their accelerated breathing. Holding her gaze, Ben then slid his hand around to the nape of her neck and then into her hair, entangling his fingers, pulling her to him. Eyes on hers, he nudged her up against the waist-high row of cabinets lining one wall.

Ben pressed her into the wall and lowered his mouth to hers, almost but not quite touching. Either he expected her to shove free, or he was building the anticipation. Since she had no intention of shoving him away, and the anticipation had already built to an almost painful degree, she wrapped herself around him.

His soft, knowing laugh echoed in her mouth as he

kissed her, and that made her bite his lower lip. Laughing again, he easily took control, holding her still so he could bite her back. Things went a little wild then. She arched into him, trying to make him take action as he ran his hands over her, molding and cupping her to him. Melding them together, the kiss went on and on until she was moaning, helplessly rocking, making him swear and lose some of his tight control. Bunching the hem of her dress in his big palms, he pulled it over her head and tossed it aside.

Her bra went next, and then her panties, leaving her in just her boots.

She went to kick them off, but he stopped her. "Leave them," he said in a rough voice that gave her a rush. Pulling back, he took in the sight of her leaning against the wall, nude except for the boots, and let out a long breath. "You are so fucking beautiful, Aubrey."

"Stop that. I said no foreplay."

"Words are foreplay?"

"When you're the one speaking the words, they are," she said.

He arched a brow.

"Oh, please," she said. "Like you don't know your voice is an aphrodisiac all by itself. Tell me you've got a condom."

He reached into his pocket and came up with one. His shirt was already unbuttoned—her doing. He smelled like the wood he'd been working with in her store. His eyes were dark and heated; his hair was messy from her fingers. A lock of it fell across his forehead.

Just looking at him was foreplay. Damn it. She unzipped him and yanked him into her, kissing him slow and deep. "Remember," she murmured against his mouth. "Don't get attached to me."

He smiled and nipped at her lower lip again. "How about if I just sink into you?"

Her entire body quivered. "That's all I'm asking. Hard, Ben. Hard and fast."

He laughed, but it turned into a rough groan when she rolled the condom down his length. Then he wrestled the control back by whipping her around, bending her over the cabinets, and plunging into her in one deliciously perfect hard stroke. Unable to hold back, she cried out, and he stilled.

"Don't you dare stop," she gasped, already halfway there. She only needed a few more strokes. "Please, Ben. Do it. Do me."

He let out another low laugh, murmuring something that sounded like "You kill me" before giving her what she'd asked for, taking her with an urgency that she knew wasn't Mr. Fast-Isn't-My-Style's usual MO.

But Ben was nothing if not adaptable, not to mention accommodating. She'd said hard, and he gave it to her. Fisting a hand in her hair, he pulled her head back to kiss her, his hand gripping her hip to hold her right where he wanted her.

She melted back into him as he moved inside her, rubbing up against him, making him groan and laugh at the same time. "Killing me," he murmured again.

She could feel the brutal, tempered strength in his every movement, and in response, her body quivered. So damn close… "Ben—"

"I know," he said, brushing her ear with his mouth, whispering things—wonderfully wicked, naughty things

that nudged her right to the edge. And then the words that
knocked her right over that edge. "Come, Aubrey. I want
you to come." And then he slid a hand between her legs
to take her there.

She wasn't all the way back to Earth when he growled
out, "You are so hot when you let go," and, staggeringly,
she came again.

Groaning, he dropped his head to her shoulder, sinking
his teeth into her as he tensed and followed her over.

Aubrey never did make it to the AA meeting. Ben trailed
her home and then spent the long hours of the night showing her just how important foreplay could be, in slow,
torturous detail.

And then he showed her again.

And again.

He took her to places she'd never been, right there in
her loft. She liked to think that she'd done the same for
him, too, remembering how she'd given in to her desire to
kiss every inch of his hard body. Halfway down his torso,
he'd sunk his fingers into her hair and whispered hoarsely,
"Please tell me I ordered the happy ending."

He'd definitely gotten his happy ending...

She woke up with a start at six thirty the next morning.
It wasn't because Ben was leaving; he'd done that an
hour ago to go run. Her phone had awakened her. It was
buzzing on her nightstand. It was a text from a number
she didn't recognize. It read:

*Got your number from your father. I thought about
what you said and decided you and the teens de-*

serve each other, but you need to work your way up to them, because—trust me—they'll walk all over you. You're starting at the Reading Corner with the youngest terrors we have. Be at the rec center Wed @ 3:00.
—Judge Henderson

Aubrey lay back in her bed and smiled. She was so sated and boneless she wasn't sure she could even get out of bed. But she gave it the old college try and limped over to her notebook. There, she carefully crossed off number six with a satisfied smile on her face.

Except the smile might also be attributed to a certain sexy Ben McDaniel...

By seven, Ben had run with Sam, showered, and was standing at Aubrey's car, a coffee in each hand.

She staggered out the door at 7:05, and though she looked exhausted, she had a smile on her face as she came to a startled halt at the sight of him.

He didn't attempt to draw her into conversation, just handed her the coffee. She sipped.

He waited.

She sipped some more. At about the sixty-second mark, she started to show some signs of life.

"Thanks," she finally said.

"You're welcome. You're also welcome for the smile."

She choked on her coffee. "For your information, the smile is because Judge Sue Henderson has *almost* agreed to let me work with the troubled teen girls at the teen center," she told him.

"And this made you smile?" He shuddered. "That sounds terrifying."

She shrugged and then softened. "And okay, maybe *some* of the smile is because of you."

He felt his own smile slowly crease his face. "Yeah?"

"Yeah." She hip-bumped him. "As you damn well know already. And while we're on this subject, why are you here?"

"Thought you might want a driver again today."

"My car's running fine now," she said, then gave him a wary look. "Right?"

"Right. But since the jig is up and I know what you're up to…"

She didn't take the bait by responding, nor did she volunteer any new information, so he went on. "You might as well let me drive you."

"You only *think* you know what I'm up to," she reminded him.

He shrugged. "Maybe. But I've got a full gas tank and you don't. And even if you won't admit it, you like my company."

"Maybe I just like your body."

"That works, too," he said easily.

"How do you know my tank's on empty?"

"Call it a hunch," he said.

Letting out a breath, she headed toward his truck. He opened the door for her and let her in, then walked around and slid behind the wheel.

"I know what I get out of this," she said. "But what do you get out of it?"

"Your sunny and sweet disposition?"

She laughed, which made his morning.

"Maybe I like your company, too," he said.

She glanced over at him as if searching for sarcasm. He let her look, because for once he wasn't feeling sarcastic.

She pulled out her list. "I need to go to the nursery."

He headed in that direction, neither of them speaking, though the silence was easy. Five minutes later he'd pulled into the nursery parking lot.

Aubrey didn't move to get out of the truck. "Something that has nothing to do with my list—I had a crush on you in high school."

Surprised, he turned in his seat and looked at her. She looked at him right back. It just might have been the most real thing she'd ever said to him, right after what she'd so sweetly whispered in his ear last night—*Please, Ben, please don't stop, you feel so good…*

"I know."

She stared at him for a beat, and then, looking mortified, fumbled with the door handle.

He hit the AUTO LOCK button.

"Damn it. Let me go."

He'd done a lot of that in his life—letting go. He didn't feel like doing it this time.

Aubrey fought the door, but he'd been fast with the locks. When she figured out how to unlock the door, he simply hit AUTO LOCK again. He'd always been damn fast. He gave off that laid-back vibe, but he could move like lightning. His hand slid up her arm to her neck.

"Don't," she whispered. She didn't want him to be nice. She couldn't handle nice.

But of course he didn't listen. Instead he turned her to face him, his expression dialed to confusion.

Stupid male race. They never understood. "I'm embarrassed," she explained.

This appeared to confuse him even more. "Why?" he asked. "You were damn hot in high school. It's just that you were a few years behind me, and I was with Hannah."

She closed her eyes for a beat. "The way you looked at me last night? Back then, I'd have done anything to have you look at me like that."

"Nothing about that time can be changed," he said with a painful gentleness that made her want to run far and wide. "But we're here now."

"We're here now." She stared up at him, because suddenly *she* was the confused one. "What does that mean?"

"We're..." He trailed off.

She waited, but he didn't say more. She knew she should remain quiet and force him to fill the silence, but the suspense was killing her. "We're what? *Together*?" she asked, heart pounding, pounding, pounding.

He rubbed his jaw, and the sound of his stubble seemed loud in the truck interior.

And sexy.

But the movement was a tell, a rare show of uncertainty from a man who always knew his next move. "We're what?" she asked again, needing to know with a shocking desperation.

"We're..." He blew out a breath. "Hell if I know."

Fair enough, she supposed. "Wait here?" she asked, pausing while he hit unlock before sliding out of the truck. She shook the sexy Mr. McDaniel from her thoughts—as if it were that easy—and walked into the nursery, where she asked for Dusty Barren.

"He doesn't work here anymore," the guy at the check-out counter told her.

"Okay," Aubrey said. "Do you know where I could reach him?"

"I'm sorry." The clerk shifted his weight from foot to foot, looking suddenly uncomfortable. "He died last year."

Ben was only halfway through beating Jack's ass on *Words with Friends* when Aubrey came back to the truck, looking solemn.

"I need to go to the cemetery," she said.

This surprised him. He knew this had something to do with someone on her list. Sometimes she was happy when she got through with one, sometimes she would cry—which killed him. He tried to remember who else was on the list from the few brief glimpses he'd gotten, and who might have died.

He had no idea.

So he drove her to the cemetery.

Once there, she again slid out of the truck. Ben watched her vanish over the hill to the right. When she was gone, he got out of the truck, too, and headed to the hill on the left. He walked about a quarter of a mile before he got to the right headstone.

HANNAH WALSH MCDANIEL.

He crouched down and brushed some dirt off the stone. "Hey, babe," he said. "It's been a while." He blew out a sigh and waited for the usual stab of pain.

But it was only an ache. Worse, he had to strain to see her face in his mind.

Her voice had faded a long time ago.

"I'm sorry," he said, and ran his fingers over her headstone again.

He heard the crunch of the frozen ground behind him and knew it was Aubrey. She stayed back a respectful few feet, quiet, which was unlike her.

Quiet had been Hannah's style, but it wasn't Aubrey's. Aubrey was volatile. Passionate.

Hannah had never fought. Never.

And Aubrey fought for everything.

"You had a good marriage," Aubrey said.

She hadn't worded it as a question, but he knew she was asking. And the truth was, he'd always believed he'd had a great marriage. It'd been serene, calm. He'd liked that.

But now…now he wasn't sure whether quiet and calm would do it for him. Since that was a path he didn't want to go down—wondering if he and Hannah would be happy today with the man he'd become—he shrugged off the unsettled feelings the question brought and craned his neck to look at Aubrey. "We were young," he said simply.

Staring at him, she nodded. "Life sucks."

"Sometimes," he agreed, and rose. He searched her face, saw that she'd made peace with whatever she'd set out to do here, which he was glad for. He offered her a hand.

They walked back to the truck in silence.

Chapter 20

♥

Several days later, Aubrey sat at her desk, staring at her open notebook. Number seven on her list was weighing on her mind. She'd worked at the nursery for two weeks in her junior year of high school. The owner had never let her near the plants—he'd claimed to know after one look at someone if he or she had a black thumb, which Aubrey did—so instead, she'd been an all-around grunt, doing whatever had been required: sweeping, answering phones, running errands.

One of the other hired hands had been a special-needs teenager her same age. Dusty Burrows had been big as a horse, so it made sense that he'd been hired as the heavy lifter—bags of cement, manure, trees—whatever'd been needed.

He'd had a crush on Aubrey, which he'd shown by leaving flowers on her car and helping her with chores, all with a sweet smile on his silent face. He'd never spoken to her, not once. He rarely spoke to anyone, only when he had to.

Then one day he *stopped* smiling at her, stopped helping her, stopped leaving her flowers. He stopped being her friend entirely, and she didn't know why.

One year later, she'd been cleaning out her car when she'd found a birthday card, lost and forgotten deep between the seats. It'd been from Dusty, confessing his love for her.

She'd been embarrassed, both for him and for herself, and she'd thrown the card away and not dealt with it.

In hindsight, she'd always known that he most likely thought she'd ignored him or, worse, laughed at him.

She hated herself for that.

The bell over the bookstore's front door rang, and Aubrey prepared a smile. To her surprise, it was Carla. Her sister was in her usual pale blue scrubs, but looking a lot less tired than she had a week ago. "Hey," Aubrey said.

Carla leaned against the checkout counter, her expression impossible to read.

Already becoming a doctor, Aubrey thought wryly. Carla didn't fidget, didn't hedge. She got right to the point. "Do you remember that time you got in trouble at the library?" she asked. "For having sex in the reference section with Anthony, the principal's son?"

"I remember," Aubrey said carefully. "Though I'm surprised you do."

Carla closed her eyes, drew a deep breath, and then met Aubrey's gaze again. "I remember, because it was me."

Aubrey blinked. "Say what?"

"It was me. *I* had sex with Anthony in the reference section of the high school library."

Aubrey stared at her. "One more time."

Carla's smile was tight. "Yeah," she said. "And it gets worse. I knew you got blamed. That you were suspended. I knew you got in big trouble, that Dad jumped all over Mom's shit about how she'd raised you, and in return you then jumped all over Dad for being mean to Mom. It tore up the very tenuous peace between the four of us. But the only thing I felt at the time was this huge, overwhelming relief that it wasn't me who got suspended."

Aubrey was so stunned about the whole confession she could hardly speak. "*Why?*"

Carla looked pained and embarrassed, both new expressions for her. "I had a crush on him. I thought I loved him."

"No: I mean why did you let everyone think it was me?"

"Yeah. Well, that's a lot more complicated." Carla paused. "I'm not proud of it," she said quietly. "But the best I've got is that I really wanted to be brave and strong and independent—like you."

"Me," Aubrey repeated.

"Yes. I wanted to not care what people thought of me," Carla said. "I wanted to be…" She smiled sadly. "Well, *you*, Aubrey. But I wasn't. I wasn't anything close to you. I could only wish I was."

Aubrey stared at her. "Seriously?"

"Hand to heaven," Carla said, and bit her lower lip. "I'm sorry. So sorry. I was rude when you tried to apologize to me, and that was guilt. You're forgiven for that stupid internship thing; *of course* you're forgiven."

Aubrey felt a weight lift. "Yeah?"

"*Yeah*. And thanks for bringing me food and watching out for my plants. You went over and above, and I'm so grateful for you." She drew in a deep breath. "And now…well, I'm sort of hoping *you'd* forgive *me*. For not owning up to my mistake and letting you take the fall."

"It's ancient history," Aubrey said honestly. "And anyway, I did plenty of stuff in that library I shouldn't have. Karma was bound to come around and bite me on the ass at some point."

"You're not mad?" Carla asked softly.

"Trust me. In the grand scheme of my life, that incident was nothing."

"But you were grounded for three months," Carla reminded her. "And Dad…well, he never let you forget it. You took it, though—you took everything he dished out to you, always."

Aubrey shrugged. "I had Mom."

Carla hesitated, and then nodded. "So we're good?"

"We're good," Aubrey promised. And then the two of them shared what might have been their first genuine smile.

The next evening, right after the bookstore closed for the day, Ben went to work on paint touch-up. He'd spent the last few nights painting walls, and the place was looking brand new.

Aubrey came down the stairs from her loft. She was in her coat and boots, her purse over her arm, and he nearly opened his mouth to ask if she'd consider modeling just those boots again. Clearly the paint fumes had gone to his head. "Going out?" he asked.

She faltered briefly. "Yes."

He took in how carefully made up she was, and his stomach clenched. "On a date?" Not that it mattered, he told himself. He *hoped* she was going out on a date, because then it would prove that they weren't anything to each other.

Which is what he wanted.

Totally.

Completely.

Yep—that's what he wanted, all right. To be free…so it made no sense at all that he held his breath for her answer.

"Not a date," she said.

He didn't want to think about the relief that hit him like a Mack truck.

She moved to the door and then hesitated, her hand on the handle, her back to him. "I don't suppose you sabotaged my car again?"

"Nope," he said. "If she doesn't start, it's because she's a piece of shit." He put down his paintbrush and made an executive decision. "How about a ride, Sunshine?"

She glanced back, and he was quite certain she didn't realize that she looked hopeful. "You have more ass-kicking to do to Jack on your phone?" she asked.

"Always," he said. "Give me a minute to wash up."

"It's okay," she said, in motion again. "I've got this."

He caught up with her. She'd been good with makeup, but he could see the faint smudges of exhaustion beneath her eyes. She hadn't been sleeping. She was worried about something, probably whatever she was going to do tonight. "A minute," he said again, and, to be sure she didn't leave without him, dragged her with him to wash up.

The bathroom was tiny, but he nudged her into it and then crowded her up against the sink as he cleaned up.

"I could've waited out there," she said, sounding a little breathless.

He reached around her for a towel, and she sucked in a breath and then licked her lips. Ben put a hand on either side of her hips and caged her in between his body and the counter.

"What's with the he-man act?" she whispered, her gaze on his mouth.

He smiled. "You think I'm acting…he-man?"

"Yes. What I don't know is why. You trying to impress me, Ben?"

"You're already impressed."

She let out a low, almost reluctant laugh. "You think so?"

"Uh-huh." He leaned in so that they shared their next breath. Her eyes drifted closed, and her lips parted, waiting for a kiss.

But he didn't kiss her.

Her eyes flew open, and he laughed softly.

"You're such an ass," she said with no heat. "And to think I almost admitted that I was going to sabotage my own car so you'd have to give me a ride." When he laughed again, she gave him a push so she could get around him and out of the bathroom. He followed, grinning, enjoying the fact that he'd coaxed her out of her melancholy mood.

It'd started to rain as they dashed out to his truck, and he grabbed her hand to steady her. "Where to?" he asked when they were inside, shaking off the rain.

"Kingsbury."

Kingsbury was a town about twenty miles northeast of Lucky Harbor. She gave him an address in an upscale neighborhood, where the houses were big and bigger and the yards were all cared for by hired hands. "Someone from your list?" he asked.

"There. Park there," she said instead of answering, gesturing to a spot across the street and halfway down the block from the address she'd given him.

It was dusk. In Lucky Harbor, dusk lasted about two minutes, and in those two minutes between light and dark, everything turned a pale blue. When he'd been a kid, he'd always thought it was a magical time, when anything could happen. As an adult, he knew there was no magic.

Aubrey was studying the house intently, not giving much away. But he knew she knew the truth as well—that nothing happened unless you *made* it happen.

In fact, she was working on just that—working hard—and it touched him. Much more than it should have.

As dark settled around them, a car pulled into the driveway of the house. A man got out from behind the wheel and came around to the passenger side. He opened the door and assisted a woman as she got out of the car. For a moment, the man's face and the woman's face were highlighted by the porch lights.

Beside him, Aubrey gasped.

"What?" he asked.

She put a hand to her mouth and shook her head.

"It's something," he insisted.

The couple ducked through the rain together, laughing.

"Who are they?" Ben asked.

"Professor Stephen Bennett," Aubrey said, her voice soft, almost as far away as she seemed from him right now. "He was my English professor."

Ben got a very bad feeling in his gut. "And you came here to what—thank him for teaching you the classics?"

The couple had made it to the covered porch, where Professor Bennett pulled the woman in close to him and was kissing her with considerable heat.

"Time to go," Aubrey said tightly.

Ben glanced at her. She wasn't looking at the couple but rather out into the dark night, her expression pensive. "You okay?" he asked.

"I want to go home."

Ben started the truck and got back on the freeway, but he exited before Lucky Harbor, taking a winding road. When the road ended, he drove a little bit farther on a dirt fire road until he came to a small clearing. Turning off the engine, he got out and came around for Aubrey.

The night was a dark one. It'd stopped raining now, but the ground was soft and wet and smelled earthy. The trees were still laden and heavy with water, and whenever the wind kicked up, more water fell from them. "You warm enough?" he asked.

"Yes. Why?"

"Up for a walk?"

"Here? In the dark?" She looked around. "Where are we?"

"You'll see."

She stared at him for a long moment and then put her hand in his. He led her to what looked like a thirty-foot rock, then pulled his keys from his pocket and flicked on a small penlight he had attached to them. "Watch your step," he told her, but quickly realized that was impossible in her high-heeled boots. "Never mind." Taking her arm, he lifted her and twisted himself around so that he was carrying her piggyback.

"Ben," she gasped, throwing her arms around his neck so she didn't fall. "Put me down."

Ignoring that, he took the steep hill in front of them.

Her breathing hitched. "I'm wearing a skirt!" she said, sounding panicked.

"I know," he said. His fingers were intimately wrapped around her thighs, which in turn wrapped around his waist. Mmm. He let his hands slide northward until she squeaked.

He laughed, but stopped moving his hands.

"It's not funny," she said. "I'm flashing my goodies to the world back here."

"It's dark, and there's no one out here but us. But if you want me to keep you covered…" Once again his hands went on the move, sliding upward until he squeezed her sweet ass. The only thing between his palms and her skin was her panties, which—God bless them—felt thin and skimpy. His very favorite kind.

"Ben!" She squirmed, nearly climbing over his head. "I'm serious!"

"So am I. Are these lace?"

"Stop it!" She wriggled some more, still trying to climb out of his reach, which only made him crack up again. But he stopped copping a feel. Mostly because he was going straight down the incline now, and concentrating was a good idea.

Worried noises were still sounding in his ear from the anxious Aubrey, who was gripping him for dear life. "Oh, my God," she whispered, dropping her head to his shoulder. "*Oh, my God.*"

"Don't worry," he said. "I hardly ever fall here. Of course I haven't done it while sporting a hard-on before…"

She bit his ear, and he groaned. "I like that," he said. "A lot."

She blew out a breath.

"And that…"

"Oh, for God's sake. You like everything."

"True."

A few minutes later, he let go of her legs, letting her slowly slide down his back.

She quickly straightened her skirt. "You're impossible," she said.

"So I've been told." Taking her hand, he tugged her close, showing her the view in front of them. They stood on the top of the bluffs, on the far east side of the harbor. From here they had a perfect postcard view of the little Washington State beach town, cozily nestled in the rocky cove. The main drag—a quirky, eclectic mix of the old and new—was lit up. Looking at it from here never failed to be a comfort for him.

No matter how far and wide he'd traveled, this was home.

He could see the pier, also lit, jutting out into the water, lined with more shops and outdoor cafés. And the Ferris wheel. He'd loved that damn thing as a kid.

He and Aubrey sat side by side. Eyeing their scenic view of the Pacific Ocean, swirling and pounding the rocky shore three hundred feet below, Aubrey shook her head. "It's so gorgeous. I've never been up here."

"Never?" He found this hard to believe. "You're telling me through all your teenage years here in Lucky Harbor, no guy ever brought you up here to make out?"

She smiled. "I wasn't as easy as I looked."

"I found that a lot with girls back then," he said on a disappointed sigh that made her laugh.

He loved the sound of her laugh. Her eyes lit and her face softened. Not that she wasn't always beautiful, because she was. But when she smiled like that, she relaxed and…let him in.

He knew she wasn't good at it. He got that he was one of the chosen few. He had to admit he liked that and found himself wanting even more.

"How did you ever find this spot?" she asked.

"Luke found it years ago, out of necessity."

"Necessity?"

He smiled. "You were never a teenage boy."

"That is an accurate statement."

He laughed. "As a whole, the breed tends to need a lot of unsupervised time away from authority of any kind. It makes it easier to get in all sorts of trouble, which is incredibly attractive to the breed in general."

She smiled. "What did you all do?"

"Probably best to ask what we *didn't* do. For one thing, we'd steal Luke's sister's stash of pot. Or booze from Jack's dad. We weren't choosy. Whatever we could get our klepto fingers on. Then I'd tell Dee that Jack and I were going to spend the night at Luke's, and Luke would tell his grandma he was going to Jack's."

"Ah," she said. "The switch and bait."

"Yep."

"And then you would…" She arched a brow.

"Hike up here. We'd make a campfire—also illegal—and then get drunk or high and sleep out beneath the stars. We were complete idiots." But those times, just the three of them against the world, were vivid in Ben's mind. They were some of his fondest memories.

"You ever get caught?" she asked.

"Bite your tongue." He smiled. "Nope, we never got caught."

She shook her head, smiling a little bit, too, enjoying the story. "Hard to picture Detective Luke Hanover and Fire Marshal Jack Harper being juvenile delinquents," she said.

"But not hard to imagine me as one?" he asked mildly.

Now she laughed outright. "Benjamin McDaniel, you were born a delinquent."

This was true enough, and he smiled at the sight of her relaxing a little bit, enjoying herself at his expense. "Some things are in the blood, I guess," he said.

Her smile slowly faded. "I didn't mean—"

"I know." He couldn't help the genes he'd come from—he got that. And most of the time he never even thought about it, about his real parents. He'd honestly been kidding. But Aubrey shocked the hell out of him when she put her hands on his jaw and stared fiercely into his eyes. "We're *not* our parents," she said. "We're self-made."

He dropped his forehead to hers. "Is that why you're killing yourself with that list?"

She closed her eyes and laughed softly.

"Tell me about the professor," he said.

Sighing, she pulled back from him and stared out into the water. "I met him when I was in college in Seattle. He taught English there, my favorite subject."

Having hated English, Ben made a face, and she laughed again. "He brought it all to life," she said. "And it dazzled me. He dazzled me."

Ben had a feeling he knew where this was going, and he wasn't going to like it. "Tell me."

"I slept with him," Aubrey admitted out loud for the first time, glad for the dark. "It was against the rules, of course, not that I cared. All I cared about was how this smart, funny, amazing man found me attractive."

"He looks like he has twenty years on you," Ben said.

His voice was low and not nearly as calm as usual. He was mad at the professor on her behalf. But what had happened had been one hundred percent Aubrey's own doing and all her fault. "Forty didn't look so bad," she said. "Not on Professor Bennett." She pulled her knees up and wrapped her arms around them, suddenly a little chilled. "He gave me the attention I'd been seeking, and for one whole, glorious quarter, it was really great."

Ben slid close and rubbed his hand up and down her arm, as if trying to warm and soothe her. "What happened?"

This was the hard part. "One day I heard a couple of the other professors talking about him, how he liked to pick a pretty blonde every semester to be his pet, in spite of the fact that he was a married man. They said someday someone was going to turn him in and he'd lose his job." She paused, remembering the agony and humiliation. "So that's what happened. The college got a tip that he'd been screwing a pretty blonde, and he was fired, a year before he would've gotten tenure."

"Tenure doesn't mean shit when you break the rule and fuck around with an underage minor," Ben said harshly.

"I wasn't underage. I was twenty."

"And he was *forty*," he said. "You were twenty and this guy was forty, and you think this is *your* fault? Hell, no, Aubrey, it doesn't work like that. Jesus. You were just a kid. He took advantage of you."

"You're missing the point," she said. "*I* called in the tip."

He turned her to face him and ducked down a little to look her in the eyes. "You were a *kid*," he repeated.

"I got him fired, Ben."

"Good."

She stared at him. He was sitting there, vibrating tension and being pissed off on her behalf. And then it hit her, why she felt so…moved. No one had ever been pissed off on her behalf before. "I wasn't a kid. I was an adult," she said. "And on top of that, I knew the consequences of sleeping with a professor."

"Did you know he was married?"

"No," she admitted. "Not until I heard those other professors talking about him. I reacted with temper and hurt feelings. I shouldn't have made that call."

"So you went to his place tonight to *apologize*?" he asked incredulously.

"Yes, actually," she said, and then hesitated. "Until I saw him with his wife." She shook her head. "He's still married. Or maybe she's a new wife. It doesn't matter; she was wearing a big fat diamond ring. I'm not going to mess with his life for a second time just to assuage my guilty conscience."

"How about I go mess with his life by rearranging his face?" Ben muttered.

She laughed, but Ben's expression was carved in granite, and her smiled faded. "You aren't serious."

He just looked at her, eyes flat, mouth flat.

He was dead serious.

"No," she said, shaking her head. "No. I want you to forget everything I've told you tonight."

Testosterone pouring off him in waves, he looked away, out at the water, noncommittal. The queen of noncommittal herself, Aubrey cupped his face and pulled him back around. "I mean it," she said. "Put it out of your head."

"How do you suppose I should do that, Aubrey—put it out of my mind?"

Oh, listen to him, all alpha and furious with it. The man who'd made sure she knew that he didn't want a committed relationship with her. She was beginning to suspect he was full of shit about that, but who was she to tell him so? Lots of people hadn't wanted to be with her, including her own father.

But there was a lot of room between nothing and a committed relationship. "We should fill your mind with something else," she suggested, making her voice soft and sultry.

His gaze immediately went all heavy-lidded, and his voice lowered as well, to that sexy drawl that did her in every time. "Such as?"

Her gaze dropped to his mouth. "Well, to be honest, a few things come to mind."

"Tell me," he said huskily.

"Hmm…I'm more into show. Maybe we should go back to my place."

"Or…" He pulled off his jacket and spread it out behind her on the rock.

"Here?" she whispered.

"Yeah." Laying her back, he towered over her, rocking his pelvis to hers, letting her feel how hard he was. "Here."

Already breathless, her body betrayed her by quivering in anticipation. "Someone might come."

"That would be you," he said, and lowered himself down to kiss her.

Chapter 21

♥

At the next Craft Corner, Ben worked to keep his patience but he was quickly losing the battle. Within fifteen minutes, he was already having to resist the urge to bang his head against the wall. He'd made the spectacularly stupid mistake of asking the kids last week what they wanted to make, and they'd voted for a birdhouse, of all things. He'd cheated by buying the materials himself ahead of time and precutting all the plywood, effectively making "birdhouse kits." All the kids had to do was fit the pieces together like a puzzle and then glue and paint. "Right there," he said to Pink, pointing to a spot on her wood. "Glue right there."

"Why?" she asked.

He had twenty-five kids today, and every single one of them had asked him at least a million questions. A billion. Surely they all had sore throats from talking so much. "To hold the roof on the birdhouse," he said for the fifth time.

"Oh, yeah," she said. She'd lost both of her top front

teeth this past week, and she liked to press her tongue into the vacancy. She beamed at him, a toothless grin, and damn if he didn't feel his heart squeeze. Finding himself utterly helpless in the face of her sweetness, he ruffled her hair.

Her smiled widened. "You're awfully good with this stuff, Mr. Teacher."

No matter how many times he reminded her his name was Ben, she still said "mister," and now she'd taken to calling him Mr. Teacher, making him feel about a thousand years old.

"*Real* good," Pink added, clearly impressed. She cocked her head, leveling him with those heartbreaker-in-the-making blue eyes. "Are all dads good with this stuff?" she wanted to know.

Another hard squeeze to his heart. He wasn't sure if he'd survive her. "I don't know." And that was God's truth. He really didn't know jack about dads.

Pink nodded, accepting this with a wisdom that she shouldn't yet have. "I wonder if our dad is," she said softly.

"He is." He could say that much with absolute certainty, happy to be able give her at least something to go on. And then, trying to avoid another barrage of questions, he shifted his attention to her twin. "How's it going, Kendra?"

She shrugged, but her project was pitch-perfect.

"Hey, great job." He crouched down to her eye level, and she smiled the spitting image of Pink's smile—without the missing front teeth, of course. Unlike her sister, however, she didn't say a word, which had his heart rolling over in his chest and exposing its tender underbelly. He ruffled her hair, as he had Pink's. "Maybe you should come to my work and be my assistant," he said.

She nodded vehemently.

"Problem is," he said, unable to believe he was going to say this, "my assistant would have to talk."

Pink leaned in and whispered something in her twin's ear. Kendra listened avidly and then turned her head and said something in Pink's ear.

Pink nodded and looked up at Ben. "She says she wants to be your assistant, but I'd have to come along so I can tell you whatever she needs to say."

Knowing he'd been outsmarted, Ben tossed back his head and laughed. Then he met Kendra's gaze. "Smart girl."

Kendra gave him a thumbs-up.

That night after he dropped them off at their foster home—taking yet a third hard squeeze to his heart as they vanished inside the house—he drove straight to Seattle.

To Bob's Auto Shop.

He walked right past a scowling Bob and Ed. If they wanted another fight, he was perfectly willing to give them one, but neither man stopped him.

He found Dan on his back beneath a Jeep and kicked the cart to get his attention.

Dan rolled himself out and stared up at Ben. "What do you want?"

"You being a dad to your daughters, for starters."

Dan's mouth tightened. "We going to do this again?"

"You're a fucking idiot," Ben said. "You know that, right? You have these two perfect little girls, and you don't even see them. Explain that to me."

"Already did."

"Do it again."

Dan flung the wrench in his hand against the wall with shocking violence.

Ben didn't move a single inch, just arched a brow.

"Fuck," Dan said beneath his breath. He stood up, and though he still barely came to Ben's shoulders, he stepped toe-to-toe with him. "I come from shit."

"So?"

"I went to prison."

"Yeah, I looked that up," Ben said. "You told me it was a bogus charge, but I had to check for myself. The police were feeling pressure from the DA to make an arrest, and you had a juvie record that matched, so the charges stuck. But the rumor is that you really didn't do it."

Dan looked away. "Rumors don't mean dick in a court of law."

"You have a house."

"It's small and needs work," Dan said.

"It's in a good school district," Ben said, and at Dan's look of surprise, he nodded. "Yeah, I checked that, too. You've got a decent job."

"I work for ex-cons."

"Who did their time and turned things around." Ben shrugged at Dan's stare. "I'm good at research. These guys are family men, with kids. They're running this business clean and in the black, and they care about you." He paused, and then dropped the ace in the hole. "And then there's your sister."

Dan's eyes hardened. "Leave her out of this."

Ben liked the protective reaction, but he wasn't going to leave anything out. "You share your house with your twenty-five-year-old sister, who's just graduated college—thanks to you, by the way," Ben added. "She's working as a second-grade teacher. You've got a built-in support system."

Dan looked baffled. "Why do you even give a shit about me?"

"Oh, I *don't* give a shit about you," Ben said. "I give a shit about your daughters—two sweet, adorable five-year-old girls who deserve a whole hell of a lot better than being deserted in a foster home."

Dan stared at him. "I don't even know where to start, man. They must hate me."

"You start by exercising your rights to visitation. You get to know them. You'll see. Neither of them has the capacity to hate."

Ten minutes later, Ben was heading back to Lucky Harbor. Exhausted, he strode through his place, intending to go straight to bed, but there was Jack on his couch, feet up on the coffee table next to an empty bag of chips—Ben's—and two empty beer bottles, also Ben's. Jack's head was back, his mouth open. He was fast asleep. Next to him, equally sprawled out, equally dead to the world, was a snoring Kevin.

Nothing snored louder than a Great Dane.

Except maybe Jack. Ben gave his cousin's leg a nudge. Actually, it was more of a kick.

Jack sat straight up, instantly alert. "Wha—Did I miss the alarm?"

"You're off duty. And you don't fight fires anymore, remember?"

"Oh, yeah." Jack scrubbed his hands over his face. "What the hell time is it?"

"I don't know. Why are you here? Where's Leah?"

"Leah's at book club night. At your girlfriend's book-store, as a matter of fact."

"Aubrey's not my girlfriend. You ate all my chips and drank my beer?"

"Yeah. You'd gone to the grocery store and I hadn't."

Made perfect sense. Ben had certainly done the same to Jack enough times. Living next door to each other made it especially easy.

"I saw the dollhouse in the garage," Jack said.

Well, hell. "So?"

"So you haven't built anything like that since Hannah."

"Don't read anything into it," Ben said. He sure as hell didn't want to. He also didn't want to think about how he'd stalked the bluffs until he'd found the sole house with a dollhouse on the porch. Or how he'd then gone to the hardware store and spent a small fortune buying the materials for the replacement dollhouse he was making Aubrey.

Or why he was making it in the first place.

He plopped down in between Jack and Kevin. Kevin immediately crawled onto Ben's lap for a hug. Obliging, Ben wrapped his arms around the huge dog, giving him a full-body rub that had Kevin groaning in ecstasy. Then he burped in Ben's face.

"Your dog smells like my chips," Ben said.

"He might've had a few."

Ben leaned back and closed his eyes.

"You're not going to talk about what you're building in the garage?" Jack asked.

"No."

"Okay, then I'll talk. At first, I didn't approve of Aubrey for you."

At this, Ben slit open his eyes and looked at Jack. "Didn't approve? What the hell are we, eighteenth-century virgins?"

"I didn't approve," Jack said again, "because I thought she wasn't your type. You're quiet. You're introspective. You don't like flash. You've had a lot of shit in your life, and you came out on top. You're one of the strongest people I know, and whenever I need anything, you're at my back, no questions asked."

"Yeah? Maybe you could learn something from the no-questions-asked thing."

"Don't be an asshole," Jack said. "Hannah was such a great match because she was like you, very much so. I always thought when the day came that you landed yourself in another relationship, you'd need that same quiet strength she possessed, just like yours. But I was wrong. Aubrey is a force. She's not quiet. She's not easy. But in her own way, she's really good for you. She brings you out of your shell. She challenges you. She keeps you on your toes."

"Thanks, Dr. Phil."

Uninsulted, Jack smiled.

Ben didn't. "I'm not getting involved with Aubrey."

Now Jack laughed.

"Shut up. I'm not."

"Okay. But you're involved. Everyone knows it but you. Have you seen Facebook lately? Lucky Harbor's favorite son—you—has a poll up on whether or not you should settle down with Aubrey. Odds aren't in her favor at the moment."

"Jesus." Ben wasn't amused by this. By any of it. "People need to mind their own business. Aubrey could do way better than me. And we have sex," he said bluntly. "That's not the same thing as being involved. Not everyone has the future on their minds, like you and Luke suddenly do."

"I like her," Jack said, no longer amused, either. "A lot. But I'm not saying marry her. I'm saying just relax a little bit and enjoy being back here in Lucky Harbor. Enjoy having a woman who looks at you the way she does. And you look at her, too, you know. I've seen you with those moon eyes."

"Yeah?" Ben asked. "Well, shoot me next time."

Jack ignored this. "I think it's fair to say I know you like no one else does. This thing with Aubrey is different, and you know it."

Ben thought of how she'd been trying to make a difference, giving the seniors a place to go, giving anyone who needed it a place to go. Hell, she was even excited about working with troubled teens. He thought about how she felt in his arms, how she made him feel in hers—like he was the best man she knew and the only one she wanted. She moved him at every turn, without even trying.

And he knew Jack was right. This thing, this... whatever it was that they were doing, it *was* different.

And different was terrifying. And he wasn't ready to fall in love. He'd been there, done that, and it had flattened him. "I've told her, and now I'll tell you," he said. "I'm not looking for a committed relationship. I don't have it in me right now."

"Whatever you say, man." Jack rose and snapped his fingers at Kevin.

Kevin squeezed his eyes tight and pretended to be asleep.

Ben found a laugh after all. "Leave him."

"He ate chili tonight at the firehouse."

"Take him," Ben said.

Kevin sighed and jumped off Ben's lap, farting as he did so.

"Thanks," Ben said, waving the air in front of his face as he rose too.

"Yeah, should've warned you," Jack said. "He's got some serious hang time with those." Jack gave Ben a look that said they weren't closing the file on this subject.

Ben opened the door. "I'm okay, you know. I'm fine on my own."

Jack met his gaze. "Yeah. But you've been on your own a long time. Maybe it's time to try something new."

Chapter 22

Once again Aubrey woke up to a text message that was making her phone vibrate on her nightstand. But this one was from Ben and read:

In the shop.

Odd, she thought. He'd never felt the need to announce his presence to her before. In fact, he seemed to get a kick out of surprising her.

A glance at her clock told her that she had half an hour to get up and get out to water Mr. Wilford's pumpkin patch—which still wasn't growing yet, damn it—and be back here to open on time.

But the text was making her curious. Rolling out of bed, she tiptoed down the stairs to see what he might be doing that he'd found it necessary to warn her about.

He was sitting on the counter in front of the coffee and tea station, sipping from a to-go cup from Leah's bakery.

She could tell by his clothes—slacks and a button-down shirt topped by a jacket—that he was going to his job. His real job. She'd seen him in jeans and a tool belt covered in sawdust, and she liked that look a lot. She'd also seen him in nothing. *That* particular memory gave her a flash of heat, because Ben in nothing was the hottest thing she'd ever seen. That was definitely her favorite look, but seeing him like this, a little dressed up, his broad shoulders stretching his dress shirt to its limits, the top button undone, his tie still loose, as though he weren't quite ready to settle into work for the day, did something serious to her insides.

Get a grip. She tiptoed closer, wanting to catch him unawares, the way he always caught her. Two feet from him, she was grinning widely, like an idiot, her hands outstretched to scare him, when he suddenly twisted and locked eyes on her.

"Damn it," she said.

"The top step creaks."

"I should hire someone to fix that," she said drily.

He didn't answer. He was busy taking in the very skimpy tank top and tiny boy shorts she'd slept in. From the heat in his gaze, she could tell he liked the view. But when he reached for her, she took a step back, out of his range.

"Come here."

Shaking her head, she covered her mouth with her hands. "Morning breath."

"I don't care."

He wasn't scared off by much, she knew. Well, except for a committed relationship, and at that thought, her mood went a little south. "I'm going to shower," she said, and when his eyes darkened with interest, she shook her head. "*Alone*."

He took another sip of his steaming drink. "I'm really good in the shower."

Her nipples got perky, and she crossed her arms over herself, making him laugh softly.

"Go get dressed," he said. "I've started a new book club."

"What?" That's when she realized she could hear voices. *Little* voices. And then another, not little voice, but a low baritone, and she stared at Ben in horror.

He straightened, set down his drink, and pulled off his jacket, which he wrapped around her. It was warm, and it smelled like him, and it fell to her thighs. Putting a finger to his lips, he took her hand, leading her to the half wall. Then, holding her in front of him, he pressed on her shoulders until she ducked low.

He crouched behind her, cradling her body within his, stroking a hand down her back while she did her best not to notice that he smelled so good she wanted to inhale him.

And/or lick him as though he were a lollipop.

Pressing his jaw to hers, he gestured with his chin to look ahead.

Seated on one of her couches were Pink and Kendra. Their legs were short enough to stick straight out, and they each held a stack of books on their laps. In between them was a man who looked so much like them he could have been their older brother. He was reading out loud from one of Aubrey's favorite children's books, and the girls were enraptured, staring up into his face, hanging on every single word.

"That's their dad," Ben whispered against her ear. "Dan Ingalls. He's got visitation rights."

She craned her neck and looked up at Ben. Once again, he had a several-day-old scruff going on his jaw, and she wanted him to rub it over her body. "Since when?" she whispered, barely staying on topic.

"Since always, apparently. He just didn't exercise them. Until now."

There was something in his voice. Relief, she thought, and reached for his hand. "You did this," she said. "You brought them together."

He shook his head. "It's just a visit. I don't know if he's really into it." He looked at the little girls hanging on every word as their dad read the book.

Her heart squeezed at how important this was to him. The girls had seriously insinuated themselves into his heart. He was invested, whether he wanted to admit it or not.

And as wrong as it was to think it, it gave her hope. Because maybe he could get invested in something else, too. *Someone* else.

Someone like her…

Two days later, Aubrey closed the store, ran her receipts, and realized something shocking. "I broke even today," she said aloud in surprise.

Ben, who'd showed up after work, changed into jeans, and gotten busy on the back shelves, poked his head around the corner. He was covered in a layer of sawdust. "What?"

"I broke even," she marveled.

He flashed her a smile. "Congratulations." He held out a hand. "Come on. I'll buy you a drink."

They went to the Love Shack.

Aubrey was halfway through a tall, cold beer when Pastor Mike walked in the front door and headed to a table. He stopped short at the sight of Aubrey at the bar and then changed direction and headed straight for her.

Crap. She shoved her beer so that it was in front of Ben and lifted her hands the way a basketball player did when he'd just fouled but was trying to pretend he hadn't.

"Aubrey," Pastor Mike said, calm and quiet as ever, but the concern and worry were there in his eyes as he took in the two beers in front of Ben. He glanced at Ben, nodded, and then his attention came back to her. "How are you doing?"

"I'm good. *Really*," she added.

He nodded. "And you know you can call me."

"Yes," she said emphatically. "I know I can call you."

"Anytime."

"Anytime," she repeated, adding what she hoped was a confidence-boosting nod. "Thank you."

When he'd walked way, she blew out a breath, belatedly realizing Ben was looking at her. "What?" she asked.

"Anything you want to tell me?"

"Such as…?"

"Well, either you're having a fling with Pastor Mike or he thinks you're an alcoholic."

Aubrey grimaced. She wasn't sure which excuse to go with. "Maybe I found God."

Ben just looked at her.

She racked her brain, but there really wasn't a good option. "Okay, I didn't know how to tell you, but Pastor Mike and I are madly in love."

Ben shook his head. "Don't ever play poker."

Damn it. "Okay, so he thinks I'm an alcoholic."

"Well, I guess that's better than your sleeping with him," Ben said.

Interesting that *that* would bug him.

"Why would he think you're an alcoholic?" he asked.

"It's…complicated."

A laugh gusted out of him. "That doesn't surprise me."

"Oh, like *you're* a piece of cake," she said, and crossed her arms, insulted. "You know what? I don't want to talk about it."

"Do you ever?"

She rolled her eyes. "You're not exactly Mr. Talkative yourself, you know. You're always sticking your nose in my business about the list and all, but you're holding on to plenty of secrets yourself."

He tossed back his drink and set it down. Then he stood up and held out his hand. "Come on."

She looked at him, suddenly wary. "Where to?"

"Chicken?" he asked quietly.

How was it that he knew all her buttons? "Of course not."

"So then…" He waggled his fingers.

She stared at them and then, with a sigh, let him pull her up.

He brought her to his place. Jack's side of the duplex was dark. So was Ben's, until he unlocked and opened the front door, reached in, and turned on a light.

"What are we doing here?" she asked, hesitating on the front step. Nothing good was going to come of stepping inside.

Okay, scratch that. *Everything* good would come of it, but—

"I want to show you something."

"Oh, boy, I know this game," she said with a lightness she didn't feel.

He smiled. "Something else."

"What?"

He looked at her for a long moment. "Okay, but after I show you, I don't want you to get all weird and try to close yourself off."

"I don't do that."

He gave her a long look.

"Fine," she said, caving. "I totally do that. It's my thing."

"Don't do it to me," he said very seriously, very solemnly.

She stared into his eyes, butterflies bouncing around inside her now. "All right."

"Promise."

"Seriously?" She sighed when he didn't budge. "Okay, I promise not to shut you out. Jeez, I didn't know you had such tender feelings."

He out-and-out laughed at that, and then pulled her through the living room to the kitchen. There, he shoved open a door that led to his garage.

He gave her a look that made an odd feeling begin to course through her. Nerves. Then he flipped on the light, and she gasped at the beautiful handmade wooden doll-house.

Chapter 23

♥

Heart pounding, Aubrey walked to the dollhouse and ran her fingers over the meticulously handcrafted wood. It was beautiful. She wasn't sure how long she stood there before she felt Ben's hand run down her back.

"I don't have any tissues," he said, "but you can use my shirt if you want."

She let out a laugh to hide her sob. "Why? Why did you do this?"

His hand was still on her. He was stroking her as though he just liked the feel of her beneath his hand, but it didn't escape her notice that he didn't answer.

With an unsteady breath, she touched the dollhouse again. It was a three-story Victorian, as hers had been when she was a child. Unlike that one, however, this dollhouse was made entirely of wood—no plastic or cardboard anywhere—and it was of heirloom quality. If she'd been a child, she'd have spent hours having her dolls run up and down the spiral staircase, peek out the numerous windows, and swing open the front door. "Thank you," she whispered. Ali and Leah were right. Her gut was right. She needed to tell him why he was on the list.

But she wasn't ready to lose him.

A little voice deep inside her warned that the longer she waited, the worse the consequences would be, but she told that voice to shut up. She arched a little so that Ben's hand pressed harder against her back. "Ben…"

He stroked her again, slowly this time, more purpose-fully. She waited for him to speak, but he didn't. His silence was loaded now, weighted with hunger and desire. Her heart kicked into a fast, heavy beat, and everything within her tightened with need.

For him. "*Ben.*"

His hand moved on her again, stroking her hair, then softly sweeping it aside. She felt his mouth against the nape of her neck and was working at drawing in a des-perate breath when he turned her around to face him. Cupping her jaw, he kissed her, stealing away the air she'd managed to drag in. His mouth was firm, just like the rest of his hard, warm body, and so male that she melted into him. By the time he finally lifted his head and met her gaze, she'd wrapped herself around him like a pretzel.

"Your choice," he said.

There was no choice. She needed him more than she needed air. And she needed air pretty damn bad. There were a lot of reasons why she should still take the closing-herself-off option, but she knew she wasn't going to. She wanted him to put his hands and his mouth on her. She wanted him to work his magic, and he *was* magic. He was a masterful lover, intuitive and shockingly sensitive. She wanted him to do all the things his eyes were promising, and she wanted that now. "My choice is you," she said.

She'd barely gotten the words out before his mouth was back on hers. He kissed her hard and then pulled back to look at her for a beat before he kissed her again.

And then again.

And then he lifted her up so that her legs wrapped around him. He carried her from the garage to his bedroom, letting her down by his bed, slowly sliding her along his body. Then he stripped her with slow care, groaning as he bared her to his satisfaction. Lowering his head, he splayed his hands on her bare back, drawing her close. Opening his mouth on first one breast, and then the other, he teased her with his tongue, sucking and nibbling.

She moaned—a low, desperately hungry sound—as she slid her fingers into his hair, holding his head to her. She couldn't help it. She was trying to climb his body as though it were a tree when he stepped back and pulled off his own clothes in a few smooth, economical movements.

She just stared at him. His body was incredible, and she didn't think she'd ever get tired of looking at it.

He still hadn't spoken a word.

She might have thought he was entirely unmoved, except he was sporting an impressive erection that made her mouth water. She was still staring at it in awe, thinking *In me now*, when he gave her a nudge and she fell backward onto the bed.

He followed her down, and she moaned again when he kissed her, long and deep. And then he kissed every inch of her, slowly and thoroughly, until she came. Exploded, really.

He put on a condom and entered her, and she came again. Instantly. She cried out in surprise and shock as it went on and on, endless shudders and ripples of pleasure. She was vaguely aware of the sounds she was making and might have been horrified, but she realized she wasn't the only one. When her senses returned, Ben was still over her, muscles quaking, breathing as harshly as she.

After a moment, he rolled off the bed and went into the bathroom.

She told herself to get up and get dressed and then get out. She needed to do so before her heart got any more invested than it already was. Trembling like a leaf, she took a long moment to even sit up, and by then Ben was back. He stood at the side of the bed, voice low, eyes dark and direct. "Stay," he said. And then he slid in beside her, pulling the covers over the top of them, dragging her in against him.

Oh, God. God, he felt so good. But this wasn't real. She needed to remind them both of that and set some boundaries. For his sake. "Ben—"

"Sleep," he said, voice gruff.

"But—"

He tightened his grip. Her cheek was on his chest, her thigh between his. She was breathing in his scent with every breath and couldn't remember ever feeling so content in her life. She didn't close her eyes, she didn't want to miss a second of this, because it wouldn't last. It couldn't. Unable to resist, she let her hand drift over his chest. It was a beautiful chest, broad and sculpted and spattered with light hair from pec to pec. He was warm and hard, and he hummed his pleasure at her touch. "Okay?" he asked quietly in the dark, tightening his grip.

She nodded against him. She was so far more than okay that it was terrifying.

They slept some then, and she woke up in the gray light of dawn, violently aroused. Ben was between her legs, working his magic with his tongue. She came before she had all her faculties working, and then he rose over her and kissed her, slow and unrushed.

Their joining was much more leisurely this time, but no less hot. Maybe it was because they knew each other's bodies now, or maybe it was just sheer animal magnetism, but when he finally slid into her and began a series of driving thrusts, she went out of her mind. And when she climaxed, she nearly burst out of her skin as well.

Afterward, he held her for a long time, and Aubrey reveled in it, afraid of what might happen when full daylight came.

"Shh," he murmured, sounding sleepy.

"I didn't say anything."

"You're thinking so hard you're making me tired." He stroked a big hand down her back to possessively cup her ass, holding her close. "Sleep."

She didn't. Couldn't.

He made a noise like that of a rumbling lion and rolled her beneath him, pinning her to the mattress.

"What are you doing?" she asked, already breathless.

"Wearing you out so you can sleep." He kissed her mouth, her chin, her throat, her shoulder. A nipple. And as he headed further south, she gasped and arched, sliding her fingers into his hair. "Omigod."

"No," he said. "Just Ben."

She started to laugh, but then he got creative with his tongue, and she cried out instead.

He made good on his promise. A long time later, they both flopped to the mattress, breathing raggedly, sated, and completely worn out.

When Aubrey woke again, the sun was shining. She slipped from Ben's arms and stared down at him, still asleep on the bed. He looked relaxed and young. His jaw was rough with stubble, his hair wild from her fingers. And if she wasn't mistaken, he had a bite mark on his shoulder. She'd marked him. Fair enough, she thought, since he'd indelibly marked her. On the inside…

She'd done the unthinkable and started the slippery fall from lust to love.

Or maybe she'd fallen for him a long time ago…

Either way, big mistake. She began scooping up her clothes, but she was still trembling, little aftershocks of great sex. She stilled for a moment to gather herself, and then felt two warm hands settle on her arms and pull her back against an even warmer chest. And then a mouth brushed her shoulder.

"Pastor Mike?" she murmured.

A soft laugh huffed against her skin, and then he bit her. She laughed, too, but her smile fell away, and, unable to keep it inside any longer, she turned to face him. "Ben, what are we doing?"

"About to have some hot morning sex?" He reached for her, but she stepped back, her knees wobbling so badly she sank into a chair.

"But it's *just* sex," she said, meeting his gaze, trying to be as calm as he always was. "Right?"

He held her gaze but dropped his hands from her. "Aubrey—"

"I need to know, Ben. I need to know because I can't be in this all by myself. I can't. I—" God, she was such a hypocrite. She wanted him, like this, just like this. But there was the secret between them, one he didn't even know about. She covered her face.

"Hey," he said gently, kneeling beside her chair, placing his hands on her legs. "I thought you wanted it to stay simple, too."

"I do." But as he'd pointed out several times, nothing was ever simple with her. "Or I thought I did," she added.

He held her gaze, but his own was a little hooded now. "I think of you all the time. And I know an awful lot of it is sex—an awful lot," he said. "But not all."

Her heart did a funny dance. Either hope, or terror, she wasn't sure which.

Both, she decided. Definitely both.

"But," he went on slowly, still holding her gaze prisoner, because he was far braver than she was, "I didn't need this. I didn't want this in my life," he said.

"I know." She rose abruptly. "I've worked hard to keep this just sex—for you, Ben, for *your* comfort level, so you wouldn't think I was trying to drag you into a committed relationship." She turned back and found him standing right there, and she wrapped her arms around his neck. "You're not going to turn into a lapdog, Ben."

His arms closed around her hard. "No?"

"No. And even though I risk breaking my own no-emotions clause, I care about you," she admitted. "More than I wanted to. Much more."

He stared at her as if she'd just told him she was carrying a nuclear bomb.

"It's supposed to be a compliment," she said, and

backed away. "One you aren't expected to return. You know that, right?"

"Goddamn it," he said, and she started at his shocking vehemence, because he never raised his voice. In fact, unless he had his tongue in her mouth, or any of his other body parts entangled with hers, it was difficult to tell what he was feeling.

But she felt his feelings now, loud and clear. Shock. Anger.

Fear.

Sympathy flooded her. He, the guy who was seemingly afraid of nothing, was afraid of her feelings for him. Or maybe he was afraid of what he felt for her.

Not that she blamed him. He'd already given a woman everything he had, and she was gone. "My feelings aren't meant to be a burden," she said softly. "But I won't apologize for them, or take them back."

He closed his eyes. "I care about you, too, Aubrey, but…"

"But you don't want to. I get it." It shouldn't hurt. At all. "Never mind," she said. "Subject change."

"You knew my feelings on this," he said. "From the beginning."

"Yeah. Got them loud and clear," she said.

He studied her for a beat. "Caring about someone means you're open," he finally said.

"What are you saying, that you're not open?"

"I'm open," he said. "I'm an open book." He lifted his hands out to his sides. "What you see is what you get."

Suddenly she knew what he was getting at, and her heart kicked again. "And you don't think that's the case with me."

"You're smoke and mirrors, Aubrey."

Her heart started pounding. He knew. Maybe not the what exactly, but he knew something. "How so?"

"Forget it."

Forget it? Was he serious? She'd pulled on her dress. She had one boot on, the other in her hand. "Tell me or I'll throw this at you."

He shook his head, a small smile playing at the corners of his mouth. "That," he said. "That right there. You dress like you're going to some fancy tea, but underneath the clothes you're ready to brawl for anything you believe in. You want people to think you're tough and that you don't care what anyone thinks, but you do. You care. A lot." He met her gaze. "You care too much."

"Well, I'm not going to apologize for that, either!"

"So why do you keep it your dirty secret?"

"What are you talking about?"

"Your list," he said, and her stomach sank, because here it came. Doomsday. "When are you going to tell me about the list?" he asked quietly.

She looked into his eyes and knew it was a huge risk, but she had to do it or lose him right here and now. "Okay."

"Okay?"

She let out a long, shaky breath. "About a month ago, I kind of wandered into a weekly AA meeting by accident."

"How do you wander into AA by accident?"

"Well, I was—" Running from *him*, in fact. "That's not the important part. The important part is that when I was there, something happened."

"Pastor Mike."

She nodded. "No. Well, yes. Pastor Mike happened.

He thought—" She broke off with a grimace. "He thought I was an alcoholic, so he brought me into that meeting."

He stared at her. "You went to an AA meeting even though you're not an alcoholic."

"Yes. I know. But in the meeting I heard something that struck a chord with me."

"And that was?"

"Make amends with people you've wronged."

He stared at her, and then his eyes softened. "Everyone's made mistakes, Aubrey."

Some more than others... "I know," she said. "I'm just trying to own mine." She was going to have to tell him, and her knees went weak with fear and anxiety.

A frown of concern creased his brow, but just as he stepped toward her, there came the unmistakable sound of Ben's front door opening.

Ben had his jeans on in a wink. Leaving them unfastened, he headed out to the living room, eyes flat and calm, body perfectly relaxed and yet somehow braced for violence at the same time.

"Jesus, Jack," she heard him say.

By the time she finished dressing and fixing her hair, the scent of something delicious was coming from the kitchen. She followed the mouthwatering aroma of bacon and coffee and found Jack at the stove top stirring something, with Ben glaring at him.

Ignoring him, Jack smiled at Aubrey. "Hey," he said. "Sorry for the interruption. Ben here didn't mention that he was having a sleepover."

"Ben didn't mention it," Ben said, "because it's none of your business."

"Testy in the mornings, isn't he?" Jack said to Aubrey,

not looking like he was in a hurry to go anywhere. He grabbed another bowl so that there were three lined up on the counter, and then he began filling them. "Just got off duty and brought a big pot of breakfast casserole to Mr. Sunshine here. There's enough to go around, so have a seat."

"Oh," she said. "No, thanks. I have to—"

"Sit."

"Resistance is futile," Ben said drily. "He'll just wear you down."

"It's true," Jack said.

Ben reached out with his foot and nudged a chair toward her.

She picked a different chair. One that was farther away from him. He arched a brow as he also sat. Kevin, the Great Dane, immediately leaped into his lap. Ben laughed and wrapped his arms around the dog. Kevin snuggled in as though he weighed ten pounds, not 150, and sent Aubrey a look from the security of Ben's arms—*My man, not yours.*

Jack plopped into the chair that Ben had pulled out for Aubrey. "Aw, thanks, man." He blew a kiss in Ben's direction.

In turn, Ben upturned his middle finger in Jack's direction.

Jack grinned. "You're just cranky because you think I'm going to ask Aubrey some awkward questions."

"You're not going to ask a single question," Ben said.

"Seriously," Jack said. "For a guy who just got some, *how* can you still be pissy?"

Aubrey choked on her bite of the breakfast casserole.

Ben shot Jack a fulminating look and leaned over him to pat Aubrey on the back.

"We're just friends," Aubrey said to Jack, smacking Ben's hand away. "And sometimes we're not even that."

Jack grinned. "Do tell."

"Don't," Ben said to her. "Anything you say is just fuel for him. He's Lucille in training."

"Sorry," Jack said, looking anything but. "I just got excited that Ben's got a friend other than me and Luke. He's growing up so fast."

Ben sent him a look that would have had Aubrey peeing in her pants if she had been a man. She stood up and brought her bowl to the sink. She couldn't eat. She couldn't do this. They had so much more to talk about, she and Ben, but she wasn't eager to do that, because then it would be over. She might never be ready for that.

Not that Ben was exactly showing signs of being ready for a relationship either. The most likely scenario was that he wasn't ever going to be ready.

Oh, yes, she knew he wanted her in his bed.

But that wasn't going to ever be enough for her. She knew that now. It hurt, deep down inside, and she didn't know what to do. She'd promised herself she would tell him the truth—she'd very nearly done so only a few moments ago—but now she needed to think. Turning, she looked at Jack. "Thanks for breakfast. I've got to go."

Jack smiled at her. "Anytime."

She didn't look at Ben. She was halfway through the living room before she was aware of him following her, but still she kept going. When she reached for the front door, a bigger hand got there first, holding it closed. She stared at the forearm lined with sinew and strength and let out a breath. "I have to get to the store, Ben."

"You're leaving mad."

"No."

"Now you're leaving mad *and* lying."

She dropped her head to the door. "Ben—"

He put his hands on her and turned her to face him. "There," he said. "Now you can try to lie right to my face."

"I've got to go," she said again. "Please, Ben."

"Shit," he said, staring at her. "You never say 'please'—unless we're having sex."

Behind them, Jack snorted.

When both Ben and Aubrey glanced over at him, he raised his hands in surrender. "I'm going."

"So am I," Aubrey said, and turned to the door.

"We're not done with this," Ben said.

She glanced back to find him standing there in nothing but those low-slung jeans, hands up over his head and braced on the doorjamb, watching her with the expression that never failed to make her body hum. And she could only hope that he was right—that they weren't done with this.

Chapter 24

♥

Aubrey drove past her bookstore and straight to the church. It was early, but the front doors were unlocked. Maybe a church was always unlocked; she had no idea. No doubt the people here were far more trusting than she was. In any case, she let herself in and was grateful to find Pastor Mike in his office, reading.

He looked up with surprise. "Aubrey. I've been thinking about you since you missed the meeting."

Because she'd been in bed with Ben.

And in the shower.

And against the wall…"I'm sorry," she said, hoping she wasn't blushing. "Something came up. But I have"—she looked at her watch—"seventeen minutes, and I've got a problem that's really much bigger than seventeen minutes, but I thought out of everyone I know, you're probably the only one who could help me. I don't know." She blew out a breath. She was rambling. "Can I come in?"

"You already are," he said with a smile. He rose and gestured to a chair. "Tell me the problem."

"It's actually more of a question. About making amends." She hesitated, because now that she was here, she was nervous. Very nervous. What if she'd already screwed up too badly? What if there were no amends that could fix this one last thing on her list, the most important thing on her list?

THE HARD ONE.

"Sixteen minutes," Mike reminded her gently.

"Right." She drew a deep breath. "Okay, so say you have a secret, something you want to apologize for, but by coming out with it, you might hurt the very person you want to make amends to?" She stopped. "You know what? Never mind; I'm not making sense."

"Yes, you are," Pastor Mike said. "It's just a hard thing to say. You've wronged someone. You want to apologize, but in bringing it out into the open, you might hurt the very person you wanted to apologize to. Do I have that right?"

"Yes." She sagged back in her chair. "You're very good at this."

"Don't say that yet." He leaned in and met her gaze. "Aubrey, sometimes you have to go with your heart. The very soul of your heart, where all the goodness is."

"You make it sound easy."

He shook his head. "It's not. That part of your heart is usually protected by pride and stubbornness."

Aubrey let out a half laugh, half groan, and covered her face.

"Sometimes," he said quietly, "you have to do the hard thing, not the easy thing."

She dropped her hands. "But either way feels like the hard thing—on the one hand, telling him, and on the other hand, keeping the knowledge to myself."

"Okay, so what's the *right* thing?"

Aubrey drew in a deep breath and leaned back. The truth was, she'd known deep in her gut for a long time that *not* telling Ben what she'd done all those years ago was *not* the right thing.

Which meant she really did have to tell him.

She had to hurt him.

And then, once she came clean with him, when she freed herself of the burden of the truth, she'd lose him. He wouldn't smile at her anymore. He wouldn't make her day by just being *in* her day.

He wouldn't be in her day at all.

To do the right thing, she had to destroy the best thing that had ever happened to her. "Sometimes," she said miserably, "I wish there was a DELETE button in life."

Pastor Mike smiled sympathetically. "Do you want to tell me what you did?" he asked.

No. No, she wanted to *never* ever tell anyone what she'd done. How she'd broken Ben and Hannah up all those years ago, for a stupid, selfish reason that didn't even matter anymore. Thank God they'd managed to get back together two years later—that they'd had a few years before Hannah had died. But Aubrey knew it wouldn't matter to Ben. All that would matter is that she'd screwed things up for him.

And there was nothing she could do or say to make that up to him.

Nothing.

* * *

Aubrey drove back to the bookstore. As she walked through, opening the place for the day, she came to a sudden halt at the sight of the dollhouse set up in the children's section. Weak-kneed, she sat in front of it. Ben, of course. He'd done this—for her.

She spent a few long moments staring at it and then had to reapply her mascara before she greeted any customers.

That night Ben heard a persistent honking from out front of his duplex. When he opened the door to investigate, he found the local senior center dial-a-ride van out front. The door slid open, and a bunch of blue-haired ladies peeked out and waved at him.

The driver was his aunt Dee, though her hair wasn't blue but a bright, shiny platinum blond. He'd long since stopped being surprised by her colorful wigs. He was just happy she was past the worst of the chemo and clearly no longer depressed.

"Get in," Dee said, waving him over. "Tonight's the Winter Festival, remember?"

He remembered, but he shook his head in the negative. Lucky Harbor reveled in its traditions, and Winter Festival was one of them. It involved a lot of beer and wine and dancing on the pier, made possible by stands of portable heaters that kept everyone warm—as though the festivities and alcohol wouldn't do that on their own.

But Ben didn't feel the need to go. Luke and Jack were both working the event, so he figured he'd stay home with Kevin and a movie.

"Ah, come on," Dee coaxed. "We need a designated driver."

"Where's your boyfriend?" he asked. "Why can't he be the DD?"

At that, several male heads popped out, one of them being Ronald, Dee's boyfriend. Another was Edward, Luke's grandfather.

Shit. Everyone was looking at Ben hopefully. He didn't want to do this. He wasn't in a festival kind of mood. He'd worked hard this week, and he was physically exhausted. Mentally, too.

And Aubrey was avoiding him.

And maybe he'd been avoiding her, too, after she'd revealed her feelings. He had feelings, too, and not only wasn't he ready for them, he didn't want them. Fat lot of good that was doing him…

Relenting, he drove them to the festival. "Hey," he said, holding down the door locks before anyone could escape. "This party is over in two hours, you hear me? You must be back at the van in two hours, or you're walking home."

This was met by a chorus of moans and groans. Dee released her seat belt and hugged Ben from behind. "That's only ten o'clock, sweetheart. We aren't pumpkins, you know."

"Don't you all need to get home to take your Metamucil?" he asked desperately, as Dee continued to hug him. There was no rushing a hug from Dee. He'd learned that years ago, when he'd first been dumped on her doorstep. She'd hugged him hello, she'd hugged him good-bye, she'd hugged him whenever she'd passed him in the hallway, and he'd squirmed over every single one. He knew she loved him. Just as he knew that sometimes she hugged him just to torture him and to amuse herself.

That's what family did—fuck with each other. And sweet as she was, she could give as good as she got.

"Midnight," she said now, in her soft but steely voice. "Okay, baby? We'll owe you."

Since he couldn't imagine needing a favor from the seniors of Lucky Harbor, he just disentangled himself and unlocked the doors. "Midnight," he agreed reluctantly. "Be here. I mean it."

As Lucille padded by, she patted his shoulder. "Saw your girl yesterday at the rec center. She was volunteering at Reading Corner."

"Reading Corner?"

"Sure. Craft Corner is Tuesdays and Fridays; Reading Corner is Wednesday. Volunteers come in and read to the kids. She was good, too—did all the voices just right. The kids ate her up."

Ben looked into Lucille's eyes and saw something sly. "What are you up to?" he asked warily.

"Who, me?" she asked innocently.

When the van was empty, Ben stared out at the pier, which was lit up like the Fourth of July. Yeah, the people of Lucky Harbor took their Winter Festival very seriously. The last time he'd been here for the festival, he'd had Hannah with him, and at that thought he braced for the usual stab of agony through his heart. But there was no sharp pain at all, just a sweet ache and the memory of Hannah dragging him out onto the dance floor, which made him smile.

But he still didn't want to go. So he put the van in gear and hit the gas. There was really only one place he wanted to be tonight, and only one person he wanted to be with.

* * *

Alone, Aubrey sat on her bed in a big T-shirt she'd stolen from Ben. Every other item of clothing she owned was either at the dry cleaner or in her laundry basket, waiting for a trip to the Laundromat. Her grand-opening party was only a few days from now, and she was working on the plans. The store calendar had filled up so nicely, with something happening just about every day of the week, that she actually had a shot at making this work.

Too bad she didn't have a shot in hell of making her private life work nearly so neatly. She'd promised herself that the very next time she saw Ben she'd tell him the truth. That he was on her list. She was pretty sure how things would go from there.

South. Fast.

Restless, she rose and started a game of darts. If she got a bull's-eye, she told herself, she'd tell Ben now. She'd get into her car, drive straight to his place, and just spit it out.

Which would effectively ruin the best thing that had ever happened to her…

She got a bull's-eye on the second try. Damn it. "Two out of three," she said out loud, and gathered the darts.

She startled when the single knock sounded at her door. She knew that knock, and even if she hadn't, the way her nipples hardened told her exactly who was on the other side of the door.

He didn't knock again. This was because, as she'd learned, he had the patience of a saint.

Not that there was anything remotely saintly about him.

Still, she glanced through the peephole. Though she hadn't made a noise, Ben looked right at her, brow cocked.

If you open the door, you have to tell him.

On the other side of the door, Ben lifted the bag he held. It was from the Love Shack.

Her head said, *Danger, Will Robinson, danger!* But her stomach growled, and apparently her stomach was the boss. She pulled open the door. "Ben. I—"

He pushed inside as though he owned the place. "Why aren't you at the Winter Festival?"

"I'm…busy."

He glanced at the darts in her hand. "Yes, I can see that." The corners of his mouth quirked but his eyes remained serious. "You up for a game?"

"With me?"

"Three darts," he said. "Highest points combined wins."

"What does the winner get?" she asked.

His gaze ate her up. "Winner's choice."

Her heart took a treacherous leap. Her choice would be to never have to tell him what she'd done, but she knew that was no longer a choice at all. "Are you any good?" she asked.

He shrugged and made himself at home, setting down the bag he'd brought and turning to the dartboard. "Ladies first," he said.

"I stole your T-shirt," she said inanely.

"I can see that." He eyed her from head to toe and back again, lingering, making her very aware of how thin and see-through the shirt was, a fact he was clearly enjoying. "It looks better on you than it ever did on me," he said, voice low and sexy. "Play, Aubrey."

She threw her darts. Two hit the twenty, the last hit the bull's-eye. Trying to hold back her smug smile, she turned to him. "Sixty-five points."

"You're good." He slid his hand around to the nape of her neck and tugged her in for a quick, hard kiss. "But I'm better," he said silkily against her lips.

Every erogenous zone in her body stood up and danced. "Why don't you put your money where your mouth is?"

"Don't tempt me." He kissed her again, and then nipped at her lower lip. Then he pulled the darts from the board, stood at the line, and shot.

For a moment her eyes were on him, on the long, lean, hard lines of his body, and she didn't see his first throw. But his second throw caught her attention.

Triple twenty, just like his first. Uh-oh.

Turning his head, he looked at her, and then threw the third dart. Another triple twenty. He hadn't gone for the bull's-eye. He'd gone for the maximum points on the board. One hundred and eighty, to be exact.

"Hmm," she said. "You're better than good."

"Yeah." He gave her another kiss, this one a little longer, a little deeper, and a whole lot hotter. She was completely melted into him when he pulled back and gave her a light swat on the ass. "Hungry?" he asked. Without waiting for an answer, he grabbed the bag of food and sat on her bed. He pulled out a burrito and unwrapped the foil, making steam rise. He wafted it in her direction.

Her stomach growled again.

He smiled and patted the bed.

"What about your spoils?" she asked.

"Later."

She crossed her arms. "Now. I want to know what devious angle you're working."

"Devious," he repeated. "Wow. I'm wounded."

"Is it going to be sexual?" she asked, unable to keep the hopeful tone out of her voice. "Because I should have specified—if it's something sexual, it can't be from my taboo list."

He laughed. "Sunshine, we obliterated your taboo list the other night."

Oh, yeah. Damn.

"Come eat."

She sat next to him, carefully tucking the shirt around her for modesty, which cracked him up again. "You're full of laughs tonight," she said.

He shrugged. "I like being with you."

Her chest tightened. She'd wanted this, oh, God, how much she wanted this. And now she was going to have to ruin it.

You ruined it a long time ago...

"You were at Reading Corner," he said, halfway through his burrito. "Lucille told me."

"Yes," she said. "Your girls were there. They're so smart, Ben."

"I know. Dan's working on custody."

Her breath caught. "Really? How wonderful for all of them." She paused. "You did that. You brought them together. You gave those girls a real family."

He shrugged.

"It's amazing," she said. "You're amazing."

"No. I just couldn't stand it, them not having anyone. I had my aunt Dee." He ran his thumb over the backs of her knuckles. "Without her and Jack..." He shook his head. "I'd have fallen through the cracks. I probably wouldn't even be here."

Her heart squeezed. "You saved them from falling through the cracks. You gave them so much, Ben."

He busied himself with cleaning up the trash and shoving it back into the bag the food had come in. Then he balled it, aimed for the trash can twenty feet across the room, and shot.

The bag swooshed into the can.

And still he stayed quiet.

"Did I upset you?" she asked.

"No. I like the way you care about stuff," he said. "You aren't quiet about it, and though you're reserved, you aren't shy. When you have your heart and soul in something, you're in it."

Her breath caught. Had anyone ever gotten her the way he did? No. And that's when she knew. Truth was, she'd known for a damn long time. She had her heart and soul in something, all right—*him*. She closed her eyes and gave herself a lecture. *Don't you sleep with him. Don't you dare. Not until you tell him...*

He turned his hand over and entangled his fingers with hers. "I like the way you care," he said again. "I like the way you care about me."

"Is that why you're here?" she asked, heart pounding. "And not at the Winter Festival?"

"I'm the seniors' ride, but wasn't in the mood for a crowd. I have to go back to get them later," he said, and he rose. "I'll take my spoils now."

Oh, God. "We should play another game," she said quickly, and jumped up, heading to the dartboard. "We'll make it the best of two out of three—"

Strong arms wrapped around her from behind, and he turned, effectively caging her in between the hard wall and his harder body. "You reneging?" he asked, mouth against her ear.

"No, but—" She sucked in a breath as his hands roamed over her, molding the shirt to her curves. "I was just thinking it might be more fair if—"

He whipped her around to face him and then backed her to the kitchen counter, lifting her to it.

Her bare ass touched the cold surface, and she yelped.

"I claim *you*," he said, and his lips descended on hers.

She wrapped her arms around his neck and traced her tongue over his lower lip, knowing it drove him wild.

Pinning her with his big body, he let her feel what she did to him. "I've got a question," he said. "A serious one."

Her heart skidded to a stop. Oh, God. "Okay," she whispered tentatively.

"What are you wearing beneath my shirt?"

She stared at him. "Not much," she confessed.

This made him swear roughly, reverently. She laughed again and then realized that whenever she was with him, she was laughing, or smiling.

Or having an orgasm.

It'd been a long time since she'd had someone like him in her life. Maybe since…ever. But even as the warm fuzzies washed over her, so did fear. Because this was all an illusion; he wasn't really hers. And at that thought, her smile faded.

His did, too. "Should I go, Aubrey?"

"You mean…leave? Now?"

"If you want."

"No." She knew she should be embarrassed by how quickly she answered, but she felt only panic at the thought of him leaving. "Don't go."

There. She'd said it. She'd put it out there and couldn't, wouldn't, take it back. Tomorrow would be a different story, and she'd face that then, but for now, right this very minute, she knew what she needed.

Him.

Inside of her.

Ben caught her close and slowly lowered his head to hers, giving her plenty of time to stop him.

Fat chance of that. Not only did she not stop him, she grabbed him and pulled him even closer.

He was smiling when he kissed her, his lips fitting smoothly over hers. Then he straightened and kicked off his shoes and tore his shirt over his head. "It's only fair to even the score," he said.

"So you're being a gentleman by stripping?"

"Exactly."

"I'll help," she said, and unbuttoned and unzipped him so she could slide her hand inside his jeans.

Ben groaned, the sound echoing in the otherwise silent loft, a hotly erotic sound. "Ben?"

He cupped her face and deepened the kiss, and when she was completely lost, he slid his hands beneath the hem of the big T-shirt and cupped her bare bottom. "Mmm," he said, low and husky. Tugging her closer, he continued moving against her so that she could hardly breathe. "Aubrey?"

"Yes?"

"Be sure." Pulling back, he looked deep into her eyes, probably searching for a sign that she was going to regret this. "If I stay tonight," he said, "I'm going to be in your bed in about five seconds. I'm going to make love to you until neither of us can walk."

The words brought a rush of heat. "Was that supposed to scare me off?" she asked.

The faintest of smiles crossed his mouth as he pulled the shirt off her, tossing it behind him, leaving her bare to his gaze. He looked his fill with a groan, and then looked some more.

She was shaking for him. "Ben, I want—"

"Want? Or need?"

He was going to tease her now? "*Need*, damn it. I need—"

"Me." His fingers skimmed up her inner thighs and then in between, making her forget to worry about what exactly he would decide to claim as his spoils, making her forget her stupid list, making her forget just about everything, including her own name. "Say it, Aubrey." He was at her ear, the words hot along her skin. His lips grazed her earlobe, and a rush of heat shot hard and fast southward.

"Yes," she managed as he took her to the bed, pinning her to the mattress beneath his delicious weight. "You. I need you." *Only you...*

"How?" he asked, voice husky as the tip of his tongue played with her nipple before sucking it hard between his hot tongue and the roof of his mouth.

"Th—that," she said on a moan.

"Me kissing you?" He switched to her other breast and gave it the same torturous teasing. "Is that what you want?"

His questing fingers were inching closer and closer to where she needed them, close but not...quite...getting there. "And your fingers!" she gasped, giving up and arching into him.

He rewarded her with both, kissing her hard as his fingers traced their way up her thighs, and then between. The touch nearly levitated her off the bed, would have for certain if she hadn't been anchored by his body. Applying pressure in the exact right spot, his lips—God, those lips, doing diabolical things to her as well—combined the sensations so that her head spun, and she cried out.

"Anything you want," he murmured against a breast. "You want me to touch you? My mouth on you? My hands gripping your hips as I sink in and out of you until we're both screaming each other's name?"

She let her eyes drift closed as her lips parted on a "*God, yes...*" He was still just playing with her, but she was done playing. Fisting her hands in his hair, she pulled his mouth to hers. He let her control the kiss, and another, and another. Finally he lifted his head, gave her a wickedly naughty smile, and took over, shifting down her body, kissing every inch he passed. He didn't stop until he'd made himself at home between her legs, holding them open with his shoulders.

"So beautiful," he whispered, nipping first one inner thigh, and then the other, and then...in between. "Say the magic words, Aubrey. Tell me what you want now."

"Your mouth, I need your mouth."

He gave it to her, and her breathing hitched, and then stopped altogether. Her blood seemed to flow through her veins like liquid fire. White-hot, pulsing need ripped through her as he gave her exactly what she wanted.

When she'd stopped shuddering, he was resting his head on her belly, watching her recover.

"Now you," she said, reaching for him. "I want to feel you inside me. Please, Ben. Inside me now."

He rose up. "Wrap your legs around me." His voice was rough, his hands gentle, as he slid his hand up her legs and directed them around his hips. He sank into her, hard. *Perfect*.

Their groans of pleasure commingled in the air. Leaning over her, he bent low and kissed her—fervent, erotic, rough, and wild.

Her body, already on fire for him, erupted again. Ben's hands slid to her hips, cupped her ass, and, lifting her up against him, he thrust deep. It was enough to have her crying out, arching against him in an attempt to draw him even deeper. "Yes," she moaned, clutching at him. "Like that."

He growled low in his throat as he gave her what she wanted, on his terms. Slow. Purposeful. Taking her to the point of no return and beyond, to a place where she couldn't have said what she wanted next if her life had depended on it.

It didn't matter. Ben seemed to know exactly what she wanted. That was the thing about him. He instinctively knew when to be aggressive, when to be gentle and coaxing, and, best of all, he knew how to drive every last worry right out of her mind.

Chapter 25

A long time later, they collapsed on the bed, gasping, sweaty, breathing like lunatics. Ben threw a hand over his eyes as he tried to catch his breath, because though he could lie smooth as silk when he wanted to, he never lied to himself.

This wasn't just sex between him and Aubrey. This was love.

"I need to talk to you," she said.

"Okay."

She was quiet so long that he dropped his arm from his eyes and turned his head.

She was looking at him, eyes shimmering with a suspicious sheen. "It's about my list," she said softly. "You're on it."

Ben stared at her. "You said I wasn't."

"I...misled you."

He took this in for a full minute, running through his

memories and coming up completely blank. "I don't understand. What did you ever do to me?"

She sat up and reached for his shirt again, pulling it back over her head and down to mid-thigh.

Covering herself from him.

He wasn't liking this much. "Aubrey."

"Don't you want to put something on?" she asked.

"After you answer me."

She ran a hand over her eyes, and he realized her fingers were shaking. "I'm trying," she said. "I've been trying for a while." She shook her head. "No, that's a lie. I didn't know how to tell you. It's been killing me slowly, but I—" She broke off and let out a long breath. "I screwed up."

He pulled her hand from her face. "Just say it."

"Okay." She drew a deep breath. "Do you remember when Hannah broke up with you?"

"Yes." It had been the summer after he'd graduated high school, and he had been night surfing. Alone. It'd been a dangerous, reckless thing to do, but he'd been stupid back then and had often pulled such stunts. It'd been some sort of teenage testosterone-driven dare, a challenge between him and life, and he hadn't been too particular about who might win.

When he'd come back to shore, Hannah had been waiting on the beach for him. She'd stared at his feet and told him she was breaking it off because they were going to college in a few months, and they needed to spread their wings.

He remembered feeling blindsided. He'd told her that he didn't need to spread his fucking wings, and she'd smiled a little bit sadly and said she was setting him free anyway.

He hadn't seen her for two years. He'd finally run into her by sheer accident on spring break, and they'd reconnected. And though she'd never asked and he never told, he'd spent the two years away from her having a damn good time spreading his wings.

"What about it?" he asked Aubrey now.

"I told her you slept around with other girls, one of them being me. It was why she broke up with you."

It took him a moment to find words, and even then he only had one. "What?"

"Yeah." She nodded, chewing on her lower lip. "I caused her to…break up with you."

He shook his head. She was making no sense. "You were two years behind us in school. You didn't even know Hannah."

"We were in after-school tutoring together. I was there for Spanish Two. She was in danger of failing Spanish Four."

"You're lying," he said flatly. "Hannah was a straight-A student."

"She'd always been, yes," she agreed. "But Spanish flattened her. She had to get her grade from an F to a C or lose her upcoming college scholarship. She came to tutoring every day for an hour."

He stared at her as the first inkling of doubt began to creep in. Hannah had been busy every day after school, but she'd told him she was working at the optometrist's office where her mom worked. More than that, the college scholarship thing was setting off alarm bells in his head. Hannah had been all set to go to the University of Washington at Seattle—with him. But after she'd dumped him, she'd gone to a community college instead. He'd always assumed it'd been so that they wouldn't be at the same school. But what if that hadn't been it at all? What if what Aubrey was saying was true—that Hannah hadn't brought her grade up enough and she'd lost her scholarship? "I don't get it," he said. "Why did you tell her we slept together?"

"I'd like to tell you the whole thing," she said, "but the short answer is that I was jealous."

"Jealous."

"Yes." She clasped her hands together and kept her eyes on them. "I'm not proud of that. I'm sorry, Ben."

Was she serious? A "sorry" was supposed to make it all okay? He jerked upright and yanked on his pants.

"Wait," she said, jumping up, too. "Let me tell you the rest—"

"I don't give a shit about the rest." He shoved his feet into his shoes and turned back to her. "Just tell me one thing—why now? Why are you telling me this now?" Then it hit him, and he let out a harsh laugh. "The damn list. You need to clear your conscience. Well, congratulations, Aubrey, you did it. Job well done." He snatched up his shirt and, without putting it on, stormed to the door. Needing to know one more thing, he whipped back. "Wait. Why did she believe you?"

Aubrey stood there before him, pale, eyes filled with regret and other things that he didn't want to see, wearing *his* damn shirt, looking devastated. "I can be very convincing," she said softly.

"Yes," he agreed, staring down at her bowed head. "You can."

She winced as the barb hit, and he told himself he didn't care. "So what was this between us? Amendment?

You fucked me to make up for lying about fucking me?"

"No. *No*," she said. "You saw my list. FUCKING BEN was not on it."

"Well, BEN was on it. Don't tell me you're also fucking the pumpkin man."

"Don't you get it?" she cried. "I didn't plan to sleep with you at all!" She tossed up her hands. "And trust me, this"—she gestured to the bed—"was *not* how I planned to make amends."

"Okay, so out of morbid curiosity, how *were* you going to do that? How were you going to give me back the two years I missed out on with my wife?"

"I didn't know!" she said. "I still don't!"

Suddenly drained, he moved to the door. "You let me know when you figure it out."

When he was gone, Aubrey's legs gave way, and she slid down the wall. Hugging her knees, she dropped her head to her chest and fought the tears.

She remembered that long-ago night as if it were yesterday. She'd been at a party where she hadn't belonged. It'd been for seniors, so she'd been lying low when she saw Hannah and a girlfriend get in Hannah's car to leave. Talking and laughing, Hannah had pulled out into the street without looking and caused a wreck. With the cars still smoking, and horns and alarms going off, Aubrey had watched in disbelief as the two girls had switched spots, crawling past each other in the front seat so that Hannah was no longer behind the wheel.

When the police arrived, Hannah's friend—the sober one—had saved Hannah from getting a DUI.

Aubrey couldn't believe it. As the girl who had always gotten in trouble for every little infraction—and some that weren't even hers—she had been infuriated.

The next day at tutoring, Aubrey had told Hannah that she knew what she'd done. At first, Hannah had pretended not to know what Aubrey was talking about—until Aubrey told her she'd seen it herself. Hannah had paled but rallied quickly, telling Aubrey that no one would ever believe it.

Their tutor had broken up the heated whispered exchange, yelling at them to be quiet and work. Hannah had told him that Aubrey was trying to cheat.

Aubrey had gotten detention.

"You see?" Hannah had whispered. "No one will ever believe you over me. The girl who dresses like a prom queen when she's not. The girl who needs tutoring in all her classes. The girl no one wants. Even your own dad picked your sister over you."

Horrifically wounded by this, her secret and humiliating hot button, Aubrey's mouth had disconnected from her brain, and she'd said, "Ben has no complaints about me every time we meet in the woods." Not about to stop herself—her biggest regret—she'd gone on. "And I'm not the only one he's doing it with, so obviously he's not getting off on *you*."

Hannah had stormed out, earning herself detention right alongside Aubrey. But she'd dumped Ben.

And then eventually fate had stepped in and gotten them back together, though Hannah must not have told Ben about Aubrey's tale.

But he knew now…

* * *

Ben didn't sleep. Every time he closed his eyes he saw Aubrey's face as he'd left. The regret and fear and misery in her expression haunted him, making him want to toss aside his hurt and anger and soothe hers.

So he stopped closing his eyes because he *needed* to hold on to the hurt and anger. He needed that badly, and as to the reason why—well, he didn't want to study that too closely.

When dawn came, he went for a run. He beat Sam to the pier, but not by much. When Sam came up level with him, he stopped and frowned. "You okay?"

Ben grunted in response and took off. Sam caught up with him but didn't ask another question. Ben ran hard and fast, and Sam kept pace, never slowing until Ben did.

Just before they got back to the pier, Sam spoke. "You know where to find me if you need anything."

Ben met Sam's gaze and saw nothing but sincerity. He nodded. "Thanks, man, but I'm good." Actually, he was the opposite of good, and they both knew it, but Sam let the lie go.

Ben skipped the bookstore. The work he had left to do there was minimal. He knew he needed to finish, but hell if he could face her yet. So he went to work and put in twelve straight hours on a subterranean water leak out at the dam, which was threatening the properties below the harbor. That night he stumbled into bed, exhausted, and proceeded to stare at his ceiling for hours.

The next morning he heard a polite knock at his door.

He ignored it.

He ignored the doorbell, too.

But he couldn't ignore whoever the hell was letting himself into his house. He slid out of his bed, prepared to take on the intruder bare-handed and in his boxers, thinking maybe a good old fight would loosen the two-day-old knot in the center of his chest. He was ready when he padded into the living room, but stopped short at the sight of his aunt Dee.

She was in his kitchen, unloading a bag of groceries. She had a carton of eggs in one hand and a gallon of orange juice in her other as she looked up and caught sight of him. "Hey, baby."

There were flowers in a bouquet on his table. "You brought me flowers?" he asked inanely.

"No. They were on your doorstep. I just brought them in. There's a note," Dee added. "It's sealed, or I'd have totally sneaked a peek. Although I can guess."

Ben could, too, but he didn't want to go there. "You going to the senior center today?" he asked Dee.

"Yes. It's bingo lunch."

"Take the flowers with you."

She gave him an assessing look. "Okay. Did you want to go get dressed and eat, or would you rather kick my butt for intruding?"

"I'm still trying to decide."

She smiled. "Go on. Find some clothes. I'll be done here by the time you're back."

"Done with what?" he asked.

"Breakfast, silly."

"Breakfast," he repeated, stunned into stupidity by heartache and lack of sleep.

"Yes." She beamed at him. "Remember all those mornings you got up at the crack of dawn to come make me breakfast after my chemo? Well, I'm returning the favor."

He didn't want breakfast. He wanted…Aubrey. He

wanted her sated and boneless in his bed, with one of those smiles on her face that was just for him, as though he were the best thing she'd ever seen.

At the thought, emotion swamped him. He told himself it was all anger, because she'd ruined it. She'd ruined everything. But the truth was, it felt more like sadness and regret than anger.

Dee's smile faded, and she set down the orange juice and eggs and came to him, wrapping her arms around him. "Rough morning?" she asked quietly.

He shrugged.

Just as he'd done for her all those mornings when she'd been sick and exhausted and scared and hurting, she didn't ask a bunch of questions. She accepted that some days were just shit. "You look like hell," she murmured.

He let out a low laugh. "Thanks." He went to his room to yank on a pair of jeans and then came back to the kitchen.

"Sit." Dee gestured to a chair with her wooden spoon. "You'll eat."

"I'm not hungry."

"Did I ask you if you were hungry? No, I did not." Again she pointed to the chair and when he didn't budge, she shoved him.

"Bully," he said without heat, and let the five-foot-two woman push him down to the chair.

She smiled and patted his shoulder. "I learned from the best, you know."

"I wasn't this mean," he said.

"Oh, please," she said on a laugh and affected his low baritone as she imitated what he'd said to her whenever she'd resisted him. "You will sit there and shut up and eat,

Aunt Dee, and if you don't, I'll force it down your throat."

"I didn't say it like that," he said, but surprised them both by laughing.

She smiled. "Aw, that's better. You probably want to know why I'm here."

"You're here because you're nosy."

"Yes, well, there's that." She came over with a loaded plate and the juice. She set them both down in front of him and hugged him.

"Again?" he asked.

"Hug me back or I'll keep at it."

Because she looked so worried, he let her boss him around. He hugged her back, letting her hold on for as long as she wanted, which was about a year. "I'm getting gray hair here," he finally said.

She pulled back and smacked him upside the head. Then she cupped his face and stared into his eyes. "I'm here because I got the mom feeling that something is wrong. Is it hard being back here?" she asked quietly. "In Lucky Harbor? With us? Is that it? You're going to leave again?"

"No. And it's not hard being back. I like being back," he said, no longer surprised to find that it was absolutely true. He might have started out a true city boy, but he'd also been a lost one, without people who cared. And then he'd landed here in Lucky Harbor, where everyone cared. He liked that—a lot. The place fit him; it always had. "I'm not leaving," he promised.

"Is it Hannah?" she whispered. "The memories of her?"

"No," he said, and when she just kept looking at him, he said, "I miss her. I'll always miss her. But it's not her."

"Then it's Aubrey," Dee said. "Damn. I told you that one was going to be trouble."

"I don't want to talk about it."

Dee paused, still hovering. "Can I just say one thing?"

"Could a freight train stop you?"

She smiled and cupped his face once more. "It was lovely to see you putting yourself out there again. I hope that whatever happened between you two doesn't change that."

He gave her a look. "You're fishing."

"Yes." She paused, and when he didn't fill in the silence, she sighed good-naturedly. "I love you, baby. You know that, right?"

"I know it. I've never doubted it."

Her eyes looked a little damp as she looked him over again, but she nodded firmly. "You'll get through this."

She was right about that; he would get through this. He didn't see much of a choice. Life was funny that way. When it threw him a curveball, sometimes it hit him between the eyes and sometimes it hit him in the gut, but he always kept coming back to bat.

That afternoon, Ben stood bleary-eyed in front of the Craft Corner gang. He was teaching the kids how to make the kite he'd learned to build from some kids in Haiti, when what he really wanted to do was something far more physical.

Like night surf. He was feeling more than a little out of control, but he knew he needed to keep it together, because he still had to go back to work after this. He could have sworn he was keeping his bad mood from the kids, but just as though he'd projected it out there, a fight broke out over a roll of twine between Pink and a scrappy, tough little girl named Dani. "Hey," he said, striding over and breaking it up. "Cool it. There's enough twine to go around."

"That's not what this is about," Pink said, still glaring at Dani. "She's being mean."

"Am not," Dani said.

"Both of you knock it off," Ben said.

But the girls continued to stare each other down, neither one of them speaking.

Jesus, Ben thought. Girls really were aliens. "Kites," Ben said. "Make your kites."

Neither backed down until Ben gave them each a nudge.

Three minutes later the fight was back on.

"Okay," Ben said. "That's it. You have two seconds to tell me what's going on, or we're done here." He looked down at the insistent tugging on the hem of his shirt and found Kendra staring up at him, her eyes filled with anxiety.

"You aren't going to quit, right?" she asked in a small voice.

Ah, shit. Guilt swamped him, and he crouched down to look into the eyes of the little girl who hadn't spoken once in all this time—until now. Apparently her abandonment issues trumped her social anxieties. "I'm not going anywhere," Ben promised. "We're *all* going." He took Kendra's hand in his and rose to his full height, staring at the entire class. "Get your hammers."

Ben had asked Sam for advice on what to do with the kids. Sam built boats by hand and knew his way around tools. On his suggestion, Ben had ordered and bought thirty-five small hammers from the hardware store, along with work aprons and some other tools for the kids. He figured they'd go out to the railroad ties surrounding the yard and hit the shit out of the wood until aggressions were released. It'd always worked for him. "Field trip," he said.

They got halfway down the hall before Ms. Uptight Teacher stuck her head out of the office. "Where are you going?"

"Field trip," the kids yelled excitedly.

The teacher shook her head. "No permission slips."

"We're not leaving the yard," Ben said.

The kids all sighed in disappointment.

The teacher didn't look relieved. "Why are they all carrying hammers?"

"Anger management," Ben said.

Ms. Uptight Teacher was shaking her head before he finished speaking. "No."

He wondered if she practiced saying no to everything, or if it just came to her as naturally as her pinched expression did.

"If you all need a time-out," she said, "there's a basket of kick balls in the yard."

Fine. Ben took the kids to the yard, marching them to the far end. "Okay," he said, lining them up. "New lesson. Anger management."

"What's that?" several kids asked.

"It's when you expel your pent-up negative energy through physical exertion," he said.

They all blinked in collective confusion.

"You know how sometimes you just want to hit someone?" he asked them.

"You mean like when someone tells a *lie about you*?" Pink asked, glaring at Dani.

"Or when they *steal your string for your kite*?" Dani asked, glaring back at Pink.

"Yes," Ben said, stepping between them. "Just like that. But we're *not* going to hit anyone. Instead we're going to hit *something*. Something that won't get you in trouble. In this case, the fence." He set a kick ball in front of each kid, separating them widely enough so that no one could level anyone else, accidentally or otherwise. There he stepped to an empty spot with his own ball. "Go," he said.

Everyone kicked their balls at the fence, which made a very satisfactory sound as it was hit. The balls went flying, and the kids raced after them. They lined up again.

And again.

Ten minutes later each and every one of them was panting in exertion and...smiling.

Except for Ben. He drove Pink and Kendra home and finally found something that did make him smile.

Dan was sitting on the front steps of the house, waiting for his kids.

Chapter 26

Aubrey hadn't had very many shitty days lately, not since Ben had come into her life. But the past few days had been real doozies. It was horrifying, demoralizing, *devastating* to realize how badly she'd messed up. Earlier she'd opened the bookstore determined to hold her head up high. What was done was done. She'd had the best of intentions when she'd confessed her misdeed to Ben, and though she still had to somehow make him understand that, she also had to go on.

She had a lot to look forward to, she reminded herself. For one thing, her store was doing okay. And for another, her grand-opening party was only four days away. She'd do even better after that, or so she hoped.

The bell over the door jangled, and her first customers of the day walked in. Lucille and—oh, crap—Mrs. Cappernackle, the retired librarian.

Mrs. Cappernackle gave Aubrey an indecipherable

look down her long nose. "Lucille informs me you came by my place some time ago."

"Yes," Aubrey said. "I did." She paused. "You don't remember?"

"I've had some health problems," she said, still snooty. "Affects my short-term memory."

Behind her, Lucille swirled her finger by her right ear, making the sign for "crazy."

Mrs. Cappernackle didn't catch this, thankfully. "My long-term memory, however," she went on, eyes eagle sharp and on Aubrey, "remains perfectly intact."

Terrific. Not daring to meet Lucille's gaze, Aubrey bent down to the cabinet beneath the cash register and pulled out the book she'd been saving to give back to the retired librarian.

Mrs. Cappernackle's eyes narrowed. "So you *did* have it."

Aubrey didn't bother to sigh as she handed it over. "It's not the exact same copy. I bought you a new one."

Mrs. Cappernackle opened the book and stared down at a check stuck in the first page. "What's this?"

"Overdue library fees," Aubrey said, hoping it was enough.

Lucille glanced over Mrs. Cappernackle's shoulder, looked at the check, and smiled. "Aw, how sweet. Isn't that sweet, Martha?" she asked Mrs. Cappernackle.

"Hmm," Mrs. Cappernackle said. "I do like it when a person owns up to her mistakes." She narrowed her gaze on Aubrey. "But I still want you to stay out of my library."

Behind her, Lucille made the "crazy" sign again and then nodded, motioning that Aubrey should just agree.

"Done," Aubrey promised.

Mrs. Cappernackle nodded. "I'll wait in the car, Lucille. I'm tired now."

"I'll be right there," Lucille assured her with a gentle pat, and when the door had shut behind Mrs. Cappernackle, she met Aubrey's gaze. "Thanks."

"I have the feeling I should be thanking you," Aubrey said.

"Think nothing of it." She leaned in, eyes unusually solemn. "How are you holding up?"

"Me?" Aubrey asked. "I'm fine." She had no idea what exactly Lucille might be referring to, but best to be "fine" no matter what. Besides, there was no way the world could know about her and Ben yet, or at least she hoped not. "Uh…why do you ask?"

Lucille looked at her for a long moment. "I couldn't help but notice that you're not carrying Ted Marshall's book in here anywhere."

"No." Hell, no.

Lucille nodded. "Wise choice. But you can't keep it hidden forever, honey. Lots of people in town have e-readers now, you know. They're downloading his book regardless."

"My purpose wasn't to keep people from reading it," Aubrey said. "I just didn't want to sell it here. I refuse to help him earn a single penny."

Lucille nodded. "I understand that. So I hope you understand that my book club read it." Aubrey winced. "We didn't tell you, or order the book through your store, because we didn't want to hurt your feelings. But just like with *Fifty Shades*, we were morbidly curious."

"I do understand," Aubrey said. "You don't have to apologize."

"Well, I sort of do." Lucille met her gaze. "It was my idea, you see, and I feel awful about that. Because everyone read the book, all twenty-two of us, and now they're talking about it." She paused as if waiting for a specific reaction from Aubrey.

But Aubrey had no idea what that reaction was supposed to be. "Well, that's good, isn't it?"

"I don't think so, no," Lucille said. "You know Lucky Harbor. Those twenty-two people will tell twenty-two people, and so forth." She shrugged. "People love a scandal. I didn't put it on Facebook, though. I want you to know that."

"Okay," Aubrey said, even more confused now. "What am I missing, Lucille?"

Lucille paused, staring at her. "Honey, have *you* read it?"

"Just the first chapter."

Lucille took this in while moving her lower dentures around some. "Oh, dear."

"You're starting to scare me, Lucille."

Lucille sighed. "He outed you."

"He...outed me," Aubrey repeated. "What do you mean? I thought everyone already knew I was bitchy. That can't be news to anyone."

"It's not just that. He published a picture of you—one of the less revealing pictures you'd posed for, in the grand scheme of things, but still. It's pretty revealing."

"A picture. Of me," Aubrey repeated, aware that she was beginning to sound like a broken record.

"It's the one where you were in the"—she hooked her fingers to signify quotation marks—"Sexy Kitty costume."

Oh, God. *Those* pictures. She staggered back to one of

the big, cozy chairs and fell into it, her mouth open, her heart racing. Crap. *Shit*. She'd thought things couldn't get worse, but this was worse. A part of her past she'd hoped to never revisit was back, biting her on the ass.

She should've been used to it. After all, she'd just spent a month facing her past head-on, and it'd been the hardest thing she'd ever done.

But she'd been fixing her past while concentrating on her future, and that future had just come to a grinding halt. The pictures that Lucile referred to had been taken when she'd been nineteen, during her short "modeling" career. She'd used the money to pay her college tuition. It'd been that or quit school, and she'd never been a quitter. She wasn't going to apologize for that.

But that didn't mean she wanted the pictures from all those years ago to surface now.

Or ever. "I'm going to have to kill him," she murmured.

"Or," Lucille said, "you could hit him where it hurts."

"Hitting him in the nuts might get me arrested," Aubrey said. "And I'm trying to clean up my karma, not make it worse."

Lucille smiled. "I meant his wallet, honey. Sue him."

No—she couldn't. The pictures were on the Internet if someone knew where to look, and since Aubrey hadn't retained the copyright, she doubted she had a leg to stand on.

"Now, mind you," Lucille went on, "the picture he used is nothing to be ashamed of. You have a lovely figure, Aubrey. But the link to the others…"

"He published the website address?" Why, oh, why hadn't she read his entire book?

Because he was slime, that's why.

"He did," Lucille said. "And to be honest, some of *those* pictures…well, they're not quite as…tasteful as the one in his book."

Yeah. She didn't remember a single one in the bunch being…*tasteful*.

Lucille took in Aubrey's expression and frowned with concern. "You really didn't know."

She shook her head. "No."

The older woman sighed. "I'm sorry. Honestly, those pictures, they don't bother me none. I'm a modern woman, you see. But there're *some* people in town who aren't as liberated as I am. They might view this as…well…"

"Porn," Aubrey said flatly.

"Well, only if they haven't read *Fifty Shades*," Lucille said helpfully.

Good God. This was bad. Very bad. While she sat there picturing her reputation's demise, the bell on the store door tinkled. She looked up in time to see her father stride into the store in an elegant suit, his Bluetooth headset on his ear. Clearly he was in work mode.

Aubrey couldn't imagine what had brought him here until his cold gaze met hers. And then she knew.

The pictures. From the frying pan into the fire… "If you'll excuse me, Lucille," she murmured.

"No problem, dear."

"Aubrey," her father said when she'd risen on shaky legs and walked over to him.

"Long time no see," she said lightly. "You missed the last few family dinners."

He didn't buy into the small talk. "You posed nude on the Internet."

She took a moment to try to draw in a deep breath for calm. *Try* being the operative word. "It was a long time ago," she finally said.

"So you're saying there's a statute of limitations on stupid decisions?" he asked.

Ouch. "No," she said carefully. "There's not. Of course not. But at the time—"

"At the time you were in college. What kind of serious college student poses for immoral pictures—"

"It was a legit modeling job, Dad."

"Legit? Please." He stared her down. "I'm bitterly disappointed in you."

"I paid my way through college with those pictures," she said, vibrating with frustration, heartbreak, and now anger. And actually, the anger felt good—damn good. "You were a little busy at the time with the new family, but I paid my *own* way, without asking you for a cent. So I'm sorry if I didn't turn out the way you wanted me to, but you know what, Dad? You didn't turn out the way I wanted you to, either. So consider us even."

Ben worked late. He didn't get home until seven. He'd been texted approximately a million times by both Luke and Jack, demanding his presence for dinner.

They'd clearly sensed a tremor in the force, and now they wanted to drive him crazy. He had missed calls as well, wanting to know where the hell he was.

Ignoring it all, he opened his fridge. Empty. Damn. Figuring he might as well face the music sooner rather than later, he drove to the Love Shack and dropped into a chair at Luke and Jack's table. "You called?" he asked drily.

Luke looked at Jack.

"Me?" Jack asked Luke. "I thought we'd agreed *you'd* do it."

Luke shook his head and pointed at Jack.

Jack sighed and pulled out his phone.

"Forget it," Ben said. "I don't want to see Facebook. Nor do I want to know how the hell Lucille already found out that Aubrey and I broke up."

"Uh…" Luke said, and looked at Jack.

"You and Aubrey broke up?" Jack asked Ben.

"You weren't calling about the breakup?"

Luke shook his head.

Jack tried to pull his phone back, but Ben snatched it, and then went still as a stone.

The picture on the screen was of a woman in a very skimpy kitten costume, which wasn't the problem. The problem was that the woman was hotter than hot.

And she was Aubrey.

She was clearly younger, maybe even not of legal age, posing on her knees, one hand curled like a cat with its claws out, the other holding a whip. She wore cat ears, and her "tail" was curved around her million-dollar bod, which was encased in a snug leather bodice, tiny leather shorts, and stiletto heels.

"It's from an adult costume website," Jack said. "An X-rated costume website. Near as I can tell, there are a small handful of different models, maybe five in total, modeling close to a hundred different costumes that you can order for home delivery—sans the girls, of course."

Luke snorted. "Thorough much?"

"I like to do my research, especially when it involves nearly naked women."

"That's *my* woman," Ben said, and both Luke's and Jack's brows went up.

"Thought you broke up," Luke said lightly.

Ben ignored them and flipped through the site, sucking in a breath because Jack had showed him the most PG-rated costume in the bunch. He found the same younger Aubrey as a "slutty nurse," a "slutty French maid," a "slutty bunny," and a "slutty police officer." Christ. He closed the browser window and handed the phone back. "How the hell did you find this?"

"Lucille came to me with it," Luke said. "Apparently it was in Ted Marshall's book—the one that no one in town read until the seniors got hold of it for their book club."

"Why did Lucille come to you?"

Luke smiled. "She wanted me to arrest Ted for being a 'spineless dickhead.' She's worried about Aubrey because it's already getting around. Someone tweeted about it, and someone else posted some of the pictures on Instagram, and she doesn't want this to affect Aubrey's grand opening on Saturday."

Ben stood up.

"Where are you going?" Jack asked.

"To make sure she's okay."

"Didn't you just say you broke up?" Jack asked.

"He also said she was his woman," Luke said, studying Ben's face. "And speaking of that, maybe we should hear *that* story."

"Maybe we shouldn't," Ben said, and started to walk away.

"Hey," Jack said, managing to block his way. "How come when I'm fucked up, you're all in my face about it, but when you're fucked up, you get to be alone?"

"I'm not fucked up," Ben said firmly.

"You look pretty fucked up to me," Jack said. "I'm with Luke. Let's hear the story. Or should I guess? You decided you were too happy."

"What's that supposed to mean?" Ben asked, his voice very quiet. It was the voice that usually sent men running. But Jack just looked at him, not running anywhere. In fact, he went toe-to-toe with Ben and stared him straight in the eye.

"It means," Jack said, "that ever since you lost Hannah, it's like you don't think you have the right to be happy. She's dead and buried, and you think you have to be, too. That's what running for the past five years was all about."

"It was about helping people," Ben said. "You might recognize the concept, since you've been doing it all these years as a firefighter."

"Bullshit. It was *running*, Ben." Jack punctuated this with a little shove. "I gave you the five years, but it's time to get better. It's time to let yourself have a life." A bigger shove now. "It's okay to do that; there's nothing to feel guilty about."

Ben shook his head. "I get why you think I might feel guilty, and I did feel guilty for a damn long time. But I've moved on."

Jack's gaze said he thought otherwise and that Ben was an asshole.

"You two going to need a referee?" Luke asked, still sprawled out, all relaxed in his chair. "Because if I have to arrest you, Dee's gonna kill me."

Jack didn't look like he cared, and Ben blew out a breath. "This has nothing to do with my happiness," he said. "Aubrey lied to me. So it's over, end of story."

"What was the lie?" Jack asked.

"What does *that* have to do with anything?" Ben asked.

"A lot," Jack said. "If she lied and said, 'Oh baby, that was so good,' when it was only okay, that's not exactly a breakup lie."

"It was an omission," Ben specified.

"Like I-forgot-to-tell-you-I-hate-pizza omission?" Jack asked. "Or, like, I'm-really-a-male-in-chick-clothing kind of omission?"

Ben considered swiping the smirk right off Jack's face with his fist. But then Luke would get all pissed off and call Sawyer, the sheriff, just to make a point. Plus, it was probable that even off-duty Luke was armed. "It was an *omission*, okay?" he said to Jack. "Drop it."

"Well, I would," Jack returned. "Except I'm bad at that."

Luke pulled out his phone and started thumbing through his contacts.

Ben caved. Not because he was afraid of Sawyer but because he didn't have time to be arrested tonight. "Aubrey told Hannah we'd slept together," he said. "That's why Hannah dumped me. Aubrey lied to her and cost me two years with Hannah."

Two years that Hannah deserved…Ben didn't give a shit about himself. But Hannah. She was dead and gone, and she didn't have a voice.

That just about killed him dead and gone, too.

Jack, staring at Ben, dropped the teasing note in his voice. "Well, hell."

"Yeah."

"Wait," Jack said, putting his hand on Ben's shoulder

as he turned to leave. "Wait. Are you telling me that Hannah believed her? And that she never brought it up to you? Ever?"

"So?"

"*So?*" Jack said. "Don't you have to ask why? Or put some of the blame on her?"

"She's dead," Ben said flatly.

"Yeah," Jack said. "And that sucks. Sucks hard. But think about this, Ben. So Aubrey was a bitch in high school. We were dicks. For that matter, Hannah was no angel, either. Whatever. It's old history. Don't let that be an excuse to—"

"If you say *not be happy*, I swear to God—"

"—not be happy," Jack said, the dare in his eyes.

It was an arrow to the chest, because it was the cold, hard truth. He'd done exactly what Jack had said, and he planned to continue onward, thank you very much.

"Okay." Luke stood up. "Look, I should knock both of you knuckleheads into next week myself, but I'd rather go home and be with Ali."

"Tell him he's being stupid, Luke," Jack said, not taking his eyes off Ben. "Maybe he'll listen to the voice of reason."

"I'm not telling him shit," Luke said, and met Ben's gaze, too. "Because he already knows he's being stupid."

Ben shook his head and walked out of the bar, the questions floating in his head. Why had Aubrey done it? Why had she lied to Hannah?

And even more than that, why had Hannah believed her? Why would Hannah buy into the story that he'd cheated on her so readily?

Because she'd been eighteen. Young and foolish, like

him. Of course she'd believed it. This was Lucky Harbor, where gossip was gospel.

And then there was the baseline truth: He'd fully and freely enjoyed the freedom that the two-year breakup had afforded him.

He was going to have to live with that.

He drove for a good thirty minutes before he ended up parking in the alley behind the bookstore. "You are so fucked up," he murmured to himself, and took the stairs to Aubrey's place.

He was only here to make sure she knew about the pictures. He may not have forgiven her, but he didn't want her to be blindsided. That was all. He stared at Aubrey's door for a very long moment before he knocked.

Chapter 27

♥

Aubrey opened her door to Ben and felt the shock reverberate through her. She'd wanted, desperately, to talk to him, to get the chance to explain. There was so much left to say, like how badly she'd felt all these years, and how she'd never meant for them to get into a relationship without telling him the truth, that it'd just happened…

God, it had truly happened. She'd fallen for him, hard.

And she'd blown it, just as hard. He hadn't called or been to the store.

But now here he stood on her doorstep, wearing jeans, scuffed work boots, a gray henley, and an open down jacket, hood up against the rain. Given that she could see only part of his face, and that the part she *could* see was an unshaved jaw, she shouldn't have felt weak in the knees, but she did. She nearly threw herself at him in relief, but before she could move, he said, "Do you know about the pictures?"

She blinked and began to realize that this visit might not be what she hoped. "*You* know about them?"

A muscle ticked in his jaw. "Yeah."

Oh, God. "You read Ted's book?"

"No. But I heard about them and—"

"Heard about them, or saw them?" she asked tightly.

"Saw them."

Damn it. She drew a shuddery breath and tried to figure out what the silver lining might be, but really, there was none. "Do you think a lot of people in town know?" She closed her eyes. "Never mind. This is Lucky Harbor, right? Everyone knows by now. I can't even imagine what they think."

"They think you're hot as hell, that's what they think," he said. "At least the red-blooded males do."

"The pictures are old," she said. "Nearly a decade old. And in some of them I'm in a mask. Maybe people won't recognize me…" Her words faded away at the look on his face.

"You're pretty recognizable, Sunshine."

"I was young," she said softly. "And it was an okay job as far as modeling gigs went. I didn't have to sleep with the photographer, and I made enough money to pay for college."

"Aubrey," he said, and let out a long breath. "I'm not judging you. At all. You've got nothing to be ashamed of. *Nothing*," he repeated, voice like steel, making her eyes sting. "I just wanted to make sure you knew they were out so that you weren't blindsided by them."

He was here because he cared about her, and she decided to take *that* as her silver lining. She stepped back to let him in, but he was already stepping back as well, away from her. "You're…not coming in?" she asked, hating the naked vulnerability in her voice.

He didn't take off his hood, so she couldn't really see his expression, but there was a definite edge to him tonight—and a sense of exhaustion that broke her heart.

"No," he said. "I'm not coming in."

She absorbed the hurt, just one more hurt on a pile of hurts. He gave one curt, barely there nod and started to go. "Ben, I'm so sorry. I—"

"I'm sorry, too."

She stared at him, throat burning. "Why did you come?" she whispered.

"I told you. To make sure you knew."

"*Why?*" she pressed.

He was still a moment, looking at her intently. "It was the right thing to do," he finally said.

An arrow to her heart. Her gut. Her soul. Because the implication was, of course, that *she* wouldn't know the right thing if it bit her on the ass.

"Do you need anything?" he asked.

She nearly laughed, but it would have been a half-hysterical one. And in any case, she had far more pride than sense at this point, so she lifted her chin and looked him right in the eye and shook her head. "I'm fine." She was always fine.

He paused, so she added a smile to prove it. Hell if she'd let him see her sweat. If he didn't want her, she wouldn't beg.

Oh, hell. She *wanted* to beg. Bad.

But after one last long look at her, he turned and walked away.

And she let him.

* * *

Aubrey had thought she was at rock bottom when she'd screwed up with Ben.

She'd underestimated herself.

The next day was a painfully slow day at the store. The day after that was the grand-opening party, and she was beginning to think it might also be her grand closing.

Heartsick, she closed up for the day and then dropped her forehead to the door. *Damn it.* "I'm not going to cry."

"Okay, but just in case, we have reinforcements."

Aubrey whirled around and faced Ali and Leah, who'd come in the back. Ali held a bottle of Scotch and three big red plastic cups. Leah was holding a tray of goodies. "Leftovers from today's baking," she said. "And trust me when I say you don't need anything else when you have this stuff—not even a man."

"That's good," Aubrey said, and swiped at her cheeks. "Because I don't need a man."

Ali set down the cups and poured them each a very liberal dose of Scotch. "A toast," she said, waiting for Aubrey and Leah to pick up their cups. "To us," she said. "And to Aubrey." She toasted Aubrey. "Because you look damn hot in those pictures."

"Yeah," Leah said. "There's going to come a day when you yearn to look like that again." She paused. "And for the record, I've *never* looked that way. Bitch."

Aubrey felt herself laugh for the first time in two days.

They all drank, and Ali refilled their glasses. Leah ordered a pizza. They inhaled it and then raided Leah's bakery for dessert.

"I hate men," Aubrey said much later, out of the blue, and they drank to that, too.

"I can't exactly say I hate men," Ali said. "'Cause I sleep with one of the finest men out there. But I recognize *your* right to hate men." She hiccupped and then paused. "Wait. Why do you hate men again?"

"Because Ben broke up with her," Leah reminded her.

Aubrey nodded. The room was getting a little wobbly. They'd had three double shots each, and the booze had gone straight to her head with exponential power. "He had good reason," she said. "I wronged him."

"That's a chickenshit reason," Leah said. "I love him, I really do, but he's a pussy chickenshit."

Ali snorted Scotch out her nose. "Damn it!"

Aubrey looked at Leah. "You think so?"

"I know so," Leah said, maybe slurring her words a bit. "He's made mistakes, too, you know. Lots of them. He should forgive yours."

"Yes, but it was a doozy of a mistake," Aubrey admitted. "And when it comes right down to it, I did it on purpose, so actually, technically, I don't think that even qualifies as a mistake."

"Hey, love transcends all."

It was Aubrey's turn to inhale the Scotch and snort it out her nose. "Gah," she managed, her throat burning.

Ali was pounding her on the back. She got her breath back, but Ali continued to pound her until, with a weak laugh, Aubrey held up her hands. "I'm okay. But it wasn't love."

Ali and Leah looked at her, then at each other, and then burst out laughing.

"Okay," Aubrey admitted. "So I love him. Damn it. But he doesn't love me."

"Does so," Leah said, refilling her drink. "You just need to fight for him."

Aubrey stared at her. "What?"

"You're a fighter, Aubrey. And I don't mean like this…" Leah put up her own fists and nearly punched herself. "I mean you're not someone who gives up. You go after what you want. Yeah, you screwed up, but you know what? He did, too. He didn't let you talk about it or try to work through it. He just closed himself off."

"Hence the pussy chickenshit moniker," Ali said, and hiccupped again.

"Yes," Leah said. "Because he used what happened as an excuse to run away from what you two had."

Aubrey stared at her. This was true. So true…*why* hadn't he wanted to hear everything? Why hadn't he wanted to understand? And most important, *why had he been so willing to walk away from her?* Thinking about that last question made her stomach hurt, but more than that, it made her really mad.

"Yeah," Leah said, seeing the look on Aubrey's face. "That's what I'm talking about. Hang on, I've got an idea."

"Oh, boy," Ali said. "Those usually involve the police."

"Hush, you," Leah said. She pulled out her phone, hit a number, and put it on speaker.

"Hey, babe," Jack said, a smile in his voice as it filled the room. "More phone sex already? 'Cause I think you wore me out at your last break—"

"No," Leah said quickly, her face red, as she scooped the phone up close to her mouth. "And I'm not alone. Sheesh, I've got Ali and Aubrey here."

"Hey, ladies," he said smoothly. "What're you all doing?"

"Drinking," Ali said cheerfully. "We're commiserating about the penis-carrying race being too slow on the uptake. Present company and your BFF excepted, of course."

"Of course," Jack said. "And Ben, too, right?"

Aubrey growled, and Jack laughed softly. "Yeah, you're right. Our Ben *is* a little slow on the uptake, isn't he?"

"Yeah, *very* slow," Leah said before Aubrey could speak for herself. "And about that—"

"Wait!" Ali interrupted. "I want to hear more about this phone sex during business hours. I'm shocked. *Shocked*, I tell you."

Leah waved a "Shh!" hand at her. "Honey," she said to Jack. "We need a little favor."

"Anything," he said.

"We need a ride. Can you come get us?"

The back door opened, and he strolled in, phone still to his ear. He grinned as he walked up behind Leah, sank his fingers into her hair, and bent over her for a hot kiss.

Ali sighed at the sight. "We'll never get you to Ben's now," she said to Aubrey. "They can go on like this forever. They never run out of air."

It was true, apparently, because they kept kissing.

"See?" Ali said, and then shoved her way in between the smooching couple.

Jack lifted his head and smiled into Leah's dazed eyes. "Your wish is my command, babe."

Leah smiled up at him dopily. "Wow."

Ali sighed. "Damn it, now I miss Luke."

"Didn't you just see him at lunch?" Aubrey asked her.

"That was hours ago."

Jack grinned. "You ladies are all looking a little schnockered. Where do you need to go?"

"Ben's." Leah pointed to Aubrey. "She needs to tell him something *muy importante*."

Aubrey nodded grimly. "*Muy importante*."

Jack's grin widened. "This is going to be fun."

Aubrey understood the sentiment from his point of view. After all, it hadn't been all that long ago that Ben and Aubrey had delivered an inebriated Leah to Jack. That the situation was now reversed clearly pleased Jack to no end.

Of course that had turned out great, and this didn't have a chance in hell of ending anywhere close to great.

Still grinning, Jack offered Aubrey his arm. She took it because she was more than a little off her axis, and not just from the alcohol. Jack loaded her into his car, and Ali and Leah piled in behind her.

"We're your courage," Leah said.

"She doesn't need courage," Ali said. "She's kick-ass. She's *made* of courage."

Aubrey felt her heart swell. "Don't," she said quickly. "Don't make me cry. I'm mad, and I need to stay mad."

"This'll help," Jack said, and powered all the windows down.

"Hey!" they all protested immediately as freezing air hit them in the face.

"Fresh air will keep you ladies from tossing your cookies in my car," Jack said. "I hope," he added under his breath.

Aubrey didn't say anything, because her buzz was starting to wear off and a case of nerves was setting in.

Leah squeezed her hand. "Screw the nerves. This situation isn't all your fault."

Aubrey nodded. It *was* all her fault, but she was going to go with pretending that it wasn't, because Leah was right about one thing. The nerves didn't belong here. She needed to find her mad. After all, she'd honestly been trying to do the right thing by facing her past. Maybe she failed in the delivery, but her heart had been in the right place. She'd *needed* to do the right thing, because the only way she could be the kind of person she wanted to be now was to acknowledge the person she'd been.

Ben didn't have that excuse. He was using her screwup as a reason to hide behind his fears of getting attached again. "I'm a fighter," she said.

"That's right," Ali said.

"I'm going to fight for him."

"Yeah, you are," Leah said, and put up her fists, once again nearly hitting herself in the face.

"Careful, Tiger," Jack said into the rearview mirror. "How much did you all drink?"

"Not enough," Aubrey said as he parked in front of the duplex. Ben's truck was in the driveway, and her heart kicked up a notch at the sight of it.

"*No* eavesdropping," she said to her posse, and got out of the car.

There in the dark, she stood on the sidewalk a moment, gathering her scattered thoughts. In her peripheral vision, she saw Ali, Leah, and Jack tiptoe into Jack's house, and she breathed a sigh of relief, grateful there'd be no witnesses for this.

Chin up, she strode to Ben's front door and knocked.

No response; nothing but a gaping silence.

Aubrey knocked again, with a fist this time, matching the rhythm of her pounding heart.

More silence.

She backed up, to the grass yard. Picking up a small rock, she aimed it at Ben's upstairs bedroom window, and then heard the little *tink* that told her she'd hit her mark.

The window opened, and Ben stuck his head out. "What the hell?"

"I want to talk to you," Aubrey said.

He took this in for a beat. "There's this newfangled thing called a phone…"

Good point. Why hadn't she just called him? Her thoughts scattered on the wind. Damn that Scotch, slowing her thought process. "I know it's late," she said, craning her neck to try to see him. "But you should know something."

"That you've got a good arm?"

She wished she could see his expression. "I wanted to say that the only way I can be the kind of person I want to be is to acknowledge the person I was." Her tenuous balance gave way then, and she stumbled back a few steps, nearly toppling over. The damn boots. They didn't go with Scotch. By the time she looked up to Ben's window again, he was gone.

"Fine," she said and crouched low to look for another rock. Not a large one to bean him over the head with—though that had a *lot* of appeal—but another small one for his window. She wanted to get his attention, not get arrested.

Then, behind her, Ben's front door opened, and she nearly fell onto her butt. He was wearing a pair of low-slung black knit boxers and nothing else but sheer male perfection. His hair was mussed, his eyes heavy-lidded, and he had a way-past-five-o'clock shadow. Unable to stop herself, she let her gaze run south, over the ripples of his abs, the ridge of his obliques, which were bisected by a trail of dark silky hair that disappeared beneath those deliciously indecent low shorts.

In spite of the frigid air, she felt herself begin to heat from the inside out. She had to swallow hard to keep her heart from jumping right out of her throat. When she finally managed to look into his face again, he arched a dark brow.

And just like that, her temper kicked back in. "I have more to say to you," she said.

"You've been drinking."

She pointed at him. "Yes." She paused and tried to gather more of her wayward thoughts. "But that has no bearing on this."

He said nothing, just leaned against the doorway. He had a scar she'd never noticed before over one pec—one really great pec—and she wondered where he'd gotten it, and if it'd hurt. And if she could kiss it—

"Aubrey," he said.

She met his gaze. Right. She had things to say. "Okay, first of all, I didn't sleep with you to make amends. I slept with you because I wanted to."

He still didn't say anything, and she pointed at him again. "And you know what? It was your own damn fault. It was those jeans you wear, and the tool belt. It was the size of your hammer!"

From off to the side came a few commingled gasps of shocked laughter, and both Ben and Aubrey turned to look.

Jack's front window was open, and three faces were pressed up to the screen.

Ali, Leah, and Jack. The Three Stooges, though only two of them were drunk as skunks.

Aubrey narrowed her eyes and shooed them, but no one shooed. "I said no eavesdropping!"

"Jack's window just happened to be open," Leah said. "So really, that's not eavesdropping. At least not technically. Because technically—"

Jack put his hand over her mouth and shut the window, though none of them moved away.

Ben gave them a single hard look, and Jack grinned. But he did lower the shade on the window, leaving them alone.

Ben turned back to Aubrey. "The size of my hammer?"

Yeah…she couldn't believe she'd said that, either. She opted to try to find the moral high ground and lifted her chin. "You're missing my point."

He crossed his arms over the chest that she wanted to lick from the sternum to the edge of his boxers and beyond.

Focus, she ordered herself. "I couldn't help myself," she said. "Being with you. I knew it was a bad idea. Hell, *you* knew it was a bad idea. And yet we did it. We *both* did it, Ben."

He continued to just look at her, and this reminded her that she was mad. "Look," she said. "I'm tired of you not saying anything. So stop being quiet and speak up."

"I'm used to quiet."

"Well, that's just great," she said, tossing up her hands. "Because I'm so not good at quiet."

"No kidding."

She refused to let him get her off track with his pissiness, even if he had good reason for it. "Ben," she said, stepping closer. "I'm so sorry I hurt you. And I'm sorrier than I can say about what I told Hannah. I was a horrible bitch back then. But I'm not that person anymore. I have no excuse except that I was miserable and Hannah had everything I wanted, including you. But that's not who I am now."

He still didn't say anything, but she could tell he was processing what she'd said. She should just shut the hell up, but she had this chance to talk to him. She didn't know if she'd get another, so she needed to put everything out on the table. "And I never meant to keep the truth from you," she said. "I honestly didn't know how to tell you, much less fix it."

"It can't be fixed," he said.

There was another gasp from Jack's duplex. At this, Ben swore under his breath and yanked Aubrey inside. He slammed the door and faced her, hands on hips.

"It can't be fixed?" she repeated shakily.

"Well, what did you think, Aubrey? You stole two years of my life with Hannah. How did you expect me to react? And you slept with me before you told me. And you kept sleeping with me." He paused, and she wondered if he was remembering how little sleeping had actually been involved.

And how good it had been between them…

"I can't get past that part," he said quietly. "I was on your list so that you could make amends, not mess up further."

"I wasn't with you because of her," she said. "Or the list. That part…just happened."

He closed his eyes and swiped a hand over them.

Not exactly the reaction she'd been hoping for. "We have something, Ben. You know it, and I know it. Here, in the present, we have something. I don't want to walk away from that, or go quietly into the night. That's not who I am."

"No," he murmured, meeting her gaze, his unfathomable. "You're the one who waits until midnight, decides she has something to say, and can't contain it."

She was pretty sure that wasn't exactly a compliment, so she ignored it. "I'm in this, Ben. You're important to me. It's why you were on my list."

"You and that list." He inhaled, long and slow, and then shook his head. "I just want to forget it. Get over it."

She was standing there, helplessly struggling to overcome her past, fix her present, *and* secure her future all in one fell swoop. But she was watching Ben's face, and it told her the truth, the terrible truth. "I'm willing to fight for you, for us," she said slowly, taking in the devastating realization. "But you're not." She staggered back a step, feeling like she'd been hit by a train. "You're not," she repeated to herself softly, trying to make it sink in.

It didn't want to sink in. "You're not willing to fight for us at all," she said. "You're really going to use this as an excuse to get out."

"There's nothing to get out of," he said. "There was no us."

Rubbing her chest, she stared up into his eyes, which were wiped of emotion, just completely blank. And that hurt the most, she thought dazedly, in shock that he could do this, just walk away. She couldn't fight that. She didn't know how. And though she hated it, she had no choice.

She had too much pride to be the only one in this, the only one fighting.

"I'll be by to finish the wood trim," he said.

He didn't finish the rest of that sentence, which was clearly "and that's it." He didn't have to.

"Forget it," she said.

"It was a gift," he told her. "And I finish what I start."

She had to laugh. It was better than crying. And she'd cried her last tear over him, she promised herself. "Are we seriously having some stupid conversation about the trim after you just dumped me?" she asked in disbelief.

"I didn't dump you," he said. "We were never exclusive."

And the hits kept coming, even if it was the utter truth. "You're right," she said. "This was never a relationship—which we were both perfectly clear about from the get-go." She really hadn't meant to get involved, but she had, and the damage was done. He'd been it for her, the only man she wanted to be with. Not that she'd ever fully allowed herself to believe…

Okay, she had. She'd let herself believe. Her mistake. But she'd been there; she *knew* she wasn't the only one who'd fallen, damn it. He'd done it, too. He'd shown it in every look, every touch. Every kiss. "You can pretend this is about the past, but it isn't," she said. "I think you fell for me, too. And I think it scared you. I get that you've been hurt. But that's life, Ben. Life is one big fat gamble, and the odds are *never* in your favor. So you either go for it anyway and toss the dice or you don't play. But not playing?" She jabbed him in the bare chest with her finger. "That's the coward's way out. And I hadn't pegged you for a coward. Figure your shit out."

Chapter 28

Ben was still standing there in the butt-ass-cold doorway of his place in nothing but his boxers when Jack opened his own door. "You're an idiot," he said, and then ran down the sidewalk after Aubrey. Grabbing her, he redirected her 180 degrees and poured her into his car.

Ali and Leah came out of Jack's house, both taking the time to glare at Ben as well.

"What he said," Leah told him, gesturing her head toward Jack.

And then they were gone, leaving Ben alone to wonder when the hell everyone had gone from wanting him to steer clear of Aubrey to wanting them to be together.

The next morning, Ben got up early to head into work. It was a Saturday, which was perfect. He could catch up a little bit. He swung by to pick up Pink and Kendra and give them a lift to their rec ball soccer practice.

Because five-year-olds didn't judge. Things were

black and white for them. They didn't give a shit that maybe he was afraid to be happy.

The girls were in their yard playing with...Dani. Proof positive that the logic of women was far beyond him.

At the school field, he stopped and put the truck into park. He unbuckled the girls and held on to the back of Pink's jacket when she went to slide out of the vehicle. "Hold on a sec," he said. Christ—he was going to do it; he was really going to ask. "I thought we didn't like Dani."

Pink shrugged. "She said she was sorry for being mean."

Kendra nodded, her pigtails flying.

Just like that, just that easy. Ben looked into their sweet, innocent faces and felt something shift within him. They were so damn resilient. So easy to please. So completely full of life.

And so full of forgiveness.

He wished like hell he could be five again, when a "sorry" fixed everything. But it couldn't now. Nothing could.

The girls hopped out of the truck, but not before pressing sloppy wet kisses on his jaw in thanks.

Bemused, Ben sat there for a long moment, absorbing the fact that he'd just been schooled on life and forgiveness by a couple of five-year-olds. God, he was tired. So fucking tired. But every time he closed his eyes, he could see the pain in Aubrey's gaze. It haunted him.

He'd hurt her. She'd finally opened up to someone—him—and he'd tossed it right back in her face.

She was trying to right her wrongs, trying to be a person she could live with, and he'd used her past against her. Which meant this wasn't about Aubrey at all. It was

about him and his own fears of letting someone in as far
as he'd let Hannah—which hadn't worked out so well for
him.

But what had happened to Hannah hadn't been his
fault, and Aubrey was right. Life was a risk. He could
hide from that or…live it.

The choice was his.

Figure your shit out. That's what Aubrey had told him,
and at the time that had just pissed him off because he'd
thought she'd been the one who needed to figure things
out.

But he'd been wrong about that, too.

The news of what Aubrey had done to Lucky Harbor's
beloved Ben McDaniel spread like wildfire. That on top
of the nudie pictures pretty much did her in.

Foot traffic to the store on the day of her grand-
opening party was practically nonexistent, and Aubrey
knew in her gut she was sunk. "No one's going to come
to the opening tonight," she told Ali and Leah as they arrived to help her set up.

"That's okay," Leah said. "We'll eat the cupcakes our-
selves."

"Not exactly the point," Ali murmured.

Leah took in Aubrey's obviously devastated face.
"Right," she said quickly. "We'll buy a bunch of books,
too."

The bell above the door pinged, and they all turned in
renewed hope as Carla walked in. She wasn't in scrubs
today but was wearing a dress, and at the sight of her,
Aubrey's anxiety ratcheted up a couple of notches.

"Wow," Ali whispered. "You have a look-alike."

Aubrey ignored her. "Hey," she said to her sister.

"Am I early for the grand-opening party?" Carla asked, looking around.

Aubrey found her voice through her surprise. "No. We're it. We're the party."

Leah held out a tray of cupcakes as Carla looked around in confusion.

"Long story," Aubrey said.

"Cupcake?" Leah asked.

Carla took one and moaned. "Oh, my God."

Leah beamed. "Better than an orgasm, right?"

"I don't remember what an orgasm feels like," Carla admitted, and they all laughed.

Aubrey poured her a hot tea. "Thanks for coming and supporting me."

Carla met her gaze. "Well, we are sisters."

Aubrey felt some of her anxiety drain away as she nodded, unable to speak. But though her anger had drained as well, she was still flatlined by an unbearable sadness. She'd handled things wrong—all of it. "The party wasn't my smartest idea. Who really opens a bookstore these days?" She shook her head. "No one, that's who."

"Well, that's a piss-poor attitude, missy," Lucille said, coming into the store, carrying a stack of papers. "I'm surprised at you. You're supposed to be all kick-ass— Wonder Woman. Did you ever see Wonder Woman give up?"

"Lucille," Aubrey said. "You know how much people loved Hannah. You know I can't compete with that. Not after what I did."

"What you did," Lucille said, "was human. All of us have stuff we're ashamed of. Every single one of us. And if people don't remember that, well, shame on them."

Carla looked at Aubrey. "What happened?"

"She was human," Lucille repeated, and patted Carla's hand. "And nice to see you here, honey."

Aubrey shook her head at Carla's questioning gaze. "Later," she said.

Or never…

"What is all that?" Ali asked Lucille, gesturing to the things she'd brought.

"I made flyers to help bring people in for the party." Lucille held them up. It was a cartoon of a blond Wonder Woman. Her hair was drawn to resemble Aubrey's own smooth mane and was held back by a gold crown with a star in the middle. She was standing among stacks and stacks of books, hands on hips, looking pretty kick-ass. In the background were brownies, a teakettle, a laptop, and a tool belt.

"A tool belt?" Aubrey asked.

Lucille smiled. "I see Ben in here pretty regularly, so I wanted to make sure people knew that this is a hot-guy magnet. Nothing says 'hot guy' like a tool belt, you know." She pulled three automatic staplers from her huge purse and handed them out. "Okay, girls, time to get busy."

"Me, too?" Carla asked, holding a stapler, staring down at it.

Aubrey shook her head. "No, you don't have to—"

"Sisters," she said to Aubrey. Lucille handed Carla a stack of flyers, and Carla took them.

Aubrey smiled past the lump in her throat. "Thanks."

Lucille had grabbed a cupcake in each hand and was

sinking into a couch. "Hustle, ladies," she said around a full mouth. She licked chocolate off her lips. "Go on, now." She waved a cupcake. "No time to waste. I'd planned to put up a notice on Facebook, but as it turns out, I'm grounded from my account."

"How do you get grounded from your own Facebook page?" Carla asked.

Lucille shrugged unrepentantly. "One too many pictures of hot guys not wearing enough clothes. But I started an Instagram account, so it's all good."

Ben sat at his desk. Because it was a Saturday, employees who happened to be in the building kept to themselves, making it quiet. Usually his favorite state.

I'm used to quiet, he'd told Aubrey, and he'd meant that. But today it haunted him. Because he also liked Aubrey just the way she was: fiery, passionate, tough. It was bothering him that he'd let her think he didn't like those things about her.

There was a lot bothering him. He was a first-class asshole, as Jack had made clear. Jack was a lot of things, but as much as Ben hated to admit it, one of the things Jack almost always was was *right*.

Yes, Aubrey had taken away two years of time that Ben might have had with Hannah. Might. Because the truth was, he'd made the most of those two years. He'd enjoyed the hell out of himself, and an even bigger truth was that he wouldn't want to take that time back. He'd been too young for a serious relationship with Hannah back then, and only in hindsight could he see that. If they'd stayed together, he'd have blown it anyway.

All on his own.

And then there was Hannah herself. Ben had loved her—he'd loved her with everything he had, and she'd loved him. But she'd never have come to his house in the middle of the night and thrown rocks at his window to demand his attention. She'd never have yelled at him or made a scene. And she sure as hell wouldn't have fought for him. She *hadn't* fought for him, when it had come right down to it.

Instead she'd let him go without so much as the truth. Or any words at all. She'd tossed him away.

As he'd done to Aubrey.

He dropped his head and thunked it on his desk a few times.

"Careful, you'll shake something loose."

Ben lifted his head and found Lucille standing there watching him. "What are you doing here?"

She showed him a flyer for Aubrey's grand opening, and he had to smile at the image of Aubrey as Wonder Woman.

It fit.

"I'm making sure people remember to go to her grand-opening party," Lucille said.

Ben nodded. "You're a good person, Lucille."

"I am," she said. "And I thought you were."

"What does that mean?"

She just looked at him with her rheumy, knowing eyes.

"You're going to have to give me a hint," he said.

"How about a couple of hints?" Lucille said. "Such as since when do *you* judge someone for making a mistake? You've made plenty yourself, Benjamin McDaniel. Remember when you and Jack and Luke broke into the Ferris wheel's machine room and set it running in the middle of the night? Or how about when your aunt had the entire search and rescue team looking for you when you'd gone night surfing? Everyone thought you'd drowned, but there you were on the harbor, right on the beach, sleeping through your own rescue."

He winced. "I was young and stupid."

She gave him a baleful stare.

"I'm not going to discuss Aubrey with you," he said flatly.

"No, of course not. We're discussing your stupidity. Your assness. Your—"

"I got it," Ben said tightly.

"Yeah? Then do something about it, big guy."

"For the record," he said, "I was just getting ready to handle this situation."

"Well, could you speed things up a little bit?" she asked. "Our girl doesn't have all damn day. Right now she's all alone in her shop surrounded by nothing but books and cupcakes that no one's eating."

He didn't like that image. "No one came?"

"Her friends Ali and Leah came," she said, with an emphasis on *friends*, as though he should be ashamed of himself for not being one of them. "Her sister showed up, too," Lucille added. "But no one else. Lucky Harbor thinks it needs to be mad on your behalf."

Hell. That was not what he wanted. "It's none of anyone's business. What happened is between me and her."

Lucille crossed her arms. "Are you referring to way back, when she got mad at Hannah and told her a lie about the two of you? Are you seriously going to tell me that when you heard *why* Aubrey did it that it didn't make a difference to you?"

Ben went still, thoughts spinning in his head so fast he felt whiplashed.

Lucille was staring at him. "You didn't even ask Aubrey why she told Hannah that lie, did you?"

"I asked," he said. But she hadn't answered.

And he hadn't pushed.

"Oh, for Peter, Joseph, and Mary's sake!" Lucille said, exasperated. "I need to be paid for this job."

"What job?"

"Matchmaking. You young people don't even know how to communicate. Listen to me very carefully. Aubrey caught Hannah in a lie—a big one—that caused someone else a lot of problems. It pissed Aubrey off, because at that time she wasn't getting away with diddly-squat."

Ben shook his head. "What lie could Hannah have possibly told that would have upset Aubrey? They weren't even friends."

Lucille was clearly over this. "Remember that car accident she was in?"

Ben did remember. Hannah had been in the passenger seat when her best friend had gotten in an accident. Later that friend had been sued by someone in one of the other two cars involved. Thankfully, Hannah had been unhurt, but she was devastated over her friend's troubles from the fallout. "Yes. I remember."

Lucille's expression softened. "Honey, this isn't easy to say. I don't like to speak ill of the dead. *Hannah* was driving that night. The two girls switched places before the police came because Hannah had been drinking. She'd had a scholarship to lose and a father she was terrified of. A DUI couldn't happen for her."

Ben stared at her. "That's crazy. Hannah would never have let someone else take the blame."

"But that's exactly what she did," Lucille said quietly. "And Aubrey saw it."

"How do you know this?"

"Because that someone else is my granddaughter." Lucille patted him on the arm. "She said that Aubrey confronted Hannah about the accident, and Hannah denied it." She gave Ben a long look. "Hannah used Aubrey's bad reputation against her, to discount anything Aubrey might say. And then Aubrey let her mouth run off with her good sense when her temper got the best of her."

Ben didn't know what to make of any of this, and he wasn't at all sure that the details mattered at this point. It was in the past, and it would stay there. It didn't matter—none of it mattered; he knew that now. Standing, he headed to the door, but then he stopped to go back for the flyers. Lucille plowed into the back of him. Her hands came up, and because she was scarcely five feet tall they ended up on his ass. He craned his neck and looked down at her.

"Sorry," she said, but didn't remove her hands. In fact, if he wasn't mistaken, she gave him a little squeeze.

"Lucille," he said ominously.

"I know." She pulled her hands away—rather reluctantly, he thought—and sighed. "It's just been a long time since I had my hands on buns that firm."

Shaking his head, he grabbed the flyers and strode out of his office. He stopped at every person he saw, thrust out a flyer, and demanded that person's presence at the bookstore. "There's going to be stuff to eat," he said, and glanced at Lucille for confirmation.

She nodded. "Goodies from the bakery. And also hotties with buns of steel."

After Ben got everybody to leave their desks and head down the street, he took a picture of the flyer with his phone and attached it to a text message, which he sent to everyone in his contacts list who lived in Lucky Harbor—and to a few who were close enough to get their asses in a car and drive here. Then he hit up the fire station, not surprised to find that Jack had already sent everyone down to the bookstore.

Then Ben headed that way as well, stopping at every place in between. He even hit up Sam, who was working alone in his harbor warehouse, sanding away on a gorgeous boat.

"You want me to go to a party?" Sam asked in disbelief, straightening. He was covered from head to toe in sawdust.

"Yeah," Ben said.

Sam stared at him, and then let out a slow smile. "So the rumors *are* true. You've fallen for the bookstore chick."

"Shut up and get your ass to the party."

By the time Ben walked into the Book & Bean, it was filled, the crowd noisy and happy. The best sound of all was the sound of the register steadily ringing.

He was stopped by Mr. Wilford, who was shocked to report that he actually had pumpkin plants growing—in late winter.

Dee was there, too, and gave him a big hug. Just about everyone he knew was there, except the one person he wanted to see. He strode quickly through the store, completely ignoring anyone else who tried to talk to him.

He finally found Aubrey behind the coffee and tea station, serving a line of customers. She was flushed, looking relieved to be serving at all. She wore a pretty dress, her hair was up, and she was smiling.

She hadn't fallen apart. She'd picked herself up and carried on. He loved that about her.

He loved *her*.

Chapter 29

♥

At the hush in the crowd around her, Aubrey looked up, her smile slipped, and all the air vacated her lungs.

"Hey," Ben said, eyes calm and on hers, his voice quiet. "I'm looking for a book recommendation."

"A book recommendation," she repeated, heart pounding so loudly she couldn't hear herself think. Their rapt audience didn't help much. "You want a book recommendation."

"Yes. I need one on male groveling. I thought maybe there might be a *Relationships for Dummies* or something."

She wasn't sure what to make of this, so she lowered her voice. "Listen, about the other night. I wanted to apologize—"

He shook his head. "You already apologized. Several times, in fact."

"But—"

"It's enough," he said, and lithely vaulted over the

counter. "And now it's my turn." He stepped closer and put his hands on her hips. I'm sorry, Aubrey." His fingers tightened on her. "I'm sorry I was such an ass that I couldn't see past my own insecurities and fears."

Around them, their audience gave a collective "Aww," but Aubrey ignored them, not taking her eyes off Ben. "Go on," she said cautiously.

"You said you fell for me."

She flushed, thinking about everything she'd flung at him that night, including rocks. "Ben—"

"You also said *I* fell for *you*. I blew that off, but you were right, Aubrey. I did fall, hard and fast, and"—his mouth twisted wryly—"a little bit against my will."

She tried to pull free, but he held tight. "I liked it," he said. "Too much, to be honest. So when you told me about your list, I used it to back away from you. You were right about that, too. Probably we should start a new list now, of all your rights."

Thoughts rolling in her head like tumbleweeds, heart aching, she shook her head, afraid to hope. "Where are you going with this, Ben?"

"I want you," he said. "I've wanted you every single minute of this entire winter. I also need you. From the bottom of my flawed heart."

Their audience "aw'd" again, but Ben paid them no more mind than Aubrey did, his gaze still on her. "I can remember every single smile you've given me," he said, "every word you've ever said to me."

She melted a little at the sweetness of his words, but shook her head, unable to give up the doubt, the fear that this wasn't going where she so desperately hoped it would.

Unperturbed, he smiled. "I also remember every eye roll. And every single time you went toe-to-toe with me and drove me crazy."

A few people tittered and giggled.

Aubrey tried to free herself again, but he held on to her with shocking ease, even laughing softly, the bastard. He gestured to the store around them. "Hell, Aubrey, I dragged this job out to twice as long as it should have taken," he said, "just so I could keep seeing you."

"Well, that's good to know," Lucille whispered to someone. "I was beginning to think the boy didn't know what he was doing."

Ben slid Lucille a look before turning back to Aubrey. "I loved watching you work. It might've been the pretty dresses that promised a softer side to you, a side only I got to see, but I loved watching you run this world—your world. I loved watching you find your place. I loved watching you take me on and calling me on all my shit." He ran a finger along her temple and gently tucked a loose strand of hair behind her ear. "I love your spirit, your passion. I love everything about you. I love *you*, Aubrey."

The crowd sighed in unison, and as if they were watching a tennis match, their heads all turned toward Aubrey for her reaction.

She had plenty of reactions, the biggest being the fact that her heart suddenly didn't fit inside her rib cage. But she wasn't one hundred percent ready to believe. "You said you liked quiet," she said. "I'm not quiet."

"I said I was used to quiet. But I've learned something about myself. I also like *not* quiet." He smiled. "A lot."

And just like that, the little kernel of hope she'd so ruthlessly tamped down finally found room to breathe and grow. "Yeah?"

There was a smile in his eyes now. And relief. "Yeah."

Lucille leaned over the counter toward Ben and stage-whispered, "I don't think you need a book recommendation at all. You're doing pretty darn good."

"Thanks," he said.

"But the two years I stole," Aubrey said. It hurt her to even say it, but she had to get it out, all of it. There could be no more secrets. "What about them?"

He shook his head. "I mentioned I was an ass, right? I never should've blamed you for that—"

"But I—"

"Yeah, you did," he said. "And then I went on to make the most of those two years. It's over and done, Aubrey," he promised. "And anyway, I'm hoping if I play my cards right, you're going to give me a lifetime."

This cause a huge gasp from the crowd, and Aubrey matched it with one of her own. "What?" she whispered, certain she'd heard wrong.

He dropped to a knee.

"Oh, my God." She put her hands to her mouth and stared down at him.

"You're everything I need," he said. "Everything I'll ever need. And I've needed you, Aubrey, for a long time. Every single second since you threw that drink in my face."

She choked out a half laugh, half sob. "You never said—"

"I should have. Another mistake," he said, his expression serious. "The good news is that I learn from my mistakes, always. Marry me, Aubrey. Marry me and give me forever."

She felt her eyes go wide. Felt her heart kick hard. From her peripheral vision she was aware that the entire crowd had surged forward to peek over the counter in order to get a look at Ben McDaniel on one knee.

"Are you going to reject me in front of at least one hundred of our closest friends and family?" he asked lightly.

She looked into his eyes and realized he wasn't nearly as calm, cool, and unruffled as he was pretending to be, and it squeezed her heart. "No," she said.

His expression grew very serious, and there was absolute silence in the room. "No," he repeated, clearly trying to figure out what exactly she was saying no to—the proposal or rejecting him.

Letting out a laugh, Aubrey dropped to her knees in front of him, eyes burning as she met his gaze. "I mean yes."

"So…yes you'll marry me, or yes you're rejecting me?"

"Yeah, honey," Lucille piped up, leaning over the counter. "There's a pretty big difference there."

"Yes, I'll marry you." Leaning into him, Aubrey wrapped her arms around Ben's neck as their audience broke out in applause.

"Shh!" Lucille snapped above them. "I can't hear; I want to hear!"

"There's nothing more to hear," Aubrey said, eyes on Ben. "It's all been said."

Ben's eyes smiled first, and then the smile spread to

his mouth. And then he lowered that smiling mouth and kissed hers.

"You've given me so much," she said against him. "What do *you* get?"

His eyes soaked her up, as though maybe he'd never get enough of her. "You."

Commercial jingle writer Becca Thorne is looking for inspiration in Lucky Harbor.

Sam Brody might be just what she needs…

Please turn this page for a preview of

It's in His Kiss.

Chapter 1

"Oh, yeah," Becca Thorne murmured with a sigh of pleasure as she wriggled her toes in the wet sand. The sensation was better than splurging on a rare pedicure. Better than finding the perfect dress on sale. Better than...well, she'd say "orgasms," but it'd been a while, and she couldn't remember for sure.

"You're perfect," she said to the Pacific Ocean, munching on the ranch-flavored popcorn she'd bought on the pier. "So perfect that I'd marry you and have your babies if I hadn't already promised myself to my e-reader."

"Not even going to ask."

At the deep male voice behind her, Becca squeaked and whipped around, spilling some of the precious popcorn.

She'd thought she was alone on the rocky beach lined with stacks of mossy sandstone towers. Alone with her thoughts, her hopes, her fears, and all her worldly possessions—which were stuffed into her car parked in the lot behind her.

But she wasn't alone at all, because not ten feet away, between her and a huge Ferris wheel on the pier, stood a man. He wore a skintight rash guard T-shirt and loose board shorts, both dripping wet and clinging to his very hot bod. He had a surfboard tucked under a bicep like it weighed nothing, and just looking at him had her pulse doing a little tap dance.

Maybe it was his unruly sun-kissed brown hair, the strands more than a little wild and blowing in his face. Maybe it was the face itself, which was striking for its features carved in granite and its set of sage-colored eyes that held her prisoner. Or maybe it was that he carried himself like he knew he was at the top of the food chain.

It didn't matter because the wary city girl in her didn't trust anyone, not even a sexy-looking surfer dude. Taking a few steps backward, she thought about the Swiss Army knife she'd left in her car.

The man didn't react, didn't seem bothered by her retreat at all, other than the slightest tilt of the corners of his mouth. "You okay?" he asked, voice a little gruff but not aggressive.

Was she okay? The jury was still out, but that he'd asked at all meant she needed to work on her poker face. "I'm good," she said, not adding the automatic "thanks" as she would've in the old days, back when she'd still been a people pleaser. Of course, being "good" was more than a bit of an exaggeration, but what she really happened to be was none of his business.

He met her gaze and held it, and she knew that he knew

she was full of shit. But after a beat, he gave her a short nod and left her alone. Becca watched him stride up the pier steps and then vanish from sight before she turned her attention back to the ocean.

Whitecaps flashed in the last of the day's sun, and a salty breeze blew over her as the waves crashed onto the shore. Big waves. Had Sexy Surfer really just been out in that? Was he crazy?

No, *she* was the crazy one, and she let out a long, purposeful breath, and with it a lot of her tension.

But not all…

She wriggled her toes some more, waiting for the next wave. There were a million things running through her mind, most of them floating like dust motes through an open, sun-filled window, never quite landing. Still, a few managed to hit with surprising emphasis—such as the realization that she'd done it. She'd packed up and left home.

Her destination had been the Pacific Ocean. She'd always wanted to see it, and she could now say with one hundred percent certainty that it met her expectations. The knowledge that she'd fulfilled one of her dreams felt glorious, and she was nearly as light as a feather.

Nearly.

Because, of course, there were worries. The mess she'd left behind, for one. Staying out of the rut she'd just climbed out of, for another. And a life. She wanted—*needed*—a life. And employment would be good—something temporary, a filler of sorts, mostly because she'd become fond of eating.

But standing in this cozy, quirky little Washington State town she'd yet to explore, those worries all receded a little bit. She'd get through this; she always did. After all, the name of this place nearly guaranteed it.

Lucky Harbor.

She especially liked the "Lucky" part, since she was determined to chase some *good* luck for a change.

A few minutes later, the sun finally gently touched down on the water, sending a chill through the early July evening. Becca took one last look and turned to head back to her car. Sliding behind the wheel, she pulled out her phone and accessed the ad she'd found on Craigslist last month.

Cheap waterfront warehouse converted into three separate living spaces. Cheap. Furnished (sort of). Cheap. Month to month. Cheap.

It worked for Becca on all levels, especially the "cheap" part. She had the first month's rent check in her pocket, and she was meeting the landlord at the building. All she had to do was locate it. Her GPS led her away from the pier, to the other end of the harbor, down a narrow street lined with maybe ten warehouse buildings.

Problem numero uno.

None of them had a number indicating an address. After cruising up and down the street three times, she admitted defeat and parked. She called the landlord, but she only had his office number, and it went right to voicemail.

Problem number two. She was going to have to ask someone for help, which wasn't exactly her strong suit.

It wasn't even a suit of hers at all. She hummed a little to herself as she looked around, a nervous tic for sure, but it soothed her. Unfortunately, the only person in sight was a kid on a bike, in homeboy shorts about ten sizes too big and a knit cap, coming straight at her on the narrow sidewalk.

"Watch it, lady!" he yelled.

A city girl through and through, Becca held her ground. "*You* watch it," she yelled back.

The kid narrowly missed her and kept going.

"Hey, which building is two-oh-three?"

He called out over his shoulder, "Ask Sam! Sam knows everything!"

Okay, perfect. She cupped her hands around her mouth so he'd hear her. "Where's Sam?"

The kid didn't answer, but he did give a jerk of his chin toward the building off to her right.

It was a warehouse like the others—industrial, old, the siding battered by the elements and the salty air. It was built like an A-frame barn, and both the huge front and back sliding doors were open to the elements. The sign posted did give her a moment's pause.

PRIVATE DOCK
TRESPASSERS WILL BE USED AS BAIT.

She bit her lower lip and decided her need to find her place outweighed the threat. Hopefully…

The last of the sunlight slanted through, highlighting everything in gilded gold, both the skeleton of a wooden hull in the center of the space and the guy using some sort of planer along the wood. The air itself was throbbing with the beat of the loud indie rock blaring out from some unseen speakers.

From the outside, the warehouse hadn't looked like much, but as she stepped into the vast doorway, she realized the inside was a wide-open space with floor-to-rafters windows nearly three stories high. Lined with ladders and racks of stacked wood planks and tools, it was neat as a store. The boat hull, centered in the space, looked like a piece of art.

Just like the guy working on it. His shirt was damp and clinging to his every muscle as it bunched and flexed with his movements. It was all so beautiful and intriguing—the boat, the music, the man himself, right down to the corded veins on his forearms—that it was like being at the movies during the montage of scenes that always played to a soundtrack.

Then she realized she recognized the board shorts hanging dangerously low on the guy's hips.

Sexy Surfer.

Though he couldn't have possibly heard her over the hum of his power tool and the loud music, he turned to face her, straightening. And as she already knew, the view of him from the front was just as heart-stopping as it was from the back.

"Me again," she said with a little wave. "You Sam, by any chance?"

He didn't move a single muscle other than a flick of his thumb, which turned off the planer. His other hand went into his pocket and extracted a remote. With another flick, the music stopped.

"No one's allowed in here," he said.

And just like that, the pretty montage soundtrack playing in her head came to a screeching halt. "Sorry," she said, and started to say more but he turned back to his work, and with another flick of his thumb, his tool came back to life. And then the music.

Hmm. A real people person, then.

From somewhere within the warehouse, a phone rang, accompanied by a flashing red light, clearly designed in case the phone couldn't be heard over the tools. One ring, then two. Three. The guy didn't make a move toward it, though you'd have to be blind to miss the light.

On the fourth ring, the call went to a machine, where a preprogrammed male voice loudly intoned, "Lucky Harbor Charters. We're in high gear for the summer season. Coastal tours, deep-sea fishing, scuba, name your pleasure. Leave a message at the tone, or find us at the harbor, northside."

A click indicated that the caller had disconnected, but the phone immediately rang again.

Sexy Surfer still made no move toward it.

Becca glanced around for someone else, *anyone* else, but there was no one in sight.

Of course there was no one in sight, because God forbid anything should ever come easy. Her first instinct was to run out of there with her tail between her legs. But the hell with that. She was tired of running with her tail between her legs. So she lifted her chin, stepped farther inside, and raised her voice to carry over the sound of the planer, the music, and the phone, which was now ringing for a third time. "Um, hi," she called out. She might've decided to live life instead of letting it live her, but she could still be polite while doing it. "Excuse me?"

Nothing.

Looking around, she followed the cord of the planer to an electric outlet in the floor. She walked over to it and pulled the plug.

The planer stopped.

So did her heart when Sexy Surfer turned his head her way. He took her in—the fact that she was still there and that she was holding the cord to his planer—and a single brow arched in displeasure, and also a good amount of disbelief as well. Probably, with that bad 'tude, not many messed with him. But she was exhausted, hungry, and out of her element. Which made her just enough of a loose cannon to forget to be afraid.

"Sam," she repeated in what she hoped was a firm but polite tone, moving closer to him so he could hear her over his music. "Do you know him?"

"Who's asking?"

"Me." She tried a smile. Having come from a family of entertainers, most of them innate charmers to boot, she knew how to make the most of what she'd been given. "I'm Becca Thorne. I'm new to town. And I'm not looking to be bait, I'm just looking for directions..." She smiled again.

He didn't.

She cleared her throat. "I'm lost. I can't find 203 Harbor Street. I think I'm on Harbor Street, but the buildings don't have numbers on them. Some kid on a bike told me to ask Sam, because apparently Sam knows everything. So, are you Sam or not?"

Sexy Grumpy Surfer didn't confirm or deny. "You're looking for the building directly to the north," he said.

She nodded, and then shook her head with a laugh. "And north would be which way, exactly?"

Holding her gaze for another beat, he let the planer dangling in his big hand slowly slide to the floor by its cord before letting go and heading toward her.

He was beautiful, as rugged and tough as the boat

he was working on—though only the man exuded testosterone—a bunch of it.

Becca didn't have a lot of great experience with an overabundance of testosterone, so she found herself taking several steps back, to the doorway.

He didn't stop; not until he was crowded in that doorway right along with her, taking up an awful lot of space.

Actually, *all* of the space.

He was six-foot-plus of lean, hard muscle, with a lot of sawdust clinging to him, and for some reason instead of being a threat, it was the opposite. It made her warm, it made her heart pound. It made her…ache.

Eyes locked on hers, he lifted an arm and pointed to the right. "You have to go around the corner to get to the front door of that building," he said, his voice a little softer now, like maybe he was feeling some of the same heat. God, she hoped so. It'd be embarrassing to be hanging out here in lust-ville on her own.

"Around the corner," she repeated, inhaling his scent, which was fresh wood, something citrusy, and a lot of heated male skin. The combination was pretty damn heady. Too bad he didn't have much of a personality to go with it. "Thanks," she said. "I'm the new tenant there. Or one of them, anyway."

He looked at her, and she wasn't sure but she thought maybe he disapproved.

"I think there are three apartments in total," she said inanely, not sure what he disapproved of exactly—the idea of her living so close, or that she was rambling. The rambling, she couldn't help. It was another nervous tic, like the humming.

Without another word, Sexy Grumpy Surfer walked

back inside, proving her point about the personality. Heading directly for the electrical outlet, he plugged his planer back in.

"Nice talking to you," she said, unable to resist.

He glanced back at her, and though his green-grey eyes narrowed, there was a very slightly amused quirk of his lips that told her he was indeed in on the joke.

So at least he knew that he was an abrupt ass.

"I take it you haven't seen it yet," he said.

"The loft?" she asked. "No. Why? Is it that bad?"

"Depends on how long you're staying. More than five minutes?"

She laughed. "I don't actually know. Lucky Harbor is filler for me at the moment."

He stared at her, then something changed in his face. His expression softened, turning his features from hard and ungiving to—*wow*—open and almost friendly-but-not-quite friendly.

It was nearly enough to distract her from what he'd implied about the building she'd rented in.

He'd flicked the planer on again, and the music, too, bending over the hull of the boat and going back to work.

So much for the wow factor. But hey, she'd certainly been invisible before. In fact she was real good at invisible. And if that thought caused a little pang of loneliness inside her still-hurting heart, she shoved it deep and ignored it, because she knew better.

Leaving the warehouse, she turned right.

To her new place.

To a new beginning.

VISIT US ONLINE AT

WWW.HACHETTEBOOKGROUP.COM

FEATURES:

**OPENBOOK BROWSE AND
SEARCH EXCERPTS**

•

AUDIOBOOK EXCERPTS AND PODCASTS

•

AUTHOR ARTICLES AND INTERVIEWS

•

**BESTSELLER AND PUBLISHING
GROUP NEWS**

•

SIGN UP FOR E-NEWSLETTERS

•

**AUTHOR APPEARANCES AND TOUR
INFORMATION**

•

SOCIAL MEDIA FEEDS AND WIDGETS

•

DOWNLOAD FREE APPS

BOOKMARK HACHETTE BOOK GROUP
@ WWW.HACHETTEBOOKGROUP.COM